Conrad Turner
and the Quest for Trinity

JAMES LEE

DEDICATION

To my Muse. Thank you for sticking with me through it all.

Contents

Chapter One

Conrad Turner was sleeping soundly in his fifth new bed this year. Since his mother's death, it was his eleventh. The people with whom he lived now were not related to him in any important or connective way. Once, he had heard that Joanne Suchuk was a distant cousin; third cousin twice removed was the general consensus. He once was told they had a great-grandparent in common. Actually, it might have been a great-great-grandparent, but then again, does anyone really understand the removal protocol?

Conrad lived with the Suchuks in their little house on Mulberry Hill Road. There were nine people all told living in the little home, including Conrad. Mr. and Mrs. Suchuk and their six unruly children also inhabited the domain. It was amazing that anyone could sleep in the house since the ambient noise level was generally in the eardrum-piercing range. However, most of the inhabitants dropped into slumber relatively rapidly when the lights were put out.

It was a strange phenomenon. From the outside world, and from inside as well, the little house on Mulberry Hill Road would seem to jump from its foundation from the ruckus generated by the Suchuk brood. Many neighbors had sent the police to investigate in the past, but since Mrs. Suchuk acted as the town justice of the peace, only a simple warning was ever issued.

No sooner were the lights turned off in the house than silence befell the Suchuk residence. It was eerie. As if the entire clan had disappeared from the face of the Earth. Silence ensued every night at nine o'clock. You could set your watch by it. This evening in particular, though, Conrad was not sure he would be able to fall asleep.

This evening, just before bedtime, Dean Suchuk, the patriarch of the household, was speaking softly with Joanne, his wife.

"He needs to go," Dean said.

"Where will he go?"

"He's not even family, really. He could go into a nice foster home, don't you think?"

"Absolutely not! He's been through enough."

Conrad was listening from the den and stretching his body to get his ear closer to the door. As he leaned forward to hear better, he bumped into a table just next to the kitchen door.

His body shoved the table just enough to upset several items resting on the top. Out of the corner of his eye, he saw a crystal candlestick holder fall off the top of the table.

Conrad watched it fall in slow motion, and in the brief moments of its descent, he knew his fate was sealed. He was going to move again. He couldn't bear the inevitability of packing, moving, and unpacking yet again. He closed his eyes and thought, *please, just take me from this place.*

The glass holder hit the floor with a sickening crunch, and shards scattered toward the four corners of the Earth. Conrad kept his eyes closed, and he waited for the imminent confrontation. He knew what was coming, and although the anticipation caused him anxiety, he also had the strange sensation that his level of stress was diminishing.

It was an odd feeling: anticipation with a slight hint of relief. He was fifteen, after all. In three years he would be on his own, in any event. Heck, at sixteen, he could become an emancipated minor, if he so chose. It was not the end of the world. Simply put, this was his path. Or so he thought.

After several minutes had passed, Conrad opened his eyes. He expected to see Dean and Joanne Suchuk standing before him, glaring, but that was not the case. Conrad was alone. He quickly scanned around the den to find them. Again, there was no one else around. In fact, the house was eerily silent. This was not at all right. There should be some sort of retribution for his act of spying, let alone for the destruction of property.

Perhaps this was the new custom; perhaps the Suchuks had devised a new method of torture. Conceivably, they conspired to feign ignorance of Conrad's transgressions. They may have agreed to wait until Conrad thought there would be no consequence for his misdeed and then all at once pounce on him in order to catch him unguarded.

These thoughts and scenarios made Conrad angry. The Suchuks hadn't seemed to be the torturing type. They were unloving toward him, but intentionally cruel? Conrad summoned a resolve within himself. He was going to confront the Suchuks and face his punishment. He walked around the corner of the room separating the kitchen from the den. His fists and eyes were clenched as he entered the kitchen. His eyes popped open as he blurted, "I did it. It was me." Conrad became confused. He had just confessed to a phantom.

He was alone in the kitchen. The dishes had been washed and were drying in the rack, but neither Dean nor Joanne was present. Could he have earned such a break as this? Would there be no reckoning? A slight smile crept upon his face.

He retrieved a broom and dustpan from the closet and swept up the tiny bits of crystal. After depositing all the remnants into the trash can, Conrad went to his room. He removed his blue jeans, T-shirt, sneakers, and socks, folding them all neatly and placing them on the trunk at the foot of his bed. He then put on his pajamas. They were not really pajamas. Just a pair of gray sweatpants and an overly large pale-yellow T-shirt. He walked across the hall to the bathroom and flossed and brushed his teeth.

When he was finished, he stood quietly at the sink and listened. There was nothing but silence. Usually, at this time of night, there was lots of activity. Nine people living in a small house generated lots of noise, but now there was none.

"Good night," Conrad shouted to the emptiness. Still, silence was the only response.

Conrad shook his head as he walked back to his bedroom. *Fine*, he thought. *I can deal with the silent treatment.* He slammed his door as he entered the bedroom, hoping to get some reaction. There was none.

He got into bed. He turned off the lamp on his nightstand and laid his head on his pillow. In the dark, he quietly listened to the silence around him. *I am truly alone in this world*, he thought. The funny thing was he didn't feel lonely. For some reason, a great contentment had welled up within him, and the feeling confused him. Here he was on the brink of another in a long series of relocations, and yet, he was content. Was he finally accepting his lot in life, or was he losing his mind? Conrad gravitated toward the latter. How could he be content? Moving, resettling, readjusting, and all that went with the process was stressful. Only an ignoramus would be content under those circumstances. Right?

Additionally, how could this house with its brood exist in a state of silence? Wasn't his mind simply playing tricks on him? Perhaps he wasn't really lying in his bed. Maybe he was actually in the den being browbeaten by Dean Suchuk. As he thought about all the iterations involved, Conrad gained some appreciation for his perception. Whatever was actually happening at this moment, he was content. And that was enough for him. He simply wanted to move on. He wanted to have it over with. He closed his eyes and went to sleep.

Chapter Two

What seemed like only minutes later, Conrad awoke coughing. Actually, he was choking. He opened his sleep-filled eyes and saw a light haze enveloping the room. He glanced around, trying to get his bearings and to clear his mind. *Am I dreaming*, he thought. There was an acrid smell in the air. At first, he gave little thought to the odor. Soon, however, he could taste the mist as he breathed it into his nostrils. It was smoke. His bedroom was beginning to fill with it.

Conrad sprung up in his bed. The house was on fire! It was this thought that lead to him beginning to hear what was going on around him. The house was silent as before. In the distance, he could hear a faint sound. It resembled a vibration, a constant ringing. Conrad turned his head slightly to listen closer. Now he also detected faint voices. Although he couldn't make out whose they were or what they were saying, he was sure it was members of the Suchuk family. And they were no longer in the burning house. They all left the inferno and forgot about him.

Conrad jumped out of his bed and stood for a moment. The smoke was thickening around his head. He couldn't breathe and resumed choking. He remembered the advice given to him in a school assembly some years back: When one finds his or her self in a smoke-filled room, do not stand. Crawl along the floor where more oxygen can be found.

He jumped flat to the floor where he found breathing easier. He crawled toward the bedroom door. He reached up instinctively to turn the doorknob. Another flashback to the same assembly entered his thoughts: Never open a door in a smoke-filled room without first touching the door itself. The purpose of this exercise was to determine if the fire was just beyond the barrier. Hot was bad; cool was good. Conrad thought for a moment: *What if the door is hot? What is the next escape route?* He looked over his shoulder toward the window. Surely a one-story jump wouldn't kill him. *What if the outside of the house is ablaze?* "Stop it," he said aloud. "Focus." He placed his hand gingerly on the door. It was cool. He reached up to the knob and opened the door.

The hallway outside the bedroom was empty but filled with smoke. Conrad looked up. The smoke was rolling slightly along the ceiling. He knew that as the fire intensified, the smoke would roll faster. "Billowing" it was called. He knew he needed to get out of the house and FAST! He crawled along the floor toward the staircase. On the landing, he looked out over the stairs down toward the foyer, but the smoke was obscuring his view. He crawled down the stairs as quickly as he could. His breathing was hitched because the volume of smoke was increasing. He was having trouble breathing.

Halfway down the stairs, he heard the sound of a distant siren. Conrad smiled slightly. *They are coming to save me*, he thought. He continued his descent. Reaching the first floor, he stood up. Although this caused him to inhale more smoke, he wanted to give one last look at this place. He turned around and took it in. *Good riddance*, he thought. *They don't want me, never did.* He glanced back up the stairs toward his room. He saw the smoke, now billowing, collecting in the upper floor. But there was something else that caught his attention. He wasn't quite sure what it was. He squinted slightly to try to get a better view. It looked to be some sort of illumination coming from his room. It was very small but very intense. *What is that?* he thought. He wondered if the fire had somehow managed to break through to his room first. Without thinking, Conrad began to walk back toward the stairs to investigate. As his foot touched the bottom step, an arm grabbed him from behind. He felt himself being pulled backward toward the front door and out into the night.

The fireman sat Conrad on the sidewalk. There were three fire trucks parked at the curb. A frenzy of activity filled the night air. Firefighters were unrolling rubberized canvas hoses. The closest hydrant was across the street in front of the Pickwick house. Conrad knew this because when he first moved here several months ago, Dave Pickwick was sitting on the hydrant watching. Conrad remembered this because he said hi to Dave, but there was no reply. Later, Conrad and Dave had become great friends.

Several firefighters laid out the unrolled hoses. With a precision Conrad had rarely observed before, they connected the hoses together and to the hydrant. The captain was directing the action, but it seemed everyone knew what he or she was supposed to do. Conrad was impressed.

Several men and women were near the house breaking the windows with fire axes. Others were walking around the perimeter observing the progress of the fire.

"It looks like it started in the kitchen, Cap," said one. "Should we set up another line from the next block?"

"What do you think, Tracy?" the captain asked a young woman.

"Not necessary," Tracy responded. "The back half of the house is gone. Frontally, we can protect the rest."

The captain smiled. "Do it," he said.

Two firefighters were placed at the nozzle end of the connected hose. The captain signaled to another one stationed at the hydrant. With one fluid motion, the hydrant valve was actuated, and the two nozzle men braced themselves. The water shot out of the nozzle in a torrent. The nozzle men directed the flow onto the roof of the house. Then they brought the flow into the house through the windows.

Conrad was watching in awe at the intricate performance, a firefighting ballet of sorts: everyone a purpose and a purpose for everyone. It seemed to him, at the moment, an idyllic state of being: having a specific reason to do something, anything, and then simply doing it. That is what he aspired to.

A young paramedic walked over to him. "Were you in the house?" she asked.

"Yes," Conrad replied. "I was asleep in my bed."

"I need to make sure you are okay," the paramedic said. She placed a mask over Conrad's nose and mouth. "This will help you breathe easier." The paramedic unrolled a blood-pressure cuff and placed in on Conrad's left arm. Conrad looked up at her from the curb. Her hair was pulled back tight into a neat and even ponytail. Even in the florescent streetlamp illumination, he could tell her skin was flawless. He also noticed her name tag. It read, *Reason*.

"What's your name?" he asked.

The paramedic looked into his eyes and said, "It's Harriett, but call me Harri." She smiled as she said "Harri."

As Harri pumped the rubber bulb, the cuff contracted, squeezing Conrad's upper arm. *What is this thing called?* he thought. He remembered it was some strange medical term—sigmoid, sphygmo, something.

"Excuse me, Harri. What is this thing called?" he asked.

"Sphygmomanometer" was the reply.

Right, thought Conrad.

"Blood pressure is perfect," Harri said. "Any pain anywhere?"

"Not really," replied Conrad. "Hurts to breathe a bit."

"Smoke does that. Keep that mask on for a few more minutes. I need to test your blood-oxygen saturation. I'll be back in a moment."

Harri stood up and walked toward her partner who was standing beside their red emergency vehicle. Their conversation was animated. Harri gestured toward Conrad several times. Her partner shook his head "no" on each occasion. Harri folded her arms to her chest and walked back toward Conrad.

"How are you feeling?" she asked Conrad.

"I'm okay."

Harri attached a small plastic clip to the end of Conrad's left index finger. A wire ran from the clip into a box no larger than a Casio calculator. The box had a small display screen. Harri watched the screen as numbers flashed on and off. After a few moments, the box emitted a tone. A small smile crossed Harri's face as she removed the clip from Conrad's finger.

"Your oxygen level is back to normal," she said. "Looks like you'll be good as new." Then her smile retreated.

Harri removed the oxygen mask from Conrad's face. She picked up the small oxygen bottle with the mask attached and placed it into a large black Cordura bag. Harri wrapped the wire around the box she'd used to measure Conrad's oxygen level. She knelt down and placed the device into the bag also. She remained kneeling for several seconds, after which she turned toward Conrad and looked directly into his eyes penetratingly. There was pity in her observation, and he did not like to be pitied by others. In fact, it generally made him furious. But coming from Harri, who had been so briefly kind to him, it was almost palatable.

Harri said, "Someone will want to speak with you about the fire."

"Okay," replied Conrad.

"Tell them all you know."

"I don't know anything," said Conrad. "All I know is I woke up and the house was on fire. I don't even know if my fam—if everyone else in the house got out or what." There was a long pause, and the air between them acquired solemnity.

"There was no one else in the house."

"What?"

"I'll let Captain Miller talk to you about it. Take care of yourself." Harri patted Conrad's knee, picked up the black Cordura bag, and walked over to where her partner was loading all the equipment back into their truck.

Conrad watched as Harri returned to her emergency vehicle. She placed the black bag into the truck while she said something to her partner. Her partner held a two-way radio near his mouth and spoke into its transceiver. Conrad continued watching as Harri and her partner exchanged words again. This time Harri seemed less agitated, but she still wanted to get her point across. She pointed her right index finger at her partner, then threw her head back, gesturing in Conrad's direction. Her partner responded in a manner for which Harri had little tolerance. She waived her arms wildly in front of her and then, folding them across her chest, began tapping her left foot, waiting for her partner's response. When he did respond, it was a meek acknowledgment of Harri's superior logic and analysis. He shrugged his shoulders and got into their vehicle.

After several moments, the captain joined Harri and her partner. The three would talk for several minutes amongst themselves, and then one of them would gesture toward Conrad. This pattern repeated several times. Finally, the Captain walked over toward Conrad. As he approached, Conrad stood up.

"I'm Captain Miller," he said with his right hand extended.

Conrad shook the substantial hand; it was calloused and rough in texture. "Conrad Turner, sir," Conrad said.

"Mr. Turner, I need to ask you a few questions."

"Okay, shoot."

"Do you know how the fire started?"

"No, sir, I was sleeping."

"Do you know why your family was not in the house at the time?" Once again, Conrad couldn't believe he heard correctly.

"Pardon me?"

"Your family was not in the house at the time the fire started. You were alone."

"They're not my family. I just live with them."

Conrad thought about the ramifications of the information Captain Miller had relayed. The Suchuks had abandoned him to the fire. Maybe one of them set the fire to rid themselves of a problem. These thoughts filled Conrad with great, but not unknown, sadness. Every family he had lived with since his mother died eventually got rid of him. He was like a deformed appendage. You knew it was there, but you also wanted it gone. Why had his mother left him alone in the world? She had no other family to speak of. But she abandoned him. She didn't protect herself. She didn't take adequate precautions to ensure he would be cared for in the event she could not protect him herself. Conrad placed his head in his hands. He wanted to cry, but he would not let the tears come. Not now.

"Where were they?" Conrad asked.

"From what we know, it appears they went out for a meal."

"In the middle of the night?"

"We don't have all of the details, but that does appear to be what happened. They were located at the Denny's on Laurelwood. They are on their way back here now." Captain Miller placed his giant hands on each of Conrad's shoulders. "Are you going to be all right?" he asked.

Conrad looked up into his eyes and said, "Yeah, I'm always okay." Conrad managed a meek little smile.

Captain Miller returned the gesture. "Okay, then," he said. "I know you are tired and need some rest. We will contact you again if we need more information." Captain Miller tousled Conrad's hair as he walked away.

They were not even in the house, Conrad thought. *A meal? They all went for a meal and didn't take me?*

Conrad thought about the end of each of his foster home stays in the past. Each time there was a defining moment that stood out in his recollection, almost as if that specific point in time were predetermined for him. And it seemed to occur around the time he started to become comfortable in his surroundings.

Just previous to his landing on the Suchuk doorstep, he lived with the Petrarcas. Bob Petrarca had dated Conrad's mother when the two were in college together. When Conrad entered his life as a foster child, Bob was married to Beverly, and their son Danny shared a bedroom with Conrad.

The end of that episode happened when Danny claimed Conrad had attacked him. There Conrad was standing before Beverly and Bob defending himself. Danny's nose was bleeding profusely, and Conrad was intact. He told Bob that Danny had been the instigator; he wanted to believe Conrad, but Beverly would have none of it. She was not going to have the kid of one of Bob's former girlfriends beating up on her child. She didn't care that he was an orphan.

Beverly and Bob fought for days afterward. Conrad couldn't help but hear what was said from time to time. Beverly wanted him gone, but Bob had developed some affection for Conrad.

"It was just a fight," Bob said to Beverly. "Boys will be boys."

"Boys will be boys? He nearly took Danny's nose off. Do you want him to hurt one of the other kids next?"

"That's not his nature. He's a lot like his mother in that." As those words left Bob's mouth, Conrad knew his fate was sealed.

"Like his mother? I see what this is all about. Listen to me, Bobby. He's going. Either find him a place to live or I will." Then Beverly moved closer to Bob, her face but inches from his. In an ominous tone, she said, "And if I find him a place, you're going, too."

Conrad didn't blame Bob Petrarca. What choice had he? Beverly had always resented Conrad's presence; she secretly suspected that Conrad was actually Bob's offspring, but although she came close to presenting the accusation, she withheld it due to lack of evidence. Though suspecting her jealousy, Bob offered to have Conrad and his DNA tested, but Beverly backed down because the thought that Conrad might become a permanent resident in her home, being Bob's biological child, was more than she could handle.

Bob went through his memorabilia looking for someone connected to Veronica. Joanne. Yes, Joanne Campbell. Joanne and Veronica were best friends in high school. In fact, Bob recalled there was some level of familial relationship between them, too. But how would Bob find her today after all these years? He searched the online site for Peninsula High School. After cross-referencing for several hours, he found her. She was married now to Dean Suchuk.

Bob called Joanne and they talked for nearly half an hour. Joanne didn't hesitate to accept an additional child into her home. "The more, the merrier!" she exclaimed. Also, she missed Veronica terribly, and she still regretted their falling out. Bob was relieved. He had thought Joanne would be the perfect person to care for the young progeny of the former Veronica Harper, the love of Bob's youth. But things rarely turn out as we expect.

As Conrad sat remembering, the firefighting team was finishing up at the Suchuk house, or what remained of it. Most of the neighbors were standing around watching the commotion. Conrad looked around and saw Dave Pickwick standing just outside the yellow-caution-tape perimeter. Conrad motioned for Dave to come over. Dave shook his head and held each of his hands out.

"Just get over here," Conrad said out loud.

Dave lifted the tape and walked over toward Conrad. "What the hell did you do, Connie?" Dave said with a smirk.

"Nice," replied Conrad. "It's always my fault. When did you become a Suchuk?" Both boys laughed at this. "Speaking of which, where are they?" said Dave.

"You're not gonna believe it," Conrad replied. Conrad explained what he knew. For some reason or another, the Suchuks had decided to go out in the middle of the night to eat at Denny's. He didn't know what caused the fire, but he's lucky to be alive. *Lucky is relative*, Conrad thought.

"So where are they now?" asked Dave.

"Probably finishing their Rooty Tooty Fresh 'N Fruity," Conrad said.

"That's IHOP, dork," Dave laughed. "Denny's has the Grand Slam." Conrad smiled. His smile faded, though, as he looked down the street.

A black SUV had just turned onto Mulberry Hill Road from Second Street. It was speeding down the block toward them.

"They're back," Dave said, trying to relieve the tension in the air. The black Chevy Tahoe pulled toward the curb diagonally and stopped hard. All four doors opened together, and the Suchuk clan poured onto Mulberry Hill Road. Dean ran over to a firefighter who was rolling a hose. The firefighter pointed toward Captain Miller, and Dean walked in that direction.

Meanwhile, Joanne and all the Suchuk kids—Damon, Denise, Dora, Dallas, Deidra, and Donald—were standing beside the open Tahoe staring at what remained of their home. Their mouths were all agape. After several moments, Damon, the oldest of the Suchuk brood and a real great guy, yelled in Conrad's direction.

"What did you do now, a-hole?"

Joanne slapped Damon on the shoulder. She then looked over at Conrad. He could see a slight and sad smile in her expression. She said something to all the kids and started walking in Conrad's direction.

"Should I go?" Dave asked.

"No," replied Conrad. "I could use your support."

"Hello, boys," she said as she arrived. "Quite a lot of excitement going on here, don't you think?" There was an awkward silence. It hung in the air for what seemed like hours.

"Not really," Dave interjected. "I saw on the news that several people were shot in downtown today. Excitement is a matter of opinion."

"Thank you, David," Joanne said. "Would you give us some privacy?" Dave looked at Conrad for a clue. There was none because Conrad was staring at Joanne intently. "Okay, then," said Dave. "I'll see you later." As Dave walked away, he glanced back over his shoulder once.

"So what happened, Conrad?" Joanne asked.

"You abandoned me. That's what happened," Conrad replied.

"I'm talking about the fire. What did you do?"

"I was sleeping. I was sleeping, and I nearly died in my bed—alone. Where were you?"

"We needed to talk as a family, so we left."

That was it in a nutshell. Conrad was never going to be part of this or any other family. He had no family. He was an orphan. His father ran off when he was a baby, and his mother was killed by a drunk. He was all alone in the world, and he would never be accepted by anyone. The sooner he faced that, the better off he would be.

"So where am I going now?" Conrad asked.

Tears began to stream down Joanne's face. She wiped them aside with the back of her hand.

"I'm not sure yet," she said. "I'm sorry. I wish it could be different."

Conrad thought about that. He wished it could be different, too. He wished he had his mother back. He wished there was another place for him. Somewhere he was accepted.

Somewhere he was somebody. Somewhere he was important, at least to someone.

"It's okay," he said. "I'll be fine. What do we do now?"

"Well, I think for the next few days we all need to stay in a motel," Joanne replied. "Come on, let's go." She threw her arm around Conrad's shoulder, and they walked to the Tahoe together.

Dean was done talking with Captain Miller and had also returned to their vehicle. "The fire was electrical," he said. "They think the wiring in the kitchen was bad. They will know more in a few days."

"So I guess we all stay in a motel for a few days until they get this sorted out," Joanne said.

"Well, it's going to take longer than a few days to get the house back together," Dean replied. "But, yes, for the next few days we can stay in a motel. Let's go." They all piled into the Tahoe. Each door slammed shut, and they drove off down Mulberry Hill Road toward Second Street.

When Conrad climbed into the Tahoe with the rest of the Suchuk clan, he faced his usual dilemma—where to sit. Unfortunately, when Dean Suchuk ordered his version from the local Power Chevrolet dealer, he did not order the optional ninth passenger seating. Every time, including this night, when every soul living in the Suchuk house was to be transported together, Conrad had to squeeze beside Damon.

Damon, as the oldest member of the minor group, resented the fact that Conrad always squeezed next to him.

"Mom!" Damon yelled. "Why does dork-boy always have to sit next to me?"

"Behave, Damon," Joanne scolded. "Where else do you expect him to sit? We don't have enough room in here."

"I don't give a crap," Damon cursed. "I just don't want him near me."

"Damon!" Dean barked, "Language, young man. Watch it."

"I'm the oldest, you know. I shouldn't have to put up with this."

Joanne looked back at Damon, glaring. When his eyes met hers, he saw her mouth the word *behave*. Damon responded by shaking his head. That was the relationship she had with all of her kids. She was genuinely respected by each of them due to her endless patience and compassion.

Damon tried to move closer to the window to minimize his body-to-body contact with Conrad. It was difficult in the close quarters of the third-row seat. Once he got adjusted, he looked at Conrad and said, "Arsonist," under his breath. Conrad ignored the comment.

When the overloaded Tahoe pulled into the parking lot of the Best Western on Pacific Coast Highway, Dean stopped in front of the main entrance. He asked Joanne how many rooms they needed. Initially, she replied with her standard answer of two rooms. Whenever the Suchuks traveled, they generally stayed in two rooms since two members of the group could fit in each bed, and each room usually had two beds. Even with Conrad added to the mix, Joanne had calculated mentally that an additional folding cot would suffice.

"Get three rooms," Joanne said. "The insurance company will be paying. We might as well be comfortable." Joanne smiled and winked at Dean. They would finally have their own room.

Dean smiled back. "You're the boss," he said and leaped from the Tahoe. Joanne watched as he hurried into the building.

Joanne turned around in her seat to face the back of the truck. "Okay, kids," she said. "Girls, you will all be in the same room. Damon, you will share a room with Donald and Conrad."

"Great, Mom," Damon replied.

Dallas said, "Mommy, shouldn't you stay in our room? You used to be a girl, too."

Joanne smiled. "No, honey, Daddy and I will be in our own room."

"Why isn't Daddy sleeping with the boys?" Dallas asked.

Denise, the oldest Suchuk girl, said, "Daddy wants to sleep with Mommy, just like they do at home."

"That's right," Joanne interjected. "Mommy and Daddy sleep together."

Dean walked back around the front of the Tahoe and got into the driver's seat. "Three rooms," he said. "All are on the first floor." Dean started the Tahoe and drove away from the main entrance. He parked in front of room No. 110. "Okay, everyone," Dean said. "I'm sure your mother told you about the sleeping arrangements. We have rooms one-ten, one-eleven, and one-twelve. Let's go."

The four big doors opened and the entire contents of the SUV evacuated. The girls all went to room 110. Damon ran to room 112. Dean used one of the plastic access cards to open room 110 first. He handed the card to Denise.

"You're in charge," he said to Denise. "And be responsible."

"Yes, Dad," she replied.

Dean walked over to room 112.

Denise held the door for Dallas. When Dora approached, Denise let the door close. Dora grabbed it just before it fully closed.

"Thanks," Dora said.

Denise just smiled.

Dora held the door as Deidra walked through. The door closed behind them, and they were in for the night.

Dean opened room 112 with its card. Donald and Damon ran into the room. Conrad watched them speed through the door. He walked toward the doorway, and as he reached the door, he looked up at Dean. There was a slight look of sadness on Dean's face.

"Go on," he said to Conrad.

Conrad walked into the room.

Dean called to Damon. "Here," he said, handing Damon the access card. "You are responsible for this." Dean leaned down and said quietly, "He's not long for this family. Be nice." Damon nodded with acknowledgment. Dean closed the door behind him as he left.

"Okay, boys," Damon said. "I'm taking the bed near the window."

"And I've got the other one," Donald replied. Conrad looked at both boys for a moment.

"Come on, guys," he said. "Those are pretty big beds. We can share them."

"I don't think so," said Damon. Damon walked to the closet near the bathroom and opened the door. In the closet was a folding cot with what loosely could be described as a mattress. He wheeled the cot out of the closet and over toward the door to the room. "Here's your bed," he said to Conrad. "Portable, just like you like it."

Damon and Donald gave each other a high five and each boy removed his street clothes. When they were in their T-shirts and underwear, they drew back the bedspreads, blankets, and sheets, and each boy jumped into his respective bed. Then they each pulled the covers over themselves.

"G'night, bro," Donald said.

"See ya in the morning, kiddo," Damon replied. Damon then reached over to the nightstand near his bed and switched off the light.

Conrad was standing in the semidarkness. There was limited light streaming into the room between the seams in the curtains. This light was accented periodically by flashing red-and-green neon from the road sign.

"Hey," Conrad said. "Can you leave the light on for a minute so I can set up my bed?"

Damon said, "We need our sleep. Can't you open that thing with the available light coming from outside?"

Conrad shook his head in disbelief. He uncoupled the containment bar on the top of the bed. He moved the first side of the bed down. When he did, the bed emitted an enormous, rusty squeak.

"Jesus!" Damon shouted. "We're trying to sleep over here."

Donald let out a snicker.

The cot spoke the same rusty language as Conrad lowered the second side. The cot had bedclothes already covering the mattress, but there was no pillow.

"Can one of you guys let me have a pillow?" Conrad asked.

Through the darkness, a pillow flew from Donald's bed, hitting Conrad in the face.

"Thanks a lot," Conrad said.

Donald snickered again.

Conrad removed his street clothes and got into the tiny cot. As he did, each spring emitted a little squeak. As he adjusted himself, the cacophony continued.

"Christ almighty!" Damon yelled. "Are we gonna have to hear that racket all night long?"

Conrad pulled his pillow under his head and settled into the thin mattress. As he drifted off to sleep, he thought to himself, *What will become of me? I wish I could leave this place and find out where I belong.* As he fell into slumber, a single tear fell from his left eye, rolling down his cheek and alighting on his pillowcase. With that, sleep enveloped him.

Chapter Three

A few hours later, Conrad was awoken by a noise. As he lifted his groggy head to listen, all he heard was the muffled snoring coming from Donald's direction. He listened more but heard nothing else. He replaced his head on his pillow and closed his eyes.

Then he heard it again. It was a miniscule sound, barely perceptible. He listened for a few moments to assure himself he was not dreaming. There it was again. Three light taps coming from somewhere. Conrad sat up in his cot. When he did, the rusty spring orchestra began a new symphony. Conrad flinched at the noise, and with the expectation of the coming berating from Damon, but it did not come. Conrad could still hear Donald snoring, and Damon seemed to remain asleep. He also heard the three taps again. Now he could identify from where they were coming. Someone was tapping on the door to the room.

He stood up and walked to the door. He looked through the peephole to see who was disturbing them at this hour. He saw no one on the other side of the door. As he pulled back from the peephole, he heard the taps again. They were coming from the bottom of the door.

With as much finesse as he could muster, Conrad gently unlatched the locks and opened the room door. He looked down. There at the foot of the doorway was a large black rat. He could see the large outline in the ambient light, but what really caught his attention were the green eyes. They seemed to glow with their own energy. Conrad's own eyes grew wide.

Just as he was about to let out a scream, the rat said, "Do not be afraid. I am here to help you."

Conrad's eyes rolled up into their sockets as he fell backward into the room, unconscious.

Chapter Four

When he awoke, Conrad was lying on the ground, and there were trees all around him. He looked up and saw the face of the most beautiful woman he had ever seen. Her face was perfectly contoured and was rimmed by the darkest black hair. It was the color of night. As she smiled down at him, her cheeks became even more pronounced. Her eyes were the color of emeralds.

"Am I dreaming?" he asked.

"No," she said. "This is no dream. But everything you know to be true is changing."

Conrad lifted himself from the ground and stood. "What are you talking about?" he said.

The woman also stood, and when she did, Conrad was even more shocked. She was over six feet tall, and she was clothed in some sort of armor. Around her waist was a large belt with several rectangular objects attached. Hanging from the belt was a metallic cylinder topped with what appeared to be a rather large diamond. Her boots ran nearly to her knees and were made of cloth but resembled metal of some sort.

"I am Tiana," she said. "I am your sentinel, and I am here to guide and protect you."

Conrad's mind was racing. Was he dreaming? Perhaps he was still lying in his little cot at the motel and all of this was part of his imagination. If it was, it was very vivid imagining. Nonetheless, he could not quite get his mind around what was going on.

"This is no dream, Conrad," Tiana said. "Dreams have a quality to them, no?"

"I guess."

"No, you know."

"But this can't be happening."

"Why? Because it never happened before?"

"It doesn't make sense."

"Many things do not make sense. Some simply are. But everything happens."

Conrad thought about what Tiana had just said to him. *Everything happens? What does that mean?* The phrase seemed vaguely familiar to him. He couldn't quiet recollect why, but as he turned it over in his mind, he had a funny feeling inside.

He looked up and saw that Tiana was staring directly into his eyes. Her emerald eyes seemed to be glowing brightly now. She had a curious smile on her face as she cupped her hands around his cheeks. Her smile grew.

"You know what it means," she whispered. She drew back her hands and just stood before him.

Conrad continued to look at her, not sure how she knew what he was thinking, but he now noticed that her skin seemed iridescent when any of the ambient light touched it.

"Guide me where? And protect me from what?" he asked.

"Very good questions," she replied. "If you have no other questions, then take my hand." She extended her right arm and hand for his acceptance. He stood for a moment looking at her hands. Her long, thin fingers seemed delicate at first glance, but there was also strength in them. Each one ended in a perfectly manicured nail painted black. Conrad gazed up from her hand to her face again. Tiana was not regarding him. Instead, she was staring off toward the horizon.

"What do you see?" he asked.

"Come with me. Let us find out together."

Conrad reached for her outstretched hand, but just before he touched it, he asked, "Where are we going?"

She grabbed his hand and held it tight.

Conrad heard a whooshing sound, and he felt a little light-headed. The disorientation faded quickly but was replaced with confusion. They were no longer standing in the woods.

Instead, they were now on Mulberry Hill Road. The burned-out remains of the Suchuk house stood before them.

"What…how?" said Conrad.

Tiana smiled gently. "All will be revealed," she said. "Come." She walked toward the immolated foundation.

Conrad followed her, still uncertain about many things. As they reached the former front door, Tiana removed a small rectangular device from her belt.

"What is that?" Conrad asked.

"It is my token," Tiana replied. "It is the device that brought us to this place."

Tiana stepped over some burned timbers as she entered the former Suchuk residence. Conrad followed close behind. He looked around, thinking, *I used to live here.*

They were standing where the living room connected to the kitchen before the fire ate through every wall.

Tiana said, "Almost all gone."

"What?" Conrad queried.

"Do you remember your last thought before the fire?"

Conrad thought for a moment: *What was it that was going through my head?*

"I don't recall."

"Think," Tiana demanded.

Conrad reflected back to the night of the fire. The shattered glass candlestick holder, the unrequited anticipation of his castigation by Dean and Joanne Suchuk, the complete silence in a usually rambunctious house, and his ultimate calmness and peace, all leading to his resolution with his lot in life and making him feel empty and alone.

"I just wanted it to be over," he said. "I wanted to move on."

"Yes," Tiana enthused. "And the fire destroyed your confinement."

Conrad thought for a few moments before speaking. When he did, he asked if he caused the fire. "Your intention made your situation change." Tiana said. "You did not will the fire or the disappearance of the family per se, but you did make it possible for you to "move on."

Conrad looked at her. She had a smirk upon her face, which reminded him of someone. He couldn't quite put a finger on it, but at that moment, Tiana reminded him of someone he knew.

"Are you prepared to move on to your new life?" she asked.

"What?"

"For every ending, there is a new beginning. You wanted your life here to be over, and now it is. You must be prepared to enter your new life."

Conrad was getting frustrated. "Why do you talk in riddles all the time?" he said.

"You know why," Tiana replied.

"There you go again. It's really annoying, you know. Just say what you mean!"

Tiana looked at Conrad with a severe countenance. Her eyes were now a darker green, nearly black in color, yet glowing slightly. "Take my hand," she said.

Conrad refused. "I don't even know you. Where are we going?"

"This is your destiny, Conrad, and you know who I am. Come."

She reached out her hand for him to grasp, but Conrad pulled his hand back. A look of disappointment spread across Tiana's face, and she placed her hand at her side.

"Very well," she said. She removed the token from her belt, tapped out a few keystrokes, and returned it to her belt. "Good-bye, Conrad," Tiana said.

"Good-bye?" Conrad said.

But his question lingered on the empty air where Tiana was standing a moment before. She was gone.

Conrad became confused and scared. Panic overtook him with a rush of chemicals in his veins.

"Wait!" he yelled into the empty night. "Don't leave me here!"

He looked around the charred remains of the house, searching for her. Nothing remained but the burned-out reminders of the life he lived with the Suchuks. He went out through the kitchen into the backyard. Again, nothing was there save the remnants of the previous conflagration. His entire field of vision was littered with torched timbers, sodden furniture, and melted appliances. He ran frantically to the center of the backyard. He turned around to take in the entire landscape to seek any clue to where she'd gone. The house sat before him in its partial majesty, a consumed monument to its former self. But still, he saw nothing to indicate where she'd gone.

"Tiana," he whispered into the darkness.

"Yes" was the reply.

Startled, Conrad fell to the ground. He looked up at her and saw that she was once again smiling at him, her green eyes glowing. She reached down to him, and he took her hand. She lifted him to his feet.

"You left me," he said.

"No, I did not. I will always be here to guide and protect you, but you must decide your destiny. I cannot decide for you."

Conrad studied the look upon her face. Tiana was serious but understanding of his reluctance.

"Can I come back here if I want to?"

"If you wish, you may return, yes,"

Conrad took a long last look around. There was nothing there of any importance to him, just familiarity, and in his short life, familiarity was fleeting.

"I'm ready," he said.

Tiana removed the token again. She tapped several keystrokes into its face. The air around them began to churn wildly as if a sudden storm were approaching from the horizon. She reached out her hand for Conrad's grasp, and he took hold. He looked up at her and saw her hair flying about her head and face. She was looking toward the kitchen, smiling. Conrad was looking in the same direction.

What he saw made his eyes grow wide. A small white point of light was hovering in the center of the kitchen. As he watched, it lengthened into a vertical line segment reaching from the kitchen floor to where the ceiling had been before the fire. At this point, the wind was rushing around them and was making its way toward the line of light. Conrad watched as the light line expanded sideways, finally forming a rectangular doorway. It was bright white, and it was sucking the air around them into it.

"Ready?" Tiana asked.

Conrad paused for a moment, staring at the white portal. Then he nodded his consent. Tiana pushed off the ground with both feet, and the two floated on the wind toward the doorway. As they approached it, Conrad closed his eyes.

The next moment, Conrad could no longer hear the rushing wind. He heard nothing initially. Instead, his mind was focused on another sensation—warmth upon his face. He opened his eyes and saw that the sun was shining. It was very bright, and Conrad had to squint while his pupils took several seconds to adjust. He looked around to get his bearings even though he was quite disoriented. They were standing on a ridge overlooking a vast valley below them.

The valley was lush with vegetation. There was a small river flowing through it, and Conrad saw movement through the trees and foliage, but he could not see what or who it was. He also saw down below what looked like a village in a clearing. He could not see any people or other signs of life from this distance, but he sensed there were people living there. Conrad smiled, but the longer he looked, the more his mind began to race.

"Where are we?" he asked.

"Welcome to the Overworld. This is your new home."

Tiana looked at him, smiling. Conrad smiled back, but he had so many questions swimming around in his head: *Where is this place? Are we still in California? The United States? On Earth?* None of these questions seemed appropriate to ask at that moment.

He tried to focus on the now and asked, "Does anyone live in that little town?"

"We will find out together," Tiana said. "That is where we are going."

With his hand still in hers, Tiana stepped toward the edge of the ridge, pulling Conrad behind her.

"No, wait!" Conrad cried. "We'll fall!"

Tiana stepped off the ridge, dragging Conrad. As they reached the empty space off the ridge's edge, Conrad anticipated falling to his death. Instead, the two of them floated above the valley floor below.

Conrad's head was shifting to and fro. He was trying to understand what was happening to them. He lifted his right foot and slammed it down. He felt something stop his foot. There seemed to be an invisible floor upon which they stood. Tiana just smiled gently.

"Down," she said, and as if the two were standing in a transparent elevator, they began to descend into the valley below.

When the clear elevator nearly reached the valley floor, it began to move horizontally. They were now heading toward the clearing and the village. The clearevator stopped approximately one hundred yards from the entrance to the village. Tiana stepped forward, walking toward the little town. Conrad followed but held his hand in front of him, feeling for a door. Once he was comfortable that they had exited the clearevator, Conrad dropped his arms to his sides.

As they continued to walk toward the town, he could see that, indeed, the town was inhabited. He saw several people walking about. Some were carrying things: packages, bags, tools. Others were walking, talking, and living life.

Conrad noticed there was great diversity in the style of clothing the people wore. Some of the women he saw were dressed in what looked like nineteenth-century Victorian garb. Others were dressed in modern fashion. He saw one man clothed in a simple loincloth. *Clearly*, Conrad thought, *I am not in California anymore.*

He was walking behind Tiana when she suddenly stopped short. He was about to ask her why she stopped when he noticed movement in the trees on either side of the town gates.

There was a thick overgrowth of trees and vegetation surrounding the outer walls of the village. At the sides of the entry gates were tall stands of trees that appeared to be eucalyptus except for the fact that their leaves were purple. As Conrad and Tiana approached the front gate, the eucalyptus began to move violently. Suddenly, from both sides of the entry gate, two Tyrannosaurus rexes emerged. Both T. rexes bowed, teeth gnashing, and Conrad saw there were men saddled on their backs.

"Approach," said the rider on the right, "and be identified."

Tiana walked toward the right rider and, once again, removed the token from her belt. She handed it to the rider.

"Thank you for your cooperation, but who is this one?" The rider was pointing directly at Conrad.

"He's Trinity-Two," Tiana replied.

Both of the rider's faces changed. They each looked shocked and a little scared. Here were two men riding on the backs of two dinosaurs, and they were afraid? *Afraid of me*, Conrad thought.

"You may both enter," the right rider said. "Thank you again for your patience. Be well."

With that, each T. rex lifted its head, let out a piercing roar, and then ran off in perfect synchronization.

"What was that all about?" Conrad asked.

"There is much for you to learn," Tiana replied. "For now, just know that there is evil here also. Security is important to protect the villagers from evildoers." Tiana put a hand on each of Conrad's shoulders and smiled. "I am glad you are here."

Conrad smiled back. "What's Trinity-Two?"

Tiana removed her hands from Conrad and stood straight. "It is who you are. It is why I was sent for you. It is why you are here."

"But what does it mean?" Conrad asked.

"Come," Tiana said. "All your questions will be answered soon."

They walked through the village gates. The main street was not paved, yet there were automobiles moving up and down the lane. There were horses, carriages, and buckboards, too. Along each side of the main street were shops, restaurants, and other businesses of all types. Some were familiar to him and others were not. He saw a candy store. Filligan's was the name on the marquee. Next to it was a shop called Blasto's House of Tonsorio.

"What is that place?" Conrad asked.

"Stay out of there for a while," she said. "I will explain it to you later."

Tiana and Conrad continued along the main street. As they did, a man was walking toward them. He was very tall—nearly eight feet tall, in Conrad's estimation. He was also extremely thin. He was dressed in a dark-green linen suit, and he was wearing a dark-green hat. As he approached them, he tipped his hat at Tiana. She smiled back. As the man walked by, Conrad noticed that he was indeed very thin. In fact, he was two-dimensional; as he passed, Conrad saw him virtually disappear for a brief moment. From the side, this man was merely a plane in space. As he walked farther in the opposite direction, Conrad saw him from the back. Every aspect looked in order from that vantage point. *This is a very strange place, indeed*, Conrad thought to himself.

"Yes, it is," Tiana said.

"What?" Conrad spewed.

Tiana simply smiled.

"You can read minds?"

"Yes, and so can you, if you practice, but I digress. We are expected."

"Expected? Where?"

"You will see."

Tiana led him farther along the main street in the village. As they proceeded, Conrad was exhilarated and confused at the same time. None of the people here on Overworld seemed to follow any sort of social protocol. Even a method of transportation resisted conformity.

Several people were traveling on horseback. Others were transporting themselves on what appeared to be flying carpets. As Tiana and Conrad continued, they eventually reached an intersection. The signs indicated it was the intersection of Walker and Smithson. No street, avenue, boulevard, road, or way was included in the street names. The streets were simply called Walker and Smithson.

As they reached the intersection, Tiana led him to a building located on the corner. It was a four-story building, rectangular in orientation. As he looked at the front facade, Conrad happened to move his head slightly to the left. When he did, the walls of the building seemed to flex and rebound as if they were made of rubber. He moved his head again, this time to the right, and again, they flexed, but in the opposite direction. He was amused by the effect and moved his head back and forth, smiling to himself. He did this until he noticed Tiana watching him, and he immediately felt the familiar flood of embarrassment.

Tiana then pointed above the doorway to a posted sign that read, *Zzyzx*. "Here we are," Tiana said. "Stay near me while we are here."

"Count on it," Conrad replied as they entered the establishment.

Inside, Conrad saw that they had entered a bar and grill of some sort. It was a sporadically lit place where several individuals were seated conversing with a neighbor, nursing a drink, or enjoying something to eat. There was a long bar located at the back, and there were also tables strewn throughout the interior; each had a single light located in the center of it. Walking farther into the place, Conrad noticed that each table light was not actually connected to the table's surface. Rather, each light floated just above the tabletop. Conrad shook his head in disbelief.

Tiana led them to the back of Zzyzx where the bar was located. She stopped and signaled the barkeep. *He's interesting looking*, thought Conrad. And he was. His head seemed to be slightly too large for his body. Conrad could not exactly put his finger on it, but there was definitely something not quite right about his look. Maybe one of his eyes was lower than the other. Maybe his accessory features were slightly off kilter, but there was a clear anti-symmetry. The barkeep approached them.

"You're late," he said to Tiana.

"It could not be helped. Is he here?"

The barkeep looked Conrad up and down, analyzing his existence. "In the back. I'll get him."

The barkeep walked through a small door behind the bar and disappeared. Tiana watched as he exited. Conrad touched Tiana's elbow, and she looked at him.

"There is nothing to fear here," she said, "for I am with you."

Conrad took in what she'd said. "I'm just really confused."

"I understand. When we have completed our business here, I will explain what I can."

The barkeep returned through the same small doorway. He was followed by another man. The second man's complexion was darker than the barkeep's, and his hair was the color of winter's first snow. He was wearing a moustache, and he stood about five feet tall. He wasn't exactly a dwarf since he was perfectly proportioned, but there was something uncommon about him. As he walked closer to the bar, he seemed to rise up from the floor. When he stopped, his face was even with Tiana's. He looked at Conrad, taking in all that the boy was about. He smiled.

"You found him," he said.

"Yes" was Tiana's response.

The man reached out his hand, offering it to Conrad. "Gunter Went," he said, pronouncing the "W" as a "V." "I've been looking forward to this day for a long time."

Conrad took his hand and shook it. Gunter's hand felt strange to Conrad. It did not feel the way flesh feels. It seemed denser, more durable than common skin, bone, muscle, and sinew.

Gunter retracted his hand and looked back at Tiana and said, "We need to talk—privately." Conrad's face showed grave concern. "Don't leave me," he whispered to Tiana.

"I will be just over there," she said, pointing to a small table in a dimly lit alcove.

"Stay at the bar. If you need me, I will be here."

Tiana walked away toward the alcove. Gunter disappeared for a moment behind the bar, and then he reappeared, walking to the alcove behind Tiana. Conrad watched them sit together at the table. They began talking.

Conrad looked down at the floor beneath his feet. He was trying to make sense of all of this. The only thing that did make sense was that he was dreaming, that right now he was still in his own bed, in the Suchuk house, sleeping, and all of this was created in his imagination only. All he needed to do was wake up, and he could go on with his pitiful excuse for a life.

"Can I getcha anything?" the barkeep asked.

Conrad looked up. "Nothing, thanks."

"Really? It's on the house. Anything ya like."

Conrad thought for a moment. "I don't suppose you have a Coke, do you?"

A glass filled with ice-cold Coca-Cola materialized on the bar top right in front of Conrad.

"Coke it is," said the barkeep, and he walked away smiling.

Conrad reached for the glass. Just before touching it, he stopped his hand for a second. Tentatively, he continued wrapping his hand around the glass. It was solid and cold. The glass was sweating from condensation. Conrad lifted the glass from the bar, raising it to his lips. He felt the bubbles exploding from the liquid in the glass. He smelled the aroma of Coca-Cola. He took a small sip. The liquid tasted like Coke; it was cold and it was good.

Conrad pressed the glass to his lips and took another large sip. A smile grew upon his face. It was just about the best-tasting Coke he had ever had. He put the glass back down on the bar and wiped the condensation from his hand.

Conrad leaned back on his barstool with both hands on the bar. He smiled a little, thinking about the flavor of the drink. *This might not be too bad*, he thought. He looked to his left and saw a young man sitting next to him drinking what appeared to be a draught beer. Then he looked to his right.

There, sitting next to him on the right, was another man with the biggest head he had ever seen. As he examined the man closer, he realized the large dome was not an anomaly. The body to which the head was attached was just as large. Conrad now knew where the term *behemoth* came from.

"What's yer problem?" the behemoth bellowed.

Conrad backed up a bit at the sound and the smell.

"You, little man. Why are you staring at me?"

"Sorry," Conrad stuttered.

"Sorry, is it?" said the man; then he rose from his stool. His height exceeded nine feet, and his balled-up fists were the size of overstuffed Thanksgiving turkeys. He glared down at Conrad and said, "Yer gonna be sorry."

Conrad inhaled what he thought was his last breath and closed his eyes. A moment later, he heard a scream. At first, he thought, *Have I left my body, and am I hearing myself scream in pain?* He opened his eyes, and what he saw surprised and shocked him.

There, crumpled on the floor before him, was the behemoth, whimpering. He was cradling the cauterized stump of this left leg. The detached appendage was lying beside him, pulsing slightly. Standing over him was Tiana. She was reattaching the diamond-tipped cylinder to her belt.

"Come," she said to Conrad. "We must go now."

They walked out of Zzyzx into the street. Tiana turned right, walking farther toward the center of the village. Conrad followed her, staying several steps behind as they walked in silence. After several moments, she stopped and turned toward Conrad.

"You have questions?" she asked.

Conrad looked up at Tiana's face and then down at the ground. He repeated this several times trying to find the words.

"I did what I had to do to protect you from harm," Tiana said.

"You could have killed him."

"If I needed to do so, yes, I could have."

Conrad had so many questions to ask her, but he didn't know how.

"Come," Tiana said. "I will show you."

She walked farther along the road until they came to a small intersection. To the right, the road was called Coletus. To the left was an alley. Tiana walked to the left. The alley was damp and dirty; however, Conrad thought it strange that there was an absence of garbage there. Back home, in Southern California, it seemed that alleys always were littered with garbage. Conrad followed Tiana to the end of the alley.

"The man I hurt," she said, "I had no choice. He was committed to hurting you."

"How did you know?"

"I saw his thoughts."

"Saw his thoughts?" Conrad asked. "What the heck does that mean?"

Tiana reached her hand out to him. "What am I doing?" she asked.

"You are reaching for me."

"How do you know I am reaching for you?"

Conrad thought this was a very stupid question. It was quite obvious that she was reaching for him. Then it hit him, and a smile crossed his face. "Because I saw you reach for me."

"And it is no different for me when I see a thought," she said. "However, sometimes I am able to see actions in advance. You will learn to do this also." Tiana stopped to allow Conrad time to absorb what she'd said, and then she removed her token, looked at its faceplate, and returned it to her belt. "We should go now," Tiana said.

She began to walk back toward the main road but stopped after a few steps when she realized she wasn't being followed. She turned around to see where Conrad was. He was still standing in the same place he had been moments before.

"You have many more questions," Tiana broached.

"Yes," Conrad replied.

"In light of what just happened, would you be too disappointed if I answered them at another time? I want to get you to safety."

Conrad looked at her and then looked at the metal cylinder hanging from her belt. "Can I see how it works?" he asked.

She removed the diamond-topped cylinder and held it before her. An instant later, the diamond rose from the cylinder portion, pulling a glowing thread behind it. The diamond was now positioned approximately three feet above the cylinder, and it began to spin rapidly on its axis. Tiana placed her other hand on the cylinder, holding it in a combat grip. She moved into a combat stance and began to swing the device through the air. Each time the glowing thread moved through the air, a crackling sound was created.

When Tiana completed her demonstration kata, she stood straight and saluted Conrad. The diamond retracted back onto the tip of the cylinder.

"Are you satisfied?" Tiana asked.

"May I hold it?" Conrad asked.

Tiana offered the cylinder to him. Conrad reached out and took it from her. He noticed right away that it was heavier than it appeared. It was not too heavy for him to hold properly; it was just a more substantial device than he had supposed.

"It is my scepter," Tiana said.

"May I turn it on?" Conrad asked.

"It is tuned to my genetic signature," she replied. "No one else can operate it."

Conrad examined it closer. The diamond was fixed to the end. The entire shaft did not appear to have any manufacturing imperfections. It looked like it was created from one single piece of metal.

"You will have yours soon," Tiana interrupted.

"I will?" Conrad asked as a great smile grew on his face.

Tiana smiled back at him. "Yes," she said. "But let us go now."

They walked back up the alley toward the main road. When they reached the terminus, Tiana stopped.

"Where are we going," Conrad asked.

"Would you like to see where you will live?"

Farther along the road, toward the end of the town, there was a five-point intersection. Each of the divergent streets went off into a different direction. None of the roads had signs identifying a street name. From Conrad's perspective, every street looked exactly the same as the next.

Tiana stopped walking as they arrived there. She was looking at all the streets, each one winding in a different direction. Conrad looked up at her to see if he could identify her intention.

He started to ask Tiana a question when she said, "Wait and watch."

Conrad returned his gaze to the five roads diverging before them. Suddenly, a great rumbling in the ground beneath their feet began. Conrad had lived through several earthquakes back home. The sensation he felt now was similar—but different.

As he continued looking at the five points before him, he saw the roads change. Each one was changing its location and direction. Just as the streets each found its new direction and orientation, there was a small flash of light on the second road from the left.

"Did you see that?" Tiana asked.

"The light? Yes, I saw it."

"Good. That is where we are going. You take the lead."

Conrad started walking down the second road from the left, and Tiana followed close behind. The road twisted farther to the left and then doubled back to the right. There were trees on both sides of the road for portions of the trip. Finally, they reached a clearing. At the end of the road, in the midst of the clearing, was a large Queen Anne–style house. It was painted multiple colors, but all the trim was white. As they walked farther toward the house, Conrad noticed that the front door opened as if responding to a remote control. A small man was standing just inside the entrance. He was dressed in a small three-piece suit. Conrad and Tiana stepped up to the front porch and walked to the open door.

The small man smiled. "Welcome to Turner Manor," he said. "We've been expecting you, Master Turner."

Conrad and Tiana walked through the door. Conrad noticed immediately that the inside of the house was much more spacious than the exterior size of the house indicated. From the foyer, Conrad saw the room open into a much larger room. The ceiling in this great room was invisible to Conrad due to its altitude above the floor. There were multiple banisters with walkways all the way up the sides of the great room. Conrad counted fourteen floors, but he just knew there were more beyond his sight.

The small man reached out his hand to Conrad. "I am called Twix," he said.

"Pleasure meeting you, Twix," Conrad replied, shaking Twix's hand. "Conrad Turner."

At this, Twix began chuckling. "Everyone knows who you are, sir."

Conrad looked at Tiana, befuddled.

"There is much we must discuss," she said to Conrad. She then looked at Twix and said, "Twix, show Master Turner to his room. When he is relaxed and ready, please show him to my study."

"Very well, my lady," Twix replied. "Come, Master Turner."

Twix walked into the great room. Conrad hesitated for a moment and looked up at Tiana again. She gave him a slight smile and gestured for Conrad to follow Twix. Conrad smiled back and then proceeded toward the great room.

Every wall in the great room was covered with artwork. Oil paintings, watercolors, collages, charcoal drawings, they all existed in a great display. Conrad had no formal education in the arts, but many of the pieces were familiar to him. Many of the pieces were world famous. Halfway across the room, Conrad recognized an old oil painting. He knew it was painted by an artist named Van Gogh or something.

He remembered watching a television program on famous artists when he was staying with the Suchuks. The narrator pronounced the name "Van Gock," but the "ck" sound remained in the throat. He had also heard it pronounced "Van Go," which was exceedingly more palatable to him.

"There's lots of art in this house," he said to Twix. "They all look very real."

Twix stopped short and turned. "I assure you, Master Turner," he said, "every piece is an original work by the original artist."

Conrad was incredulous. *That can't be true*, he thought. *This little fidget is a liar!*

They continued across the room until they arrived at the base of a huge staircase. The stairs rose to the right and left and, one floor up, connected with the walkways up above. From this vantage point, Conrad could see that every floor, within his visual range, had a similar staircase just above where they were standing.

"What floor is my room on, Twix?" Conrad asked.

"It's the penthouse, sir. Floor thirty-five" was the reply.

"You're joking," Conrad said. "First of all, how can this tiny house have thirty-five floors?" *How could it have even the fourteen that I counted?* he thought. "Second, do you expect me to climb thirty-five floors to get there? Where's the elevator?"

"There is no elevator, sir," Twix said. "I thought you might wish to get oriented by walking around the place. Get the 'lay of the land,' so to speak. If you would rather not, there is another way."

Conrad was getting a little confused by all the doublespeak. "I'd rather just get there, thank you," he said.

There was a great flash of light. So bright was it that Conrad had to close his eyes to avert the pain. When he opened his eyes again, he was standing in a room looking out a huge picture window. Out the window, Conrad gazed upon a panoramic view of the countryside. In the distance, he saw green-and-purple mountains topped with the remnants of winter snow. There a large river running across the landscape, too. In the air, birds of all types and colors were flying within their respective groups. He also saw something that caused him to gasp involuntarily. Several pteranodons were flying in formation. On each of their backs was a person.

"What the...?" Conrad began.

"Indeed," Twix replied. "Perhaps the master should get comfortable." Twix held out a small pile of clothing and some slip-on shoes.

"What are those for?" Conrad asked.

"For you, sir. Change into them, and when you are ready, come down, and Master Tiana will explain everything to you." Twix laid the clothes and the shoes on a chair near the window and headed toward the door.

"Wait!" Conrad yelled. "How do I get down to the first floor? I don't have to climb down, do I?"

Twix smirked slightly. "When you are ready, picture me in your mind. Then think about coming to me. I will then lead you to Master Tiana's study."

With that, Twix disappeared with a crackle.

Conrad was confused, amazed, and frustrated, all at the same time. He took the clothes given to him by Twix and set them down on a small chair near the bed. He then decided to explore his room in greater detail, just in case he wanted to stay.

The room had two dressers, a walk-in closet, two bathrooms, and a fireplace with a large flat-panel television on the wall above it. In the center of the room, against the wall facing the large window, was the biggest bed Conrad had ever seen. It was nearly fourteen feet long and ten feet wide. It was topped with a beautiful white comforter, and several pillows were stacked against the headboard. Conrad moved closer to the bed. He put his hand on the comforter. It was soft, smooth, and cool to the touch. The surface, although white, seemed to shimmer slightly in the sunlight. *Nice comforter*, he thought. *But I would have preferred green.* Conrad blinked his eyes twice and shook his head in disbelief because no sooner had he thought about the color than the comforter was now a stunning shade of sea foam green with matching pillows.

"I need to lie down," Conrad said out loud.

He climbed onto the bed and crawled to the center. He repositioned two of the pillows to lie flat, and he placed his head upon them. He closed his eyes, trying to get a grasp on all that had happened to him.

Chapter Five

When Conrad reopened his eyes, sitting on the end of his bed, staring at him, was a large black-and-white cat with blazing blue eyes. Conrad was slightly startled, but with every unusual occurrence, he became less so.

"What do you want, cat?" he said.

"I'm simply trying to get a fix on you," said the cat.

Conrad nearly swallowed his tongue. Then he remembered the talking rat he saw when he opened the door to his room at the Best Western.

"Does everything talk here?"

"Don't be silly," said the cat. "Many things don't talk, at least not English."

"So who are you?" Conrad asked.

"Call me See-Two."

That's a strange name, thought Conrad. *But what isn't strange on Overworld?*

"Okay, hello, See-Two. I'm Conrad, Conrad Turner."

"Of course you are," See-Two replied. Conrad and See-Two regarded each other for several moments.

"So, are you my pet?"

"That's an awfully speciesist assumption. Perhaps you are my pet," See-Two said.

Conrad felt his face flushing with embarrassment when See-Two suddenly let out the most uproarious laugh Conrad had ever heard.

"No, no, my boy. I will be your tutor," said See-Two.

"What?" Conrad asked.

"Master Tiana will show you the way, and I will fill in the gaps."

"Clearly, I don't speak Cat because I don't understand a thing you just said."

See-Two got up from his position at the end of the bed and walked up to Conrad until his whiskers were nearly touching Conrad's face. He studied Conrad's visage and regarded him carefully. See-Two reached out his right paw, touching Conrad's forehead.

"You are more intelligent than you know," See-Two said. "And infinitely more powerful, but you must find belief first."

See-Two removed his paw from Conrad's head.

"Get some rest. You have a big life ahead of you."

With that, See-Two disappeared into a point of light.

Conrad was beginning to adjust to all that had happened recently, but he still felt uneasy. He wasn't quite sure what it was, but when he felt the apprehension, it reminded him of all the foster homes in all the counties where he was passed around. He wondered if Tiana and See-Two were right. Was his life going to be better now? Had he really found his way? He wanted to believe. He truly did, but history, his history, had proven wrong many times before. Conrad remained hopeful, though.

Conrad placed his head on a large down pillow. He pulled the green comforter over himself, leaving one leg exposed to the air. He closed his eyes and thought about the T. rex riders. He smiled and thought, *If this is a dream, I hope it never ends.*

Chapter Six

"Wake up," the voice said.

It was only a whisper, but it made Conrad stir.

"Time to get to work," the voice continued.

Conrad opened his eyes slightly. He seemed to be alone in the room. *I'm dreaming*, he thought and closed his eyes again.

"Up," said the voice.

Conrad sprung up in the bed. Not voluntarily, mind you, but he was now seated upright with the covers haphazardly thrown over his legs. With eyes wide open now, he was certain he was alone in the room.

"Who said that?" he asked the air.

For a moment, there was no response.

Suddenly, Conrad heard, "It is I, Tiana."

"Where are you?" he asked aloud even though he could not see Tiana anywhere.

"Get dressed and come down to my study" was the reply.

Conrad pulled back the covers. He stepped onto the floor and walked to the nearby chair, retrieving the clothes Twix had given him earlier. He removed his yellow T-shirt and blue jeans, folded them neatly, and placed them on top of a dresser. He unfolded the new pack of clothes. There was a pair of black loose-fitting pants and a matching top. The top was open at the front, with two long sleeves hanging from the sides.

Conrad slipped on the pants. The legs were extremely long. He had to roll them up several times just to get his feet through the bottom. He then slipped each of his arms through the sleeves in the top. The sleeves hung nearly to the floor. Conrad slid the sleeves up until his hands peeked through the cuffs. He folded the right side of the blouse over the left. When the right side touched the left, the blouse instantly shrunk to a perfect fit, as did the pants.

Conrad looked at himself in a long mirror. He thought he looked presentable in the new outfit. It was very comfortable, and although it was a perfect fit, it was loose enough for freedom of movement.

Conrad pictured Twix in his mind. He then thought, *Take me to Twix.* Conrad felt all the air rush out of his body as if someone had punched him in the solar plexus. When he landed, he stumbled forward slightly. His disorientation caused him to fall to the floor, gasping for air. Twix gently lifted him from the floor.

"It gets easier with practice," Twix said.

As Conrad regained his composure, he looked around. They were standing in a room much smaller than Conrad's. The ceiling was only half as high. The furnishings were made of some sort of reddish-gray wood that appeared to be very dense, and all were designed for someone of a diminutive stature. There were several standard-size chairs in the center of the room. They were set in a circular configuration. At the top of the circle they created was a smaller chair clearly meant for the host, Twix.

"Is this your room, Twix?" asked Conrad.

"Yes, sir," Twix replied. "It's small, quaint, and mine."

Conrad felt a flush of slight embarrassment. Had he interrupted Twix's privacy by appearing unannounced?

"I'm sorry for coming to your room like this," Conrad said.

Twix smiled slightly. "Master Turner, you have much to learn. Let us begin."

Twix and Conrad walked out of the room into a long corridor. They turned left and walked past several doors. Some were closed, but others were open. Conrad saw something looking at him as he passed one particular door. When he turned to look closer, there was nothing there. In another room, several beings were creating frameworks from a material that resembled plastic. Upon the frames, the workers were attaching a transparent material. Conrad looked at the open door. The sign read, *Wing Works*.

"Master Turner," Twix called from farther down the hallway. "No time for dawdling."

Conrad sprinted to catch up to Twix. They reached the end of the hallway together. It ended in a T-intersection with additional corridors extending to the right and to the left. There was a great double door at the terminus. Twix knocked on the door. Not a standard greeting knock, mind you, but rather, he knocked in a sort of code: *Rap-rap. Rap-rappidy-rap.* Twix stepped back from the massive wooden-and-metal doors after knocking. Within seconds, the doors swung open. Twix and Conrad entered.

They were both standing in a room that appeared to be a personal study space. There was a desk near the back wall with a high-back leather chair placed behind it. On the left side, behind the high-back chair, was a recessed alcove. Against the right wall was an ornate grandfather clock, which stood from floor to ceiling. In front of the desk were two smaller reception chairs. Between the two reception chairs was a small round table with a globe on top. It was not a globe of the Earth. Rather, it was inscribed with a strange writing Conrad did not recognize.

Twix was standing silently with his small hands behind his back. Conrad wanted to say something to cut the deafening silence but thought better of it.

Finally, after what seemed like many minutes had passed, Conrad said, "Are we waiting for something?"

"Shhh" was Twix's response.

Oh great! thought Conrad. *This is ridiculous!*

Conrad was getting anxious. At first, he wasn't sure why that was, but then he thought about the Suchuks.

There were many times in his past when he had committed some minor infraction. Prior to Conrad being read the riot act, there was always silence. Some might call it a pregnant pause. It was more than a pause to Conrad. In a house where the standard protocol was cacophonic sound, silence was less than golden because it foreshadowed a coming berating. At least that was Conrad's view.

Now he was mired in another silence. His heart began to race and a small bead of sweat began trickling down his right temple. He wiped it away, instinctively, with the back of his hand. *I've got to get out of here*, he thought. Then, with a flash of light and a crackling, Tiana appeared behind the desk. She was dressed in a black outfit nearly identical to Conrad's. There seemed to be only one difference: Tiana was also wearing a belt. The belt was made of the same material as the blouse, and it was the same color—black. The ends of the belt were emblazoned on both sides with red chevrons. Conrad counted seven chevrons on each end.

"Thank you, Twix," Tiana said aloud. A few moments elapsed before Twix bent slightly at the waist in a perfunctory bow. Then he turned and left the room. The twin doors closed behind him as if helped along by an invisible hand. Twix's hesitation seemed awkward to Conrad.

It was Twix's habit to show respect. He had been raised as a domestic servant since he was a youngster. Everyone in his clan was trained in the nearly lost art and science of domestic servitude. In fact, Twix and his kind were happier when they were serving others than when they were only engaged in self-fulfillment. To be a good servant was the ultimate goal for Twix. It was as natural a reflex for him to bow to someone worthy of respect as it was for another being to respond when spoken to. The challenge, and Twix's hesitation, stemmed from Tiana's disdain for any form of respect directed at her. Her feelings were not based upon a lack of self-esteem; Tiana had that in abundance. Rather, Tiana felt she should earn shows of respect through current deeds, not by reputation. She had told Twix years before, "Many people want commendation for deeds done so long ago that they forget to complete new ones worthy of the esteem of others."

Tiana was looking past Conrad. She was concentrating on the closed twin doors. Conrad regarded her, and the uncomfortable interlude with Twix, with a stark curiosity.

Again, with the silence, he thought. Tiana did not avert her stare at the door even though Conrad knew, or thought he knew, that she knew what he was thinking at that moment.

"I have a question," he blurted.

"Shhhhh" was her reply.

"Don't *shhh* me," he said, irritated.

Tiana drew her emerald eyes upon him. With a stern countenance, she whispered, "You must learn the lessons of the silence."

"What?" he demanded. "What was that you said? I couldn't hear you."

Tiana smiled slightly. "Thus begins today's lesson," she proclaimed.

Tiana clapped her hands together. Almost instantaneously, a grinding sound arose from the alcove behind the desk. Conrad watched intently as the wall in the alcove receded back, leaving a black hole. Then the entire wall behind the desk shifted. The configuration of the room changed rapidly around them both until everything stopped. The small waiting room had changed into a large room with padded mats on the floor and some parts of the walls. Sitting in the center of the room on the floor were four other boys and girls dressed in outfits identical to Conrad's.

"Let us meet your classmates," Tiana suggested.

Tiana walked and Conrad followed her. As they approached the children sitting together, two of the girls whispered to each other and began to giggle. Conrad was positive they were laughing at him for some reason. He reached down unconsciously with his hands to check his nonexistent fly for closure. Tiana stopped before the children.

"Class," she said, "this is your new classmate. Will you all please welcome Conrad Turner?"

With mention of his name, each of the other student's eyes grew wide. One of the boys' mouths dropped open slightly in a mute display of shock and awe. The slighter of the two girls, however, seemed to have no reaction at all. She stood up and walked over to Conrad with her hand extended in a gesture of welcome.

"It's about time you got here," she said. "I'm Mindy, Mindy Taylor."

Conrad reached out to return Mindy's handshake, but he also noticed that Mindy's speech was odd. It sounded more nasally than it should for a girl with a cute button of a nose. *She almost speaks like a deaf person*, he thought.

"Hearing impaired, please," Mindy responded.

Conrad was dumbstruck. "You can hear my thoughts, too?"

"Not really, but I knew what you were feeling. I am empathic, so I can sometimes feel your emotions."

It was then that Conrad noticed two nearly invisible hearing aids in each of Mindy's ears.

"Sorry," Conrad apologized. "I meant no offense."

"None taken," Mindy replied with a smile.

Conrad wanted to think about how beautiful she was, but instead thought about his many fights with Damon Suchuk. Damon thrived on tormenting Conrad. Every emotional jab he could take, he took with relish, and it caused Conrad much pain and sadness. The last thing he needed now was to have his every intimate feeling broadcast to this cute little girl whom he would have to see in class for the next…Who knew how long?

"Thank you for beginning the introductions, Mindy," Tiana said. "Let us continue. Atticus?"

A slightly overweight boy about Conrad's age stood up. He towered over Conrad at nearly Tiana's height.

"I'm Atticus Norman," he said. "Glad to make your acquaintance."

The boys shook hands. As they did, Conrad noticed that Atticus had a difficult time making eye contact with him. His eyes shifted around as they faced each other—first to the floor, then to the ceiling, then to one wall, then to the other.

"Glad to meet you, too," said Conrad.

They released hands and Atticus returned to the mat. The remaining boy and girl both stood at the same time. As they approached Conrad, he noticed they were jockeying for the lead position. The boy ultimately led the way, extending his hand before the girl could.

"I'm Matthew Klein, and this is my sister Matilda," he said.

"Shut up, Matt!" Matilda yelled. "I can introduce myself. Hi, as my dopey brother just informed you, I'm Matilda. My friends call me Matty."

Matthew slapped Matilda on the shoulder. "Hey, square," he said. "I'm Matty."

Matilda turned around to face Matthew. She extended her right arm, bent her right hand up at the wrist, and Matthew was sent flying backward, landing twenty-five feet away.

After a moment, Matthew jumped to his feet and stood with both legs shoulder width apart. He bent his legs at the knees and began to rotate his hands around each other in the space in front of him. It looked like he was grasping for an imaginary ball floating above the floor. Suddenly, Matthew shifted his left leg forward toward Matilda and pushed both of his hands in her direction. Matilda was knocked down to the mat. She struggled to get up, but some invisible force was holding her on the floor.

After several seconds, she got back on her feet. Her eyes were narrowing and she was gritting her teeth together.

"Enough!" shouted Tiana. "Regain your composure, both of you."

Matthew straightened his legs so that he was now standing upright.

Matilda returned the gesture, and a smile grew upon her face. She looked at Conrad and said,

"You'll get used to it. Twins act this way sometimes."

Matilda moved back to the place where she was previously. Matthew also returned to his spot. They looked at each other, smiled, and hugged.

Mindy walked to Conrad and whispered into his ear, "Watch those two."

Conrad sat on the mat next to Mindy. All the students were sitting in a very neat semicircle. Tiana took a position at the open end in the center, and she began her lecture.

"Today we will begin training with a new breathing exercise. Everyone stand up."

Mindy, Atticus, Matthew, and Matilda all sprang to their feet. Conrad rose noticeably slower. As he reached his apex, Conrad felt a sharp pain in his head. He grabbed both sides of his face.

"What's happening?" he cried. The pain stopped. Conrad opened his eyes. Through his pinkies, he saw that Tiana was standing before him.

"Discipline," she said, "will save your life someday. Understand?"

Conrad removed his hands from his face and nodded his agreement.

Tiana continued as she walked amongst the class. "Everyone take position in the ground rex stance."

All the students, save for Conrad, moved their feet shoulder width apart and bent their knees at forty-five-degree angles. They also clenched their hands into fists and withdrew them to their sides at the waist. Conrad mimicked each action as best as he could, but he felt hopelessly lost. *What am I doing here?* he thought.

"You will understand," Tiana said. "Mindy, please show Conrad how to take the ground rex stance."

Mindy stood in front of Conrad. She explained each step taken to create a strong, grounded stance. Conrad followed her directions and asked, "Is this right?" Mindy smiled and returned to her previous position. Conrad watched her and smiled, too.

"Thank you," Tiana said. "Now, breathing is the key to life. And correct breathing in battle can mean the difference between life and death."

Tiana herself dropped into a ground rex stance. She began measured breathing, inhaling through the nose and exhaling through the mouth. As she did, she unclenched her fists. With palms extended in front of her, she drew her hands and arms back with each inhale. On the exhale, she pushed them forward, leaving a slight bend in her elbows.

"Remember, inhale through the nose, exhale through the mouth, and keep your tongue lightly touching the roof of your mouth."

Conrad did not understand why it was important to keep his tongue touching the top of his mouth while breathing.

"Ask me later" came Tiana's voice in Conrad's head.

So focused was he that the sound of Tiana's thought in his head at that moment caused Conrad to blurt out, *"What?"*

The entire class turned in his direction, staring. Conrad's face turned red.

"Sorry," he apologized. "This is all very, very new and very, very strange to me."

"That's okay, Connie," Matthew said. "We've all been there."

"I haven't," announced Matilda.

"Of course not, sis," said Matthew in response.

As Matilda turned her back, Matthew pointed his right finger at his temple and rotated it. He simultaneously stuck his tongue out the side of his mouth and crossed his eyes. His classmates snickered at his cuckoo pantomime.

Once the class regained its composure, Tiana ran through several more breathing drills. After a while, she told them to retrieve a training scepter.

"Conrad," she said, "I have yours here."

She handed Conrad a well-worn scepter topped with a dark-blue crystal. Conrad was disappointed, and it showed on his face. Tiana touched him, and he looked into her eyes.

"Do not be deceived," she said. "This is no ordinary scepter. There is more to it than meets the eye."

The class spread out in the training room. Matthew and Matilda paired up.

Conrad said to Mindy, "I guess we're partners."

Mindy smiled.

"Remember, class," Tiana said, "training rules apply. That means when any one of you says 'tap,' the fight is over."

Tiana turned toward Matilda. "Also, if anyone thinks 'tap,' the same applies. Understand?"

Matilda's smile faded and she nodded yes.

Conrad and Mindy faced each other.

"I don't know how this works," Conrad said.

"It's easy," replied Mindy. "Hold the scepter like this." Mindy demonstrated the correct technique by grasping the bottom of the scepter with her left hand and placing her right hand near the crystal. "Now, think 'go' and let her rip."

The crystal on Mindy's scepter arose from the base, dragging the glowing thread behind it.

"Wait a minute," Conrad proclaimed. "I saw someone's leg hacked off with this thing. We can't practice like this. It's not safe."

"Touch the thread," Mindy said.

"No way! Are you nuts?"

Mindy leaped at Conrad, striking his left shoulder. He felt an immediate sensation of heat and electricity.

"Ouch!" he wailed. "That hurt!" Conrad rubbed his shoulder where he was struck.

"You are protected in the training arena," Tiana proclaimed. "Every scepter defaults to stun in here."

He pulled the top of his blouse down slightly to see if there was any damage to his skin. There was none.

"See, you big baby," Mindy chortled. "Are you gonna fight, or are you gonna cry?"

Conrad grasped his scepter the way Mindy had shown him. Just as he thought *go*, the blue crystal spun rapidly and rose from the base. The thread following the crystal was also glowing blue. Conrad found this unusual since every other scepter he had seen had a white, glowing thread.

"So, how do we do this?" he asked.

"Eeeyaaaaahhh," Mindy screeched as she leaped toward Conrad, swinging her scepter in a wide but carefully determined arc. In the nick of time, Conrad thrust his scepter up over his head defensively. As the two threads collided, sparks flew from both filaments.

"Are you crazy?" Conrad yelled.

"You have no idea," Mindy retorted.

Mindy retracted into an attack stance: left leg extended forward with toes pointed at a forty-five-degree angle. She placed her right leg behind her, and she carefully balanced her weight over the center. She positioned her left arm with open palm facing Conrad while she held her scepter over her head with her right hand.

"If that's the way you want it…" Conrad challenged, and he ran at her, holding his weapon next to his right ear.

As he approached Mindy's position, he swung his scepter straight down, aiming for Mindy's head. She parried his strike with her scepter and recoiled into a full spin. As she unwound, she struck Conrad in the back diagonally from shoulder to waist.

"You're dead, sucker," she proclaimed.

Conrad, wincing from the shock, heat, and pain, said, "Looks like I need lots of practice. Tap."

Both withdrew their weapons and moved to the side of the battle zone. Mindy sat down first. Conrad sat close enough to her that their thighs touched.

"Oh, sorry!" he exclaimed and moved to provide some personal space between them.

Mindy smiled.

"You're pretty good," Conrad said.

"Thanks," replied Mindy.

"How long have you been here?"

"Not too long. My parents disappeared a few years ago. I lived with some relatives for a while, but they didn't adjust to my disabilities very well."

"What do you mean?" he asked.

"They were always calling me deaf and dumb. Well, not all of them. My mom's aunt Martha understood. She was losing her hearing due to age—she was eighty-nine—but the rest of them were…"

"Cruel?" Conrad offered.

"Ignorant," replied Mindy. "One morning, I heard a rapping on my bedroom window," Mindy continued. "I looked outside and there was a big black crow sitting there. He was looking at me when I noticed his eyes were bright blue. Then he spoke to me."

"Really?" Conrad asked. "Was it Tiana?"

Mindy let loose with a huge guffaw. "No, silly. I said *he*. Weren't you listening to me?" Conrad felt stupid for saying that, but for some reason, he was nervous around Mindy.

"Yes, I heard what you said. I just didn't realize that others from here went back home."

"We each have our own sentinel," Mindy explained. "You'll meet Donovan soon enough. So how did you get here?"

Suddenly, a piercing siren sounded. Conrad covered his ears with both hands. The others did nothing except stop and return to their positions in the semicircle. When Conrad saw this, he got up and ran over to his spot, too.

When the siren ended, Tiana was smiling at her students.

"Good effort today, class," she said. "Some of you need to work on basic movement, but overall, not a bad outing. Are there any questions?"

Conrad looked at his classmates. No one seemed to have any questions, yet his head was filled with nothing but. He started to raise his hand tentatively when he heard in his head, *Later*. He retracted his arm quickly.

Tiana said, "Good. Remember, tonight, before you go to sleep, picture how you want to perform each maneuver in your mind. Soon you will each perform them flawlessly. Class dismissed."

Matthew and Matilda bolted for the door.

Atticus sauntered toward the exit. As he passed, he waved to Conrad, but before exiting, he turned and said, "Conrad, I want to spar with you next time."

Mindy also walked by Conrad as she left. "See you later?" she asked.

"Yes," Conrad replied. A slight smile grew on his face. Conrad watched as Mindy walked out of the training arena. When she reached the exit, Mindy turned to see if Conrad was watching. Of course he was. He was so overcome with embarrassment about being discovered that he hadn't noticed that Tiana was standing behind him.

"She is a nice girl," Tiana said, "and a good warrior. Yours will be a fruitful alliance."

"What do you mean?" Conrad asked.

Tiana ignored the question. "Come," she said instead. "Let us return to my study. It is time to answer more of your questions."

They walked out of the arena, reentering Tiana's study. Once they were fully inside, the alcove closed and once again appeared to be nothing more than a recessed area in the wall.

Tiana sat down in her high-back chair. Conrad stood next to her desk, looking over his left shoulder.

"What are you looking for?" Tiana asked.

Conrad did not answer right away. His bottom lip began quivering slightly, and he felt as if he were going to lose it. *Don't cry, you stupid baby!* he thought.

"Have a seat, Conrad," Tiana suggested.

Conrad moved to the guest chair nearest the alcove. As he sat down, he eased himself into the upholstery, supporting himself on both arms of the chair. Once sitting, he clasped his hands together, intertwining his fingers. Tiana waited to be sure he was fully composed before beginning. Once she was satisfied, she leaned forward, placing both elbows on the desktop.

"Questions," she said. "You have them, and I am here to answer as many as I can."

Conrad sorted through all the questions in his head for a few moments. He realized that many of them were simplistic, and he could probably find the answers on his own. There were a few, however, that he felt compelled to ask.

"In the training arena, you told us to keep our tongues touching the roof of our mouths. Why?"

Tiana placed her hands on the desktop and said, "Every living being has an intrinsic energy field within them. This energy moves within your body, but if there is a broken circuit, it stops. Touching your tongue to the roof of your mouth completes the circuit and allows a warrior to access this intrinsic energy when needed."

Conrad considered what she'd said and agreed it made sense. Then his demeanor became more serious and he looked up at Tiana.

"You called me Trinity-Two. What does that mean?"

Tiana smiled. It was a brilliant question, but also one pregnant with challenges for Conrad's fortitude.

"What do you remember about your father?" asked Tiana.

Conrad had very unclear memories of his father. Just shadows of memories, really. Sometimes when he thought about it, he had the feeling that he once had very detailed memories of him. Periodically, certain images would flash in his mind's eye that fostered wonderful feelings. Inevitably, though, if he followed those thoughts, they led to emptiness. He did have one memory burned into his subconscious, however.

"I remember him walking out on my mother and me."

Tiana nodded her head up and down slightly in understanding. "Did anyone explain to you why he left?" she asked.

"He didn't love us," Conrad replied. "Isn't that why all fathers leave?"

"Conrad," Tiana began, "people leave their children for all sorts of reasons—some selfish, some noble. Your father left to save you."

"To save me from what?"

Tiana reclined back in her chair slightly as she spoke. "Your question was regarding Trinity-Two. You are one element of a powerful triumvirate composed of Trinity-One, Trinity-Two—you, Conrad—and Trinity-Three."

Conrad's youth made it difficult to grasp the gravity of what Tiana was explaining.

"I don't understand," he said. "What does it mean?"

Tiana explained. Many years ago, a great and powerful being named Myrddin was exiled by his jealous brother Dualoc. These two brothers were so adept at creating whatever it was that they desired that myths and legends grew around their abilities, and many people proclaimed them as sorcerers, wizards, and witches. Before Myrddin was cast out, though, he decreed that there would be, one day, a trinity of souls who would bring order to the chaos. So powerful would be this union of souls that all other sorcerers would be rendered powerless.

"Today," Tiana explained, "it is known that all living beings have the power to create. What was once considered magic, sorcery, witchcraft, is now known to be a universal truth: everything in the universe is creative. Some beings are simply more talented creators than others. Those who were once called sorcerers are now called incepts. You, Conrad, are one of the most powerful incepts in history, and you are part of the Alliance of Souls."

Conrad's head was swimming. *What is she talking about? I'm a weakling, loser.*

"No, you are not!" Tiana exclaimed. "Your father, Nathaniel Turner, is Trinity-One. You, Trinity-Two, and your brother…"

Conrad jumped out of his seat.

"Brother! What brother?" he shouted. "I don't have a brother!"

"Yes, you do," Tiana said calmly. "Actually, Gabriel is your half-brother, but he is your brother nonetheless."

Conrad returned to his seat, grasping the arms of the chair with a vice-like grip. He began to hyperventilate. He felt himself getting light-headed; his peripheral vision narrowed until all he could see was a light tunnel surrounded by darkness. He stood up again and staggered toward the door. Just before he fell to the floor, he heard a crackle.

When Conrad awoke, he was lying in the large bed in his room. Tiana was sitting in a chair next to his bed, looking out the window. The sun was out and there were small purple clouds highlighting the sky. Conrad felt moisture on his forehead. He reached up and removed a damp washcloth. He placed the washcloth on the nightstand. Tiana moved her gaze from the window to Conrad. Her eyes were now shining with a light-green tint. She smiled at Conrad. He returned the gesture.

"How do you feel?" she asked.

"I'm okay, I guess."

"What do you remember?"

"You told me I'm a powerful sorcerer or something. You told me my father has another son—that I have a brother I never met. Does that about cover it?"

Tiana's smile increased to a grin. "I still owe you some more answers, if you feel up to it."

Conrad thought for a few moments. He thought about when Tiana had said she was there to protect him. From what, or from whom, did he need protection? He also thought about her saying "everything happens." That really threw him for a loop. He really wasn't up for discovering there were evil incepts or some other such nonsense after him. Neither did he want to wrap his mind around a riddle. Then it came to him.

"What's Blasto's House of Tonsorio?"

Tiana rose from her seat and said, "Let us go and discover together."

Chapter Seven

When they arrived at Blasto's, there was a line of people waiting to enter. *What is going on in there?* Conrad thought. He looked up at Tiana, and he saw she was looking right back, smiling that smile. He noticed that her eyes were now violet in color.

It made Conrad uneasy knowing that Tiana knew his every thought. *I have no privacy, but what else is new?*

Tiana knelt down next to Conrad. "I don't know your every thought," she said. "If I want to see your thoughts, I need to tune in to your frequency, much like a radio." She stood up and pointed to all the people standing in line. "I can hear every one of their thoughts. Can you imagine what the noise would be like if I could not select which ones I heard?"

Conrad thought about that for a moment. He imagined it would sound like the Suchuk house—a cacophony of voices indistinguishable from one another. When he lived there, he was able to avoid the noise by gulping down his food and running to his room. Hearing such a noise in one's head would leave no place of respite.

"If it makes you uncomfortable, I will stop listening," Tiana said.

"Thank you," Conrad replied.

He smiled at her. She was the first person in a long time who truly considered his feelings. It made Conrad feel important in some small way, and it made him happy.

As the line moved forward, Conrad noticed a group of three girls. They were each more or less in their early teens—two brunettes and a redhead. The brunettes weren't bad looking, Conrad thought, but the redhead was spectacular. Her eyes were the color of robin's eggs, and she had only one freckle that Conrad could make out. It was planted just under her left eye, and it was of a very light-brown tone, barely visible.

The girls were having a conversation in hushed tones. Interspersed with their whispers were giggles, sighs, and protestations; however, he couldn't hear more than a word here and there.

"Why don't you practice your teleauditation?" Tiana asked.

"My what?" Conrad asked.

"Mind hearing," Tiana explained. "Most people call it mind reading, but that is a misnomer. There is no reading involved. You actually *hear* the thoughts."

"How do I do it?" he asked.

"Focus on one of the girls."

Conrad stared at the redhead. Several moments passed. He wasn't sure what was supposed to happen, but nothing was.

"Now what?"

"Clear your mind and her thoughts will come to you."

Conrad closed his eyes for a moment and pictured a blank screen in his head. Again, several minutes passed with no result.

"Move up, kid."

Conrad opened his eyes and he saw that the line had moved and there was a gap of nearly thirty feet in front of him. Tiana was already up ahead. Conrad walked quickly forward to close the gap, and the group behind him followed his lead.

When he reached Tiana, he said, "Why did you call me 'kid'?"

"I said no such thing."

"Then who said it?"

"I heard no one use that word."

Conrad looked around. All the people in line were preoccupied in their own groups. No one seemed to be paying much attention to anyone else, much less him.

He continued to scan the crowd for a clue as to who the "kid" user was. When he had just about completed his scan, he eyes locked onto the bluest eyes he had ever seen. It was the redhead, and she was staring straight at him. Conrad's shyness made him avert her gaze.

"How sweet, he's shy."

Conrad reacquired the redhead, and she was now smiling at him.

"You're cute," he heard, but her lips did not move.

"Tiana!" he exclaimed. "I did it!"

Tiana smiled and placed her hand upon his shoulder. "You have just stepped into a new world," she said. "But you must be cautious and always obey the three laws."

"What three laws?" he asked.

"The First Law: You must not use another's thoughts against them. The Second Law: You must not attempt to influence another by exchanging your thoughts for theirs. And the Third Law: You must not influence free will."

Conrad was staring at Tiana; he was squinting with intensity, trying hard to understand everything he'd just heard.

"You have questions?" Tiana asked.

"No" was the reply. "I think I understand."

"Do not think. The penalty for violating any of the laws can be severe. Ask."

Conrad looked down at the ground. The crowd had moved ahead in line, so he moved forward, too. He then looked back up into Tiana's eyes, which were now dark green. "I understand the first law and the last law, but I'm not sure what the second one means, exactly."

Tiana said, "Think of something you like."

"Something I like?"

"Yes."

Conrad thought for a moment. The first thing that popped into his brain was a soft-serve ice cream sundae with whipped cream, marshmallow, chocolate fudge, and dead moths.

"*What the…?*" Conrad exclaimed.

"You understand?" Tiana asked with a sly smile.

"Yes," Conrad said. "That was gross."

Tiana pointed ahead in the line. The three girls were entering Blasto's. As they walked through the doorway, each one disappeared. The line seemed to move more rapidly now as people entered the threshold and vanished.

When Conrad approached the doorway, he started to feel panic rising up within him. In his head, he heard, *"There is nothing to fear here."* Tiana's thought comforted him, but the anxiety remained.

Just ahead of him, a group of four boys were acting out as each was sucked through the doorway.

"Help me!" one boy yelped with glee.

He was then pulled through by some invisible force. Another larger boy stood in the doorway with both of his hands propped against either side of the doorframe. His arms flexed as he was being pulled through the opening. His feet were pulled off the ground by the force, and he was moving to the horizontal. As he did, his legs disappeared into the void, but his upper torso remained visible.

"Yeehaw!" the boy yelled as he released his hands from the doorframe and shot through the space.

The remaining two simply stepped through the portal and disappeared.

Conrad and Tiana were next.

"I don't think I can do this," he said.

Tiana looked into his eyes. He noticed that they were now hazel green with dark-black rings at the edge of the iris and surrounding the pupil.

"Of course you can," Tiana assured him.

"What's going to happen to us?"

"Follow and discover."

Tiana leaped through the doorway, vanishing as the others had. Conrad swallowed hard, closed his eyes tightly, and outstretched his left leg toward the opening. He began to set his foot down; however, he could feel nothing solid beneath his foot. He caught himself from falling forward, and he opened his eyes. He saw that his left leg was missing to just above the knee. He started screaming. Suddenly, he felt a sharp shove from behind as he fell through the doorway.

On the other side, Conrad found himself surrounded by a light mist. The moisture-filled air about him was glowing in oscillating tints of purple, gold, yellow, red, and blue, pastel colors barely perceptible to the naked eye. Conrad also had the sensation of falling. He thought, *When will I hit the bottom?* Although he felt as if he were falling, there was nothing around him to visually confirm this. He could not make out any vertical structures with which to measure his perceived descent. Nor did the mist around him yield any indication of descending.

Ultimately, though, Conrad did come to rest on the ground. As he did, he noticed that the surface upon which he lay was not as he would have expected. It was not solid ground. Rather, the surface felt pliable to him. His body sunk into it slightly like a memory foam mattress. It was warm, too. The faint mist enveloped him as well. Thick and moist like the coastal marine layer that permeates southern Santa Monica Bay in the summer. As he inhaled, Conrad could taste the vapor. It did not have the saline aftertaste that ocean-borne fog does. The flavor in his throat was more acrid. Not painfully so, but it was noticeable.

After breathing the mist for several minutes, Conrad began to feel a warmth moving through his system. He shook his head slowly from side to side, trying to clear his head. The room seemed to tilt slightly, and Conrad began to giggle uncontrollably.

Slowly, the mist rose and thinned itself. Still light-headed, Conrad looked around him. As he watched, he saw other people he recognized from standing in line materialize around the room. Each one giggled, laughed, and guffawed as they did. Every one of them also scanned the room, just as Conrad was doing now.

Suddenly, Conrad heard a slight snicker. Although its volume was low, he could make out its direction. It was coming from his right. He turned his head in the direction of the sound, and whom he saw sent a shot of adrenaline through his body with such force that the pleasant effects of the mist disappeared instantly. It was the redhead.

She was staring directly into Conrad's eyes. The robin's egg blue irises were twinkling slightly in the subtle lighting. She batted her eyelashes coquettishly, smiled, and said in a soft voice, "Amanda, I am." A grin grew on Conrad's face.

"Conrad," he said.

"First time?" Amanda asked.

First time? Conrad thought. Then he realized it was his first time in Blasto's.

"Yes. Yes, it is," he replied. "Why? Do I look like a beginner?"

Amanda propped herself on one arm and leaned toward Conrad. When she smiled, Conrad realized her teeth were the whitest he could recall seeing. And smile she did. A perfect smile. Not too much gum exposed, teeth glistening, and ruby lips neatly placed above and below. Amanda leaned in closer to Conrad's face.

When she was within a few inches of him, she said, "Not exactly, but you seem to be enjoying Tonsorio."

"What is Tonsorio, exactly?" Conrad asked.

Amanda backed away from him, lying back down on the soft surface below them. She spread her arms out to both sides and slapped her hands down. Each hand made slight indentations in the surface.

"This," she said, "is Tonsorio."

Conrad reached out his right hand and felt the surface. It was soft, cool, and pliable. Conrad thought it pretty unremarkable stuff to be considered such a secret. Why Blasto's House of Tonsorio? Why not simply Blasto's House of Tempurpedic or Blasto's House of Soft Stuff?

"So why is Blasto's such a popular place," he asked, "if it's simply a place to lie down and rest?"

Amanda laughed, and her laughter made Conrad feel self-conscious. Amanda noticed his discomfort. She touched him on his shoulder.

"Oh, Conrad, I'm not laughing at you. You are just really cute."

Conrad felt his face flush. Amanda smiled at him.

"Tonsorio is not only a place to rest. You remember the feelings you felt from the time you walked across the threshold until the moment you were set down here?"

"Yes," Conrad replied.

"All of those sensations are part of the Tonsorio experience."

Conrad thought about this. He recalled the light-headed feeling he had when he was dropping toward the ground. He remembered the rushing feelings in his stomach when he'd first stepped through the doorway. He also considered how he wanted to snicker while he looked around.

While he had never himself had been intoxicated or high, he thought the sensations he felt in Blasto's were similar, if not exactly the same, as being so. Then he remembered Joanne Suchuk's admonition that drugs and alcohol abuse led to permanent brain damage.

"Is there any lasting damage from Tonsorio?" Conrad asked Amanda.

"It's not a drug," Amanda said. "From the information I gathered talking to Blasto, there is no foreign body, chemical, or other agent that enters your body. The effect is psychic only. There is a field of energy that produces the various Tonsorio effects."

"What kind of energy? Nuclear?" Conrad asked, slightly alarmed.

"Not sure," Amanda said. "It is a trade secret of Blasto's."

A bright light shined in Conrad's eyes from across the room. He squinted to see. Once his eyes focused, he saw the light was coming from an open door. Remarkably, Conrad also saw dozens of people walking out the door. He had forgotten about the other people in the room with Amanda and him. This realization startled Conrad because he then took inventory of everything he'd discussed with Amanda. *Did I say anything stupid?* he thought.

Conrad looked away from Amanda because he felt his face flushing again, but this time from embarrassment. He sat there, rubbing his left thumb against its neighbor index finger; he bit his lower lip slightly, and his right leg shook up and down. Amanda reached out her hand and, with slow, firm, downward pressure, stopped Conrad's shaking leg.

Startled, Conrad quickly glanced back at Amanda. His mouth opened in a slight "O" gesture. Just as quickly, the index finger of Amanda's unoccupied hand pressed gently against Conrad's lips. He heard a sound resembling air slowly leaking from a balloon coming from Amanda's mouth, and Conrad felt comforted. He smiled at Amanda. Once again, this near stranger, a very attractive girl, made him feel special. As if he were the only boy in the whole world.

The L-word passed through his mind like a bullet, unimpeded by the gray or white matter. The thought was not of romantic love, for they barely knew each other. He first laid eyes on Amanda while waiting in line for the Tonsoratial experience. *People don't fall in love that fast*, he thought. *Or do they?* He shook off the impression. No, he was thinking more of the familial or platonic love of one human being for another. Amanda didn't know him, but she had extended to Conrad a level of compassion, understanding, and whimsy he rarely felt from anyone in his short life. Although he had a vague recollection of his mother's effect, which reminded him of Amanda's, there was no true experience on which he could touch.

"Let's get out of here," Amanda said as she rose to her feet.

Conrad followed like an android hearing his owner's command prompt. The two walked forward, merging into the diminishing river of beings and leaving Blasto's through the exit. For the first time, Conrad noticed how cavernous the interior of Blasto's was in relation to the apparent exterior dimensions.

"It's bigger inside than it appears out, no?" Amanda remarked.

Startled, Conrad replied, "Don't tell me you read minds, too."

"No, I don't," she said. "Why?"

"Well, I was just thinking how spacious it is in here, yet the outside looks puny."

"It's just a coincidence," Amanda said. "Nothing more."

As they moved through the exit, the sun was high in the sky. "How long were we in there?" Conrad asked.

"Does it matter?" said Amanda.

He smiled at her. "I guess not. It just seems like time stood still in Blasto's, yet the outside world moved on quickly."

"That's a side effect of Tonsorio—space-time contraction."

They were walking toward the front of the building to the main street when they heard someone calling Amanda's name.

She swiveled her head around to look in the direction of the voice. When Amanda caught sight of the generator of her name, she paled. Conrad instantly noticed her changed demeanor.

"What's wrong?" he asked.

"Nothing," she said. "It's just my ex-boyfriend. Let's go."

Amanda double-timed her stride. Although Conrad had no trouble keeping up, he wondered why they were nearly running from her boyfriend—or rather, *ex*-boyfriend.

Conrad looked back over his shoulder. He saw a large youth clad almost entirely in black leather. His hair was combed straight down and was longer on the sides and back than it was in the front. In fact, his bangs looked like they were not cut, but rather ripped to their staggered lengths.

"Who is that guy?" Conrad asked Amanda as they continued sprinting along the street.

"Peyton, Peyton Campbell," she replied.

"Why are we running from him?" he asked.

"It's better that we avoid him," Amanda said. "He's unpredictable."

Conrad had no idea why he did what he was about to do, but something deep inside him told him he had to stop. So he did. After several seconds, Amanda looked back to see Conrad several yards behind her. She also saw that Peyton was continuing his pursuit, and he was rapidly closing the gap between Conrad and himself. Amanda began to continue her trek away from Peyton. She turned around after about seven steps, however, shook her head in disgust, and stormed back toward Conrad, hoping to intercept the two new rivals.

"Come on, Conrad, let's go," she pleaded.

Conrad simply shook his head and continued to keep his eyes fixed on the approaching behemoth.

"Why?"

"I don't know. I'm tired of being afraid, and something tells me I need to face him."

Amanda looked into Conrad's eyes, her head tilted slightly down and to the left. The corner of her mouth pursed as she said, "Are you sure?"

She detected a minute hesitation as Conrad looked down at the ground before reacquiring his gaze on the approaching Peyton.

Chapter Eight

Peyton noticed the two had ceased their flight. A slight smile crossed his chapped lips, and he intentionally slowed his pursuit. He was going to allow this supposed suitor to wallow in fear for a little longer as he approached. As he continued, Peyton began swinging his muscular arms at his sides like a helicopter. *This is going to be fun*, he thought.

Peyton stopped less than three feet in front of Conrad. As he stopped, Amanda stepped between the two and placed an open palm against Peyton's T-shirt-clad chest.

"Easy, Mandy," Peyton said. "This doesn't concern you."

"Yes, it does, Peyton," she replied. "We're just friends."

Peyton turned his gaze to Conrad, who was looking up at Peyton. "Not anymore," Peyton chortled.

Conrad wanted to formulate a clever retort, but all of his attention was drawn to the great size disparity between the two. Peyton stood at nearly six feet four to Conrad's five seven. And it was clear that Peyton spent much of his time in a gym. Nevertheless, Conrad exercised every bit of restraint he could muster to remain where he was and not bolt into the next county.

He thought about all the humiliations and abuse he had been subjected to by foster parents, foster siblings, vindictive peers, and assorted dregs of society during his short lifetime, and he realized there was nothing left to fear. He was mistaken, however.

Conrad offered his right hand to Peyton. "Hi, I'm Conrad. Amanda's right. We are only friends."

Peyton smiled. "Really? Well, then I guess I'll be going."

Peyton turned around and, without accepting Conrad's hand in friendship, began walking back the way he'd come. *That was easy*, Conrad thought. He also turned his back and started walking in the direction of Amanda and his previous flight. Amanda opened her mouth to warn Conrad not let his guard down, but it was too late.

Before Conrad had walked three paces, he felt something crushing his right shoulder. Peyton had somehow covered nearly one hundred yards in a matter of seconds. He grabbed Conrad, spun him around, and with a single punch, sent Conrad flying backward.

Conrad landed ten feet away on his back. Before he could regain his composure, Peyton was on him again. Peyton grabbed Conrad by the collar, lifting him to his feet. He landed several blows to Conrad's abdomen, leaving Conrad gasping for air and falling to the ground again.

"Stop it, Peyton!" Amanda screamed.

Peyton looked over his right shoulder at Amanda, laughed, and lifted Conrad from the ground again to administer more beating. Suddenly, Amanda leaped onto Peyton's back, wrapped her arms around his thick neck, and tried to choke him. Peyton's attention shifted from Conrad to Amanda as he removed her arms from his neck. He pulled Amanda over his head and tossed her to the side of the road. She hit the ground with a loud thud, and a grunt escaped her lips as she impacted the curb. Peyton began to laugh out loud at the sight of Amanda's crumpled body lying in the road. In fact, he was laughing so hard he hadn't noticed that Conrad was off the ground, and a rage was growing within him.

"Are you only able to fight with girls?" Conrad taunted.

Peyton's expression changed instantaneously as he turned to face Conrad. "Haven't had enough, punk?" Peyton exclaimed. "You're dead!"

Peyton leaped up into the air, flying toward Conrad. Conrad thought about his lesson in self-defense from earlier in the day. He lifted his hands in front of his body in a defensive posture and formed them into hand swords. As Peyton landed and continued to pursue Conrad to administer a further beating, Conrad thought, *Down!* Peyton wound up his right fist, preparing to hit Conrad square in the face. As he let his fist fly forward, Conrad settled into a fighting-horse stance, placed his palms forward, and closed his eyes, anticipating the blow.

After several seconds, Conrad opened his left eye to see why he hadn't been knocked down. He fully expected to see Peyton standing over him, ready to blast him. What he saw instead surprised him to the point of disbelief. Peyton was stretched out on the ground several yards away from Conrad, supine and unconscious. Conrad looked at his hands. *Did I do that?* he thought. He shook his head, stood up straight, and dropped his hands to his side. At the same time, Amanda rose from the ground and, seeing Peyton lying there, looked at Conrad and smiled. Her lips formed the words *What did you do?* but no sound followed.

Conrad smiled to himself. He held his hands up to examine them. As he turned them fore and aft, he couldn't see how his slight extremities could have laid waste to Peyton's massive build. Then he heard Tiana's refrain: *"You intended it, so it became the truth!"*

Perhaps there was something to this.

A crowd was beginning to gather around Peyton's immobile body. Several people pointed toward Conrad. It was clear the situation was as confusing to them as it was to Conrad.

Amanda walked over. She took Conrad's hand in hers and said, "We should go now."

Conrad nodded, and the two proceeded up the main street toward the town square.

As Amanda and Conrad turned the corner out of sight, Tiana stepped out of the shadows and onto the main road. As she walked from the dark into the light, she reattached her scepter to her belt. She briefly looked at Peyton, who by this time was beginning to come around. As he lifted himself up, Tiana stood, fixed and immovable, before him. Peyton was rubbing the back of his head as he passed her. His initial instinct was to taunt her, too, but as he moved, he sensed that would not be such a good idea.

Tiana simply smiled and said, "At least you lived to see another day. Pray you are so lucky next time."

Peyton's face blanched, and he began a hobbled run away from Tiana. Tiana laughed and folded into her rat configuration. She then ran to find Conrad.

Chapter Nine

Tiana found him sitting under a large tree in the center of the town square with Amanda. Actually, large was a rather inapt description, for Conrad and Amanda were sitting beneath "Home Tree," as the locals called her. Many of the least proficient residents of the town lived in her massive branches. Home Tree grew so tall that many of her upper limbs were invisible from the ground because they were enveloped in the clouds. Home Tree was the product of an ancient incept who contradicted the old edict that "no tree grows to the sky." The creator of Home Tree was long dead, as was the knowledge of his or her identity, but Home Tree was a giant testament to the power of the incepts.

As Tiana the rat reached Amanda and Conrad, the two were sipping fuddle-juice smoothies. Amanda was explaining

Home Tree's story to Conrad. Rather, she was explaining what she knew of the story.

"And no one knows," Amanda continued, "exactly how old Home Tree is or who, or what, is responsible for her."

Conrad took his last big slurp of fuddle juice through his straw, followed by a cacophony of slurping emanating from his cup. After which he let go with an enormous belch. He was surprised when flames shot from his mouth, and he fell off the bench. Amanda began laughing uncontrollably.

"What was that?" Conrad asked from his new seat on the ground.

Amanda began to regain her poise and replied, "Fuddle juice is flammable at certain velocities. I should have warned you."

Tiana the rat shook her little rat head from side to side and vocalized a little squeak.

"Thanks a lot!" Conrad exclaimed.

He picked himself up off the ground and returned to his seat next to Amanda on the bench. Amanda watched him all the while, trying desperately not to laugh again.

Conrad saw how much effort she was expending and said, "Go ahead, laugh."

Amanda let out a tremendous guffaw. It took her nearly half a minute to regain her composure again. When she did, her eyes were watering and she couldn't stop smiling.

"I'm glad I could be the source of so much entertainment," Conrad said. "I nearly got beaten to a pulp, and now almost incinerated."

"You are entertaining," Amanda replied. "I like that." She leaned over and gave Conrad a kiss on the cheek. "And I like you, too."

Amanda stood up.

"I have to go now," she said. "See you later?"

"Sure," Conrad said. "Where?"

"I'll find you," Amanda replied.

She then snapped her fingers and disappeared in a swirl of pink, turquoise, and yellow smoke.

"This place," said Conrad, "gets weirder by the minute."

"Well, just wait," replied Tiana the rat.

Conrad looked down toward where Tiana the rat sat.

"What?" he retorted.

Tiana instantly transformed into her human form. "I mean, you have not seen anything yet. Come now, we have wasted enough time for one day."

With that, Tiana reached out for Conrad.

"Where are we going?" he asked.

Tiana looked at him with disappointment. "Really?" she proclaimed. "Does it matter?"

He took her hand in his and immediately felt all the air being sucked from his lungs as they transported to another location in this strange land.

They landed back in Conrad's bedroom in Turner Manor. Once again, he fell to the ground and vomited.

"When will I stop getting sick?" he asked.

Tiana laughed. "You will when you are ready."

Tiana walked over to Conrad's dresser. On top of the dresser were several slivers of paper, a paperclip, a few coins from home, and a stick of Juicy Fruit gum.

"You enjoyed your day today, no?" Tiana asked.

"Yes," Conrad replied excitedly.

He looked up at Tiana. She continued looking over his belongings with her back toward him. He sensed something was troubling her, so he adjusted his enthusiasm.

"It was okay, I guess."

"Do you miss home?" Tiana queried.

Conrad couldn't quite put a finger on it, but he thought something was troubling Tiana. "What's wrong," he asked.

From his vantage point of Tiana's back, he saw her raise her left hand to her face. She ran the back of her hand across her left eye. Then she turned around.

"Nothing is wrong," she said. "I am just curious how you are feeling. I can read your thoughts, but not being an empath, there is much information I do not know. I can take you home, you know."

Conrad, startled, moved forward a step. "You want me to leave?" he asked.

Tiana's visage changed to a more sympathetic one. She stepped closer to Conrad, held his face in her hands and said, "My heart would break if you left me now. I just want to be sure you are happy here because what comes next there is no turning away from."

"What comes next?" Conrad asked.

"Sit," Tiana said, "and I will tell you."

Chapter Ten

Conrad was seated near the open window of his room. Outside, the sun was sitting low in the sky. It was not yet sunset, but within an hour or so night would fall. There were several streams of lavender clouds also set in the sky. Outside the window, a group of pteranodons caught his attention.

Tiana removed her scepter from her hip, placing it against the wall next to the window seat. She sat beside Conrad and said, "Previously, you told me you only had one memory of your father. You said you remembered him leaving you. Is that correct?"

"Yes," Conrad replied.

"That's not all you remember, though, true?" Tiana said, challenging him.

Conrad felt ashamed of himself, but he couldn't quite figure out why. He was beginning to trust Tiana, but he was uncomfortable discussing his father with anyone. It had been years since he'd spent any time thinking about his father, even though he often had thoughts and dreams about his mother. The main impression he retained from childhood was the fuzzy recollection of watching his father walk out the door. There was no angry exchange between his parents. His father simply left.

He remembered hearing his uncle Peter describe his father as a "no-account dreamer" or a "snake-oil salesman." Uncle Peter even drove Conrad to tears once by saying Conrad was so much like his father that he would most likely end up dead or in jail.

Conrad asked his mother once what had happened to cause his father to leave. "I suspect," she said, "he had grown weary of this world." At the time, Conrad was only four or five years old and had no ability then to understand what she meant. Even to this day, he still didn't quite understand what being weary of this world had to do with his father leaving his family. Was his father a loser? Uncle Peter thought so. Was his father an alcoholic or drug addict? Conrad had read about other men abandoning their families. Some of those stories described how drugs and alcohol could lead a fine upstanding father to make serious lapses in judgment and simply leave, never to return. What could cause a father to leave his wife and child otherwise?

Conrad actually researched the word *weary* once. Weary, he recalled, meant exhausted, usually by hard work. That didn't sound like something from which a "loser" would suffer. Conrad smiled at this recollection because he remembered thinking Uncle Peter was wrong about his father, and by extension, about Conrad himself. *Maybe my dad was just tired and couldn't find any other way*, he remembered thinking. But as he continued thinking about his research, his countenance changed.

There was an additional definition of weary that he now recalled—impatient or dissatisfied with something. Could it be true? Did his father leave due to some internal impatience or dissatisfaction, and with what, or whom, had he lost patience or become dissatisfied? At the time, Conrad mulled over this in his brain for several minutes.

After thinking about it over and over, he concluded that his father was dissatisfied because his mother had become pregnant. This was a simple enough story: boy meets girl, boy falls in love with girl, girl gets pregnant, boy leaves girl, blaming her for everything. How could his father be so selfish? It takes two to make a baby. How could he blame his mother for the whole incident? Uncle Peter was right. He was an asshole!

But wait a minute. Maybe there was something else. Maybe it wasn't the pregnancy itself. Maybe it was Conrad. Perhaps his mother had changed the story to protect Conrad's feelings. Perhaps Conrad was born, and upon viewing the horrible little creature, his father left, dissatisfied in his only begotten son.

A tear rolled down Conrad's cheek.

Tiana put a hand on his head and said, "You do not know the true story of your father." Conrad looked up. He saw that her eyes were now turquoise blue.

"Do you?" he asked, wiping the moisture with the back of his hand.

"You said he left me to save me. What did you mean?"

She knelt down beside him. "Your father is a great man. Everyone knows him here."

Conrad's expression changed. "You said *is*!" he exclaimed. "Does that mean what I think it means?"

Tiana smiled. "I think it is about time for you to see him again, do you not agree?"

Conrad jumped to his feet so fast and hard that the toe of his athletic shoe caught slightly on the Persian Carpet at his feet. He tripped and was falling forward toward the floor when he stopped in mid-fall.

Tiana laughed slightly. "I will accept that as a yes."

Conrad rose from his downward trajectory with the aid of Tiana's will. When he reached his apex, he asked, "Where is he?"

"Not far," Tiana replied. "How would you like to go to him?"

"I'm not sure," Conrad said. "What are my options?"

Tiana began describing all the wonderful methods of transportation on Overworld.

As Tiana described each transportation mode, Conrad visualized himself making use of each one. He saw himself on the back of a Tyrannosaurus rex, the beast running, full bore, along a road adorned on each side with trees and shrubbery of various shapes, sizes, and colors. The terrible lizard king strode at great speed, responding to each command issued by it rider. In this case, the rider was Conrad.

He pictured himself sitting on the neck of a large pteranodon, its gray skin highlighted by yellow-and-gold markings. While on the ground, its folded wings belied the true scale of this flying machine. However, once airborne, the twenty-five-foot wingspan seemed much bigger. In his mind's eye, Conrad climbed aboard the pterosaur, swinging his right leg over the beast's neck, thereby straddling it, and set his behind into the saddle that was firmly affixed to accommodate a rider. The great flying reptile jumped up upon Conrad's command, leaping into the air, its massive wings flapping to create lift as the rider and mount dispatched into a sky mottled with lavender, gray, and white clouds. As the beast reached cruising altitude, it held its wings outstretched and taught as it glided toward its final destination.

Tiana continued with other methods of moving about this strange and wonderful place. In fact, she even suggested that Conrad teleport directly to his father's side.

"How can I do that?" he asked.

"Just think of your father," Tiana began, "and follow through with a thought about taking you where he is."

"But I don't remember what he looks like," Conrad said.

The melancholia hung in the air between them.

"Close your eyes," Tiana demanded.

He obliged and closed his eyes tightly. She placed a hand on each side of his head, and she closed her own eyes. Suddenly, Conrad saw an image beginning to coalesce in his mind. At first, it was blurry, but after several moments, it became sharper. It was the visage of a man. He was tall and thin with salt-and-pepper hair. He was wearing a thin and neatly trimmed goatee. The man's facial hair was darker than the hair upon his head, and Conrad even saw a slight reddish hue in parts of it. The man was smiling and walking toward Conrad. As he got closer, his smile widened to where his teeth became exposed. They were brilliant white. The man continued forward and began to open up his arms to embrace Conrad—

Conrad convulsed back to reality.

"Wha…what was that?" Conrad exclaimed.

Tiana smiled. "What did you see?"

"A…a man…a man with a beard. He smiled at me."

"Very good. And what did you feel?"

He thought for a moment. *What did I feel? What did I feel? Why does everyone ask me what or how I feel?*

In response to his thoughts, Conrad heard, *"Because your feelings, together with your intention, make everything in your world happen."*

He looked at Tiana. Her eyes were now the color of fire opals. She smiled a slightly crooked smile. Conrad thought, *Was that my father?*

"Yes" was the response. *"But not as he is."*

"What does that mean?"

"The image you saw was a projection of your father's core or essence. It was not a true representation of him now."

"Where is he? Can I meet him?"

Tiana placed her hand on his shoulder. "You will in time, but until then, you can see him anytime you want just as you just experienced."

"But why can't I go to him now?"

Tiana explained that his teleportation ability needed to be cultivated, because if he had the present ability to teleport to his father's side, he would have done so. She also said that some people never fully developed the ability without using a device to assist transit; a token worked by amplifying and aligning the energy needed to teleport.

He thought about his lack of ability, and he became discouraged. *I am a loser*, he thought. He asked if he could have a token of his own.

"Not until you are better prepared," she said.

"Why not?"

"You could very easily materialize inside a wall, a floor, or a piece of furniture. Teleportation is not like riding a bicycle. If you doubt your ability to ride a bicycle, you could merely fall to the ground. If you doubt your ability to teleport, you could be lost forever. We will work on building your ability and confidence together."

There was a loud blast from a foghorn. Tiana looked up toward the sound. There was a second blast, followed by several staccato blips. Tiana's expression changed from its former joviality to one of deep concern. Conrad also sensed some foreboding.

"We must go," Tiana said.

She removed the token from her belt, selected a destination, and held her hand out for Conrad to grasp. He did, there was a great whoosh of air, and they disappeared.

When they landed, Conrad had neither sense of direction nor equilibrium. His head was spinning from the abruptness of their departure. Opening his eyes only compounded the dissociation, and he began to fall toward the floor. Once again, Tiana reached for him with her mind, stopping his descent. Once righted, Conrad began to regain his orientation, but the urge to vomit rose in him, too.

They were standing on the edge of what appeared to be a control center of some sort. There were many people milling around—technicians, operators, consultants—and there was one man standing toward the back of the room that Conrad sensed was in charge. He was over six feet tall with a crew cut. He wore dress slacks, a button-down shirt, a tie, and over the shirt, he wore a multicolored vest. It seemed odd that such a severely dressed gentleman would accessorize with such a gaudy vest.

The man in the vest said, "Status, people. By the numbers. Logistics?"

A young man wearing a Chicago Cubs baseball cap said, "Check."

"Guidance?"

A young woman wearing black-framed glasses and a ponytail replied, "Check."

"Navigation?"

Another young man replied, "Check."

"Systems?"

A man in his forties reviewed several translucent screens covered in streaming data. After reviewing for several seconds, he replied, "Check."

"Telemetry?"

"Check."

"Procedures?"

"Check."

"Communications?"

"Check."

"Recovery?"

An alien-looking being with four arms was running its twenty fingers over a touch-sensitive control panel. "Check" was its response as well.

While watching all the synchronized activity, Conrad thought, *What is going on here?* He hesitated to ask the question aloud because when he looked at Tiana with his standard quizzical expression, her responsive glance told him not to. Still, it became more and more difficult to stifle the impulse while watching all manner of creatures—terrestrial and otherwise—milling around the control room.

Just as Conrad felt the words forming in his throat, the man in the vest walked over to them.

"Is this him?" he said.

Conrad assumed the man was addressing Tiana, but he wasn't completely certain.

"Yes," Tiana replied after several moments had elapsed.

The man turned to face Conrad, smiled gently, and said, "Hello, Mr. Turner. My name is Nash, Nash Sine, and I am very glad to finally meet you."

Nash extended his right hand for Conrad's acceptance. Conrad responded in kind, and he even returned the smile. He couldn't quite put his finger on it, but there was something familiar about Nash.

"What procedure is to be implemented, Nash?" Tiana asked.

"We're going with Questar nine-four-nine."

"Why nine-four-nine?" Tiana asked incredulously.

"We discussed the various procedures available, and the consensus was nine-four-nine had the greatest potential for success."

"And what does Alex think?"

Nash's face flushed as the anger began to seethe within him.

Tiana stared into Nash's eyes, gently placed her right hand upon her scepter, and moved her feet into a battle stance. Although no words left her closed lips, Conrad heard, *"You forget yourself, Nash. Do not force my hand."*

Nash backed down. "Alex was in the minority."

"Which procedure does Alex recommend?"

Nash looked around the control room. Nearly every human face was looking at him. "Seven-seven-six."

Tiana removed her hand from her scepter and stood up straight. "Then I recommend we follow Alex's suggestion."

Chapter Eleven

Alexander Cassius Sine was a rambunctious child. From the time he had taken his first earthly breath, his mother, Frances Amelia Sine née Kellogg, just knew he was going to be trouble with a capital "T." Alex and his twin brother, Nash—Nashville Connor, actually—were born just outside Point Lookout, New York. When they were born, Point Lookout was a sleepy little village on the south side of Long Island.

Their father, Theodore "Ted" Woodrow Sine, was a conductor on the Long Island Railroad. Seventeen days after the boys were born, a young man boarded the train in Oceanside bound for Manhattan. Strapped to the young man's chest were seven kilograms of a highly explosive material connected to a manual detonator. Just before the train entered the tunnel for its final approach to Grand Central Station, Ted Sine noticed something peculiar about the young man.

"Ticket, please," Ted said to the young man.

As he handed his ticket to Ted, his coat opened just enough to present Ted with a glimpse of the danger. Ted grabbed the man's hands and held them up so he could not grasp the detonator. Several passengers screamed when they saw the explosive vest.

"Don't panic," Ted advised calmly. "Someone pull the emergency chain."

A young girl pulled the chain, and the train came to a screeching halt. Just after it did, many passengers jumped from the train as fast as they were able. The car in which Ted was holding the would-be bomber was nearly empty when help arrived from the locomotive. The chief engineer that day was Harvey Pincus of Rockville Center.

"You okay, Ted?" Harvey asked.

"I'm just fine," Ted replied from the floorboards of the train car.

The young man was struggling to free himself from Ted's extremely strong grip.

"Settle down," Ted said. "You won't free yourself. It's over. Just accept your fate."

Approximately twenty minutes later, when the transit police arrived, Ted's grip on the suspect was as strong as it had been when the skirmish began. One of the transit officers, Officer Lewis, approached Ted.

"We'll take it from here," he said.

"Are the passengers safe?" Ted asked.

"Yes" was the reply. "You saved many lives today."

"Not enough," Ted said as he presented the suspects hands to Officer Lewis.

"Hold these well. He's a strong one," Ted advised.

Office Lewis's incredulity was evident, as was his slipshoddiness. Just as Ted relaxed his grip on the suspect, the young man pulled his hands free from Officer Lewis's grasp. The then inevitable explosion completely obliterated the train and sent shockwaves for three miles in every direction.

Later that evening, when Ted failed to arrive at home at the appropriate time, Frances just knew something had happened. Ted was a fastidiously punctual man. He walked through the front door each and every evening at five minutes after six. This was true except on nights when he knew he would be late. On those tardy evenings, Frances would receive a telephone call at exactly five minutes after six. Since she neither received a call nor had her husband of seventeen years walked through their threshold, she knew something awful had occurred.

The telephone rang at six thirty. It was Captain Joseph of the Transit Authority Police. He explained what had happened, that Ted had stopped a bomber, that everyone on the train that day, all 187 souls, would have been lost if it weren't for Ted's bravery, that Ted was a true hero, and that he and the rest of the Transit Authority were sorry for her loss.

Frances placed the receiver back into the cradle, walked into bedroom where her infant sons were lying in their cribs, sat beside the boys, and stroked their heads. Being a widow now, with two infant sons and no other family to assist, would have put any other woman into a complete and total state of panic, but not Frances. She knew her boys needed her to be strong. There was plenty of time later for grief. Now she must begin to plan for the future.

Frances did her best to raise the boys well. Nash followed instructions to the letter, was a good student, and was quite helpful to his mother. Alex, on the other hand, caused Frances no uncertain trouble consistently. He needed to be reminded constantly to complete any task, his homework was never completed timely, and he seemed to seek out adversity daily. In a nutshell, Nash was the good seed, and Alex was the bad.

However, it wasn't as black and white as all that. Alex was also fearless, whereas Nash, although no coward, avoided confrontation whenever possible. Innumerable times during their childhood, Alex came to Nash's, and others', aid. He was a skilled, instinctive fighter, and not many adversaries got the better of him.

As adults, the contrast between them remained the same. Nash went into government service, whereas Alex made his way on the fringes of society. Nash joined the Collective Alliance when he graduated from the academy. Alex was arrested once for smuggling contraband to the outer systems—not convicted, mind you. His defense was necessity. He told the panel there was a certain tribe being systematically starved to death, so he felt it was his obligation, his right, to provide food and supplies whether the regional authorities deemed it "contraband" or not.

Whatever their past conflicts and differences, Nash and Alex remained brothers. In more recent times, they worked together frequently on Overworld. Nash was a master strategist, whereas Alex's strength was tactics. The dichotomy between the men was the primary reason Tiana sided with Alex's decision to utilize Questar 776. Nash was the better man to formulate and understand the procedures needed to resolve a circumstance, but Alex was better at implementation.

Chapter Twelve

"Where is Alex now?" Tiana asked.

"Right here, you Amazon goddess," said a voice from behind them.

Conrad spun around to see from whom that response had come. He also wondered what Tiana's reaction would be to being described as an Amazon. Conrad watched the swarthy-looking man walk slowly toward Tiana, and she held a severe look on her face. When the man was within several feet of Tiana, he removed a firearm from his hip holster blisteringly fast. However, Tiana's responsive parry with her scepter was equally as fast. The two eyed each other for many moments. There was an eerie silence in the room. Conrad could feel his heart pounding in his chest. Suddenly, the man let out a tremendous laugh.

"Ha-ha," he exclaimed. "No moss grows under your feet does it, T?"

Tiana smiled back. "And you remain the same obnoxious splezak you have always been," she said.

Alexander Sine was a tall man—over six feet, at least. His hair was dark, as were his eyes. His skin seemed to be the consistency of leather. His outfit reminded Conrad of the clothes worn by outlaws in the Wild West. He remembered seeing a movie with his mother—a Western, it was—where several men wore long coats made of thick cloth. The coats hung nearly to the ground, and underneath, the men had many guns. He wondered what other guns Alex carried under his coat.

While Conrad's attention was focused on the types and numbers of firearms being carried by Alex Sine, Nash, Alex, and Tiana were speaking to each other. Judging by their individual level of passion and exuberance, they were debating an issue of grave importance. At several points during the conversation, while Tiana was speaking, both Alex and Nash looked over at Conrad. As they watched Conrad with rapt attention, each man nodded his assent to whatever Tiana was saying. Finally, after many minutes of verbal badminton, Alex shook Tiana's hand. Nash did so also. Then each brother looked at the other and, with clear ambivalence, considered whether to acknowledge their agreement with a handshake. Tiana then grasped each man's hand, placed them together, and initiated a shaking gesture from above.

The brothers continued the motion unaided, ultimately smiling to each other.

Before they parted, Alex threw his arms around Nash and said, "We're blood, Nash. Nothing is going to change that."

"Yes, but must you constantly test the limits of brotherhood?"

Alex moved in closer to Nash's face and, in a mere whisper, said, "Our bond is limitless, brother. That is what you fail to understand."

By the time the three completed their business, Conrad was also done trying to figure out Alex Sine. They walked over to Conrad, with Tiana in the lead.

"Conrad," she said, "you have already met Nash, but this is his brother, Alexander Sine. As you no doubt observed, Nash is in charge of the control room here."

Conrad waited for Tiana to explain what Alexander's role was, but she did not do so.

Instead, Nash interjected, "As I said, I've been looking forward to meeting you for a very long time."

The pleasantries between Nash and Conrad completed, the four stood silent for several moments. Each addressed the others with glances, except for Conrad and Alex. When Conrad looked over at Alex, and Alex returned the glance,

Conrad averted his eyes. *Why doesn't Tiana introduce us?* Conrad thought.

Then he remembered.

"Why don't you introduce me to him?" Conrad asked Tiana telepathically.

"Why, indeed," Conrad heard in his mind. Then, *"Introduce yourself, boy!"*

It was strange, but it did not feel like Tiana's mind was speaking to him. Although telepathy did not involve the ears, there was a different "tone" to this thought. Besides, Tiana had never referred to him as "boy" before.

"What do I say?" Conrad's mind asked Tiana.

"How about hello" was the response.

Conrad was sure these responses were not coming from Tiana. Conrad looked into Tiana's eyes. They were glowing amber now, and she was smiling brightly. He looked at Nash with a *Was it you?* look.

Nash shook his head.

When he looked at Alex, there was a great big smile on the man's face, and Conrad's mind heard, *"Bingo!"*

Conrad extended his hand. "Hello," he said. "I'm Conrad Turner, sir."

Alex grasped Conrad's hand and shook it vigorously. "Damn glad to meet you, Master Turner. Damn glad. We're going to be famous friends. I'm just sure of it. But there is business to attend to."

Tiana said, "Yes, there is, but everything has its time. We will speak on this soon."

She put her hand on Conrad's shoulder. *"I will tell you all you need to know. Trust that,"* Tiana's mind relayed. Conrad felt he could trust Tiana, but there was also a slight feeling inside him of foreboding. He wasn't sure from where it came, but he was certain it was there.

So much had transpired in the last few weeks. So many changes had occurred in his life. He knew he was on a better path, but he also sensed that, before this was all done, there was going to be some difficult times ahead. He wasn't completely convinced this air of pessimism hadn't followed him from his prior existence, but still, it remained within him, causing slight anxiety.

"How do we do this, then?" Nash asked.

Tiana looked at Nash. Conrad was certain she was using telepathy to castigate him, but Tiana's ability to filter her thoughts blocked Conrad from hearing.

"We must retire to a quiet place for reflection and discussion," she said.

She removed her token from her belt, tapped a few keystrokes, and looked up. She smiled. Her eyes were brilliant aqua as she pressed the final button on the token. A bright line of light grew in the center of the circle, formed by where the four of them were standing. A whooshing of air followed as they all funneled into the line of light.

Chapter Thirteen

Conrad was angry. Nearly every time he teleported since he'd arrived on Overworld, he became disoriented. He hated the feeling. It was like a large hook pulling from the inside of his belly, and his head felt as if it were on a swivel. *Twix is a lying fidget,* he thought. It was supposed to get easier as time went on, but it wasn't. For a moment, Conrad contemplated traveling around Overworld on T. rex-back for the duration of his time there.

Once he regained his equilibrium, Conrad looked around. They had landed in a very large room. Actually, it was a hangar of some sort, but much larger than any Conrad had seen or imagined. Alex, Nash, Tiana, and Conrad were standing before a console covered in flashing lights. Protruding from the back side of the console was what appeared to be a metal beam, and attached to the beam, extending upward at a ninety-degree angle, was a robotic torso, neck, head, and six cybernetic arms. All six arms were moving rapidly over the console, pressing buttons, flipping switches, making connections, and terminating communications.

As the robot continued to work the console, Conrad saw something he could barely believe. In the center of the hangar, several bright lights illuminated. What they illuminated was the cause of Conrad's semi-disbelief. It was a ship, a craft of some sort, poised in the center of the hangar. It was supported on three structures that grew out of the hangar floor. Each structure had three massive cylinders attached to it. There were workers moving up and down a loading ramp to the ship, and every time a worker entered or exited the craft, the cylinders compressed and rebounded in unison. Conrad had seen enough science fiction movies to know that this was a spacecraft. But what a spaceship was doing here escaped him.

"Seks, do we have a course projection?" Alex said to the robot torso.

A sound emanated from Seks's mechanical face—a series of consecutive low-frequency warbles that sounded a lot like humming.

"And neutron star activity?" Alex added.

Another round of humming.

"Fine," Alex concluded. "We need to get space borne in about fifteen minutes. Is everyone ready?"

"We're going into *space*?" Conrad exclaimed.

Alex smiled and said, "What'samatter, sport? Didn't you always wish to go into outer space?" It was true. Ever since Conrad could remember, he wanted to travel in space. He remembered the first time he watched *Star Wars*. He couldn't believe how great the special effects were. He went to the movie house with Cora Vellusi, Ty Phillips, and Donny Brownstone. It was just before his mother died. The Emporium Movie House was showing the re-mastered versions of Episodes IV, V, and VI, and Veronica Turner thought it would be good for her son to see this cinematic masterpiece on the big screen.

She asked him if he wanted to see it.

"Of course," he said.

"Why don't you invite some friends?"

In those days, Conrad's friends were few, but they were true friends. Cora, Ty, Donny, and Conrad were nearly inseparable from fourth grade on. They would spend nearly every weekend together. Well, sometimes Cora had to do "girly" things with her girlfriends. She hated when Ty and Donny teased her about being a girl. She hated it so much that she beat their butts every time they did. Cora was the muscle in their group—fearless and tenacious.

When the "Four Musketeers," as Veronica called them, watched the *Star Wars* trilogy, Conrad was transfixed. He knew it was just a motion picture, but somewhere inside, there was a small part of him hoping it was real.

"Wow," he had said. "Wouldn't it be great to fly through space like that?"

"Are you demented?" Donny asked. "It's make-believe, you geek."

"Well, it is now, but maybe someday," Conrad replied.

Donny made a face by sticking his tongue out the corner of his mouth and crossing his eyes. Cora and Ty simply laughed. Even Conrad smiled after his embarrassment had subsided.

He remembered telling his mother how much he had liked the movie, and she smiled as brightly as he did.

"Mom, it was the greatest," he said. "Do you think I'll ever be able to travel in outer space, from planet to planet, or even from galaxy to galaxy?"

Veronica bent down slightly and held her son's face between her hands. Conrad remembered her hands being incredibly soft and warm. She looked into his eyes and said, "It doesn't matter what I think, but if you believe it, it will happen for you."

"Do you really think so, Mom?"

"Everything happens," she replied.

Chapter Fourteen

Conrad was jolted back into the present when he remembered his mother's assertion. His head quickly swung to the right, and he looked directly at Tiana, who was staring at him. She had a knowing smirk on her face.

"See," he heard in his mind, *"you did know what it means."*

"But how did you know my mother said it to me?" he thought.

"There will be time later to discuss many things," Tiana replied telepathically. *"But now we must go."*

"If everyone will climb aboard," Alex announced, "we will get this adventure started."

Nash asked, "Are we fully provisioned for the journey?"

Alex seemed perturbed by Nash's lack of confidence in his interplanetary planning skills.

"We have enough for now and we can re-provision on Mercatorum if we need anything else, but we're burning starlight, so if you'll all board the *Magnum*, we'll be off."

The four walked toward the ship, single file.

The *Doppler Magnum* sat 120 feet from nose to tail, and it held a shape similar to the old NASA space shuttle, except that it had no wings and was wider along the bottom, with a semi-cylindrical shape. It also had two tail sections compared to the shuttle's one.

As they moved ahead, Conrad marveled at the machine. It sat regally upon the three struts and seemed poised to launch out of the hangar at any moment. They all walked up the gangway, entering the ship.

As they entered, Alex said, "Find the seat with your name above, be seated, and prepare for gravoff."

Conrad saw that each passenger seat had a name floating above it. The names oscillated from green to blue-green in color. Tiana's floating name was hovering above a seat directly next to the one above which hung the name *Conrad*.

Alex took a seat at the front of the ship, and Nash sat next to him. Above and in front of Alex's seat was a large blank space on the bulkhead of the ship. Conrad expected there to be a transparent windshield of some sort in the cockpit area, but there was none. There was nothing before Alex but a large panoramic portion of the interior of the ship's skin. There were not even any navigational or control instruments. Conrad started to perspire. Tiana gently placed a hand on his knee, and he began to relax again.

Alex said, "Operations."

Instantly, a control panel with instruments and gauges appeared on the vacant bulkhead.

"Visual," Alex barked.

A virtual window to the outside world appeared above the control panel.

Alex followed the two former commands with "Power" and then "Prepare gravoff."

There was a deep pulsation from somewhere in the ship, together with the sound of other automated tasks being completed.

Conrad observed the back of Nash's head moving rapidly from side to side, scanning the information being presented on the control panel. When his rapid head movements subsided, he held up his right thumb.

"Okay, everyone," Alex said. "Let's go."

Conrad wasn't sure what to expect on his first spaceflight, but what he experienced was nothing as he had imagined.

Chapter Fifteen

Several moments after Alex announced their departure, the *Doppler Magnum* slowly rose from the hangar floor. Conrad heard the landing struts disengage as the ship rose. It continued to rise, and this action caused Conrad great consternation. *Won't we crash into the hangar roof?*

"Alex is an excellent pilot," he heard in his mind in Tiana's comforting thought tone.

She was right. They continued to rise off the ground, and Conrad considered that the roof must have retracted during the prelaunch procedures.

As they continued their ascent, Conrad looked toward the backs of Alex and Nash's heads again. However, now he noticed something different. He was now looking at them on an upward angle. Through the virtual windshield, he saw the lavender clouds of Overworld. Conrad was just about to say, "Wow," when the deep pulsation in the ship suddenly changed to a sustained whine. As it did, the *Doppler Magnum* sped upward out of the atmosphere so quickly that Conrad lost his breath.

"You must exhale during planetary escape," Tiana advised.

Conrad wanted to reply verbally, but without the requisite air in his lungs, he was unable to do so. *"Thanks for the heads-up,"* he thought instead.

Tiana smiled and laughed slightly.

As the *Doppler Magnum* rose though the atmosphere of Overworld, Conrad saw the dark of space through the virtual windshield. The light of billions of stars shone brightly; his heart skipped a beat. *Am I really in outer space?* he thought.

He felt Tiana's hand touch his with a reassuring grasp. He looked over to see she was still smiling, and her eyes were glowing emerald green again.

"Prepare for supralight jump," Alex announced.

Conrad felt his retention harness squeeze his chest slightly as the mechanism seemed to react to Alex's command. Before he could say or think anything, some powerful force grabbed a hold of the ship, wrenching it loose from the gravitational force of Overworld, and flung it forward. The stars, which were previously mere points of light in the blackness of space, elongated and stretched. The star lines seemed to define a tunnel through which the *Doppler Magnum* and her passengers traveled until there was a blinding flash of light. Conrad winced from its brightness.

When he reopened his eyes, he couldn't see. Instinctively, he reached out for Tiana. *"Help me,"* he thought.

"Your sight will return shortly," she said. "You must avoid looking directly into the photic flare."

After several moments, Conrad's vision began to return. At first, he could only see things on the periphery, but soon everything came back into clear focus.

He looked out through the virtual windshield. What he saw startled him. It appeared that the ship was not moving. Where the stars were previously positioned, there was now simple darkness.

"Why have we stopped?" he asked.

"Haven't stopped," Nash answered. "You just can't see things as they are when you are moving faster than light."

"It's safe to move about the cabin," Alex announced, rising from the command chair. "We should be on Mercatorum in a little over six hours. Everyone can relax until then."

"Captain Alex, can I ask you a question?" Conrad said. Alex walked over to where Tiana and Conrad were seated and said,

"Yeah, Conrad, what is it?"

"How fast are we going?"

Nash interjected, "L-factor six."

After a brief scowl in Nash's direction, Alex replied, "Yes, L-factor six."

Conrad thought for a moment. "Is that six times the speed of light?"

"No," Alex said. "That's a common misconception."

Alex went on to explain that light-factor travel involved tenfold increases in speed at each L-factor level. Unlike the single-digit increases most people assumed, the L-factors allowed ships so equipped to travel great distances in a relatively short time.

"So we are currently traveling at one hundred thousand times the speed of light," Alex proclaimed.

"Holy sh—" Conrad almost said. "I mean, that's cool. So this planet we're heading for…"

"Mercatorum," Alex corrected.

"Right," Conrad said, slightly embarrassed. "Mercatorum. It's really far away from Overworld, then?"

"About seventy light-years," Alex replied. You are a very curious boy, aren't you?" Alex tousled the hair on Conrad's head. "I like that."

Tiana rose and said, "Come, Conrad, we have many things to discuss and much training to work through."

She walked to the rear bulkhead of the cabin, and Conrad followed obediently. Tiana opened the door in the bulkhead and motioned Conrad to walk through.

"Ladies first," Conrad said with a big smile on his face. Tiana returned the smile and walked through the door as Conrad followed. He closed the bulkhead door behind them.

Chapter Sixteen

The cabin behind the main one was festooned with seating of various sorts, several view screens that resembled flat-panel television sets were affixed to the walls, and there were counters around the perimeter that acted as support for numerous machines and gadgets, many of which Conrad had never seen before.

Halfway into the room, Tiana stopped and turned to face Conrad. Her eyes were blazing amber. She lowered herself into a battle stance and said, "Defend yourself!"

Conrad was just about to respond when Tiana thrust both her hands forward in Conrad's direction. He felt a force strike him in the chest and abdomen with such power that he was thrown to the floor. The force continued to push him along the floor until his head struck the opposite bulkhead.

Conrad rubbed the spot on his head that had impacted the bulkhead as he picked himself off the floor. *"Why did you do that?"* he thought.

"Defend yourself!" Tiana barked.

She lifted her scepter from her belt and, with a flick of her wrist, activated the weapon. The diamond tip was spinning faster than before as Tiana set her legs down into a forty-five-degree cat stance.

Conrad's head was tilted toward the floor, but he was watching Tiana through the tops of his eyes. Anger was rising in him as he thought the one person whom he believed had his best interests at heart was now about to kill him. Tiana leaped toward him with her scepter, completing a semicircle about her head, and she was about to land a fatal blow, severing Conrad's head from his body.

Conrad thought, *"No!"*

A nanosecond before Tiana's scepter landed, Conrad's scepter was in his hand, activated, and he used it to parry Tiana's strike off to the left. As if by instinct, Conrad followed through the motion, weaving his scepter through the air in a labyrinthine fashion. He stopped when the blue crystal was mere centimeters away from piercing Tiana's throat. Conrad breathed deeply, staring at Tiana through the tops of his eyes again. Time seemed to stand still for a few moments.

Then Tiana smiled and said, "Bravo, Master Turner, bravo. So you do have a survival instinct, after all."

Conrad deactivated his scepter and raised his head so that he was now looking directly at Tiana's face. With a quizzical look on his face, he replied, "You were testing me?"

"Do you have so little faith as to believe I would ever harm you intentionally?"

"But…You hit me," he said, obviously hurt by the apparent disloyalty.

"Conrad, I am your protector, mentor, teacher, and friend. You are part of my family, now and forever." She placed her hand on the top of his head and then against the center of this chest.

"What I did I was compelled to do in order to protect you."

"Protect me from what?" Conrad asked.

Before Tiana could respond aloud, the thought formed in Conrad's brain: *"There are many dangers out here. Some are corporeal and others are not. But I will train you, and you will know how to protect yourself from all of them."*

Tiana knelt down beside Conrad so that her head was below his. She looked upward into his eyes and asked, "Are you ready to learn?"

"Yes," he replied without hesitation.

Tiana rose up. "I am glad to hear it. Let us continue our work," she said. "I am impressed with you so far." Tiana smiled.

Tiana began to explain the process needed to cultivate Conrad's native ability to manifest and bring into reality whatever he wanted. She asked him to reflect and consider what would be his greatest wish. Conrad thought. After several minutes, he said he would want his mother back. Tiana explained that, one day, he would see her again but that bringing someone back from the dead was one of only a few prohibitions placed upon incepts.

"What are the others?" he asked.

Tiana began her lecture about the Code of Myrddin. This code formed the legal and moral framework within which every incept must operate, or risk facing severe consequences. The code consisted of the following:

1. You shall not interfere with free will.
2. You shall not cause an imbalance.
3. You shall not force the dead to return to life.
4. You shall not create a direct conflict with another incept.
5. You shall strive to create order.

Conrad listened intently to every word Tiana uttered. He made mental notes of each one of the codes. After she had completed the lecture, Conrad though about each one of the codes. Not interfering with free will seemed pretty straightforward, but the others left him scratching his head.

"You have questions?" Tiana asked.

"I don't get what some of the rules mean."

"Example?"

"I shouldn't cause an imbalance? Imbalance in what?"

Tiana explained that everything in the universe is connected in some way. Some of the connections run deep and others are superficial. However, all the connections are necessary for everything to proceed and continue. When an imbalance occurs, something in the universe must adjust to compensate for the imbalance. It is the duty of all incepts to bring more order to the universe, not less. So, therefore, incepts must strive not to bring disorder, imbalance, into being.

"What happens if I bring imbalance accidentally?"

"Try to avoid it if at all possible, but if you do, you must remedy it immediately."

"What if I can't?"

Tiana looked sternly at Conrad. "Then neither I nor anyone else can help you on that path. It will be one you must follow on your own."

Conrad didn't like Tiana's explanation of the rule about maintaining balance. He did not like it one bit. He was especially perturbed by the lack of clarity relating to the potential penalty for breaking the rule. *A path I must follow on my own?* he thought. *What the heck does that mean, anyway?* He was beginning to think that Tiana spoke in riddles to confuse him, which made him sad and angry. Maybe she wasn't what she appeared to be. Maybe she was not his protector, after all. Perhaps he was still, and always would be, alone.

In his mind, he heard, *"Is that what you think, or is that what you feel?"*

"What's the difference?" he replied.

"There is a great difference," Tiana said. "Thoughts are governed by the conscious mind, and it can play tricks on you. Feelings are controlled and interpreted by the subconscious mind. There is no judgment or analysis."

Tiana stepped forward quickly, startling Conrad, who moved away from her advance reflexively.

"See, your subconscious made your body move away from a perceived attack. Your conscious mind was not even aware at first that I had made an aggressive move in your direction."

"Okay," Conrad said. "But what does that have to do with the difference between thinking and feeling?"

"If you think I am someone I am not, that is most likely a result of our recent confrontation. You were hurt by what you perceived as my disloyalty. However, if you feel I am not the person you believed me to be, if you feel I am not here to protect and mentor you, and if you feel I mean you harm, then I will go away and never return."

"What are you saying?" he asked with a slight tremor in his voice.

Tiana knelt next to Conrad, and grasping his shoulders gently, she pulled him closer to her, close enough for her to whisper in his ear. "If you feel that I would ever harm you, you must follow that feeling, and I will leave your life. Your subconscious does not lie, and I must protect you, even if it means I must leave."

Tiana released Conrad's shoulders and stood up. Watching her face, he tried to discern her meaning. Her eyes were light brown in color now, and she showed no outward indication of her feelings.

Conrad inhaled deeply as he closed his eyes in contemplation. He thought to himself, *Tiana.* He saw her face in his mind's eye, but he sensed nothing else.

He opened his eyes and said, "You don't have to go. I don't think you will harm me."

"That is insufficient," she replied. "What does your heart tell you?"

While staring into her brown eyes, he thought again: *Will Tiana ever hurt me?*

Several moments passed, with silence hanging between them.

Tiana lowered her chin and said, "I see. Good-bye, Conrad."

"Wait!" Conrad exclaimed. I don't want you to go. Please, don't leave me. I know you won't hurt me. I just know it."

Tiana smiled and said, "Are you certain?"

"I'm not certain about a lot yet…but I will be…so long as you are with me."

"Fair enough," Tiana said. "Come, we have many things to accomplish, and we are nearing our destination."

Tiana and Conrad reentered the command compartment in time to see the *Doppler Magnum* exit hyperspace. On the virtual windshield, long streaks of light shortened progressively until they all became points of light—stars. At the penultimate moment before the ship slowed completely from supralight speed, the disk of Mercatorum formed as a cylindrical shape that coalesced into a planetary form.

Mercatorum hung in space, a blue-green world surrounded by an orange-hued cloud cover of sporadic densities. The clouds were tinted by the light from the orange sun at the center of this solar system, a system comprised of four planets. Mercatorum was the largest, and the only one positioned in its sun's habitable zone.

The other three planets—Kapsar, Llewwlln, and Nautiko—were thoroughly explored, but other than Nautiko, which had a surface comprised predominantly of semiliquid water, there were no settlements on them.

Alex and Nash were seated at the control console. They were engaged in a heated conversation when Tiana and Conrad reentered.

"No, Nash," Alex said. "I'm captain of this ship, and we…" Alex's voice trailed off as he became aware of the passengers' presence.

"Welcome back," he said jovially. "You'll need to take your seats for landing. We'll be on the ground in a few minutes."

"Is there a problem?" Tiana asked.

Her eyes were blue-green in color, and the irises appeared to be rotating slowly around the center of her pupil. Nash looked at Tiana resignedly, but it was Alex who responded to her query.

"Nothing unusual. We just disagree on where to land."

"What are the choices?" she asked.

Nash started to speak, but Alex looked at him, placed a hand on Nash's shoulder, and turned to look at Tiana.

"I want to land at Valposta. Nash thinks we're more likely to find him at Ammerand."

Tiana closed her eyes briefly. When she reopened them, she said, "Ammerand."

Alex was clearly not pleased with Tiana's "opinion," and his demeanor showed it. "Fine," he retorted. "Nothing I prefer to do more after a flight of seventy light-years than to go on a wild-goose chase. Prepare for landing."

Tiana shook her head as she took her seat beside Conrad.

As his retention harness retracted, Conrad asked, "Who are we looking for?"

"Your father," Tiana replied without turning to see his reaction, which was swift and powerful.

"My father! Why didn't you tell me? I can't believe you didn't tell me! What am I supposed to say to him? What am I supposed to do? What if he doesn't want to see me?"

"Silence!" Conrad heard in his mind. *"All will be as it should be. Trust in that."*

Conrad regarded Tiana sheepishly. He hated when he let his emotions get the better of him. Such outbursts inevitably caused him great embarrassment, yet many times, he felt unable, or unwilling, to suppress them.

"But my father," he thought, *"I barely remember him. What will I say to him?"*

Tiana replied telepathically: *"Your father loved you when he left, and he continues to love you now. Why do you have so little trust in that after your vision?"*

He thought about the vision, how his father had looked, what he'd felt during it, the slight anger, remorse, fear, and ambivalence. It wasn't about his father leaving a small, scared boy any longer. It was about whom Conrad was, his destiny, his connection to his father and his ancestors, because, plainly, since his mother's death, Conrad was alone.

Now, it seemed, he was going to be reunited with his father. That one thought was completely overwhelming for him to fathom. He was no longer an orphan, a foster child, dreck. Instead, he had a past, a present, and from all indications, a fine future. A smile creped upon Conrad's face as this last thought progressed through his brain. *Not too shabby,* he thought.

As the *Doppler Magnum* entered the Mercatorum atmosphere, it shook briefly. A barely perceptible tone preceded the activation of the inertial dampening system. Once activated, the inertial dampers acted as shock absorbers to buffer the substantial forces encountered during a planetary landing.

"Entry shields to fifty percent," Alex said.

Conrad saw the reddish glow of friction between the atmosphere and the invisible energy shield that surrounded the ship, and he remembered reading about spacecraft when he was in fourth grade. The textbook indicated that, upon reentry, spaceships like the shuttle heated to three thousand degrees Fahrenheit. Most of the illustrations in the book showed the shuttle entering the atmosphere with its belly more or less absorbing the brunt of the kinetic energy. The *Doppler Magnum* seemed to be entering the atmosphere of Mercatorum directly. Conrad crossed his fingers and said a silent prayer. He did not notice Tiana smiling at his newly reestablished religious fervor.

When the ship exited the white-orange clouds, Conrad saw buildings, rivers, roads, and other geographic markers of civilization. As the ground rapidly approached the ship, the *Doppler Magnum* swung its rear end wide, preparing to land in a clearing meant for spacecraft.

Conrad saw several ships on the ground, and amongst them were crewmembers and others milling around. Alex and Nash maneuvered the ship to land in between two freighters, the distance between which seemed narrower than the *Magnum*'s width. Once they were in preliminary position, however, the ship landed without incident.

"Wow!" Conrad exclaimed. "Great job landing."

"Thanks, sport," Alex replied.

"Good of you to notice, Conrad," Nash said, sounding a little perturbed. "But once inside the atmosphere, the landing computer takes control."

Conrad saw Alex turn his head in his direction and wink. Conrad shook his head in disbelief.

The landing ramp extended itself out several yards from the ship as the exit gantry opened to allow egress. Alex and Nash stood first.

"I want everyone to stick close," Alex said. "I'm not sure what's in store for us here. I wanted to go to Valposta."

Alex scowled at Tiana, who closed her eyes slightly and shook her head.

Tiana and Conrad got out of their seats next, when a strange thing caught Conrad's attention. A small bolt of red light shot into the ship through the open gantry way. The bolt shot past Alex's head and exploded into a side bulkhead.

On instinct alone, Alex drew a small weapon from his belt. Just as the weapon cleared his long coat, the barrel grew to almost a foot long. A heartbeat later, Alex crouched slightly and began leveling a fusillade of responsive shots in the direction of the attack. Conrad could feel his heart pounding in his chest.

"What's going on?" he whispered to Tiana.

Tiana held her hand up to his face. Her eyes were closed, and she was concentrating on something.

After about thirty seconds had come and gone in what felt—to Conrad, at least—like three days, the concussions of exploding energy subsided.

Alex relaxed and stood, regarding the interior of his ship. "Damage report," he said.

"Minor damage to vector projector two. No breaches identified" came the computer voice from the artificial neural network, or ANN.

"Secure and repair," Alex said, relieved there were no breaches in the hull. Holes in a spacecraft's outer skin could take weeks to repair, and he didn't want to be stuck on Mercatorum for that long.

Nash dusted himself off. "So what's the plan," he asked.

"I dunno," Alex replied. He motioned and pointed to Tiana. "It's her show."

Tiana and Conrad walked to the front of the cabin.

"Maybe you were correct about Valposta," Tiana said. "But let us ascertain why someone here finds us to be a threat."

Mercatorum was governed on a global scale by various regional governors, and order was maintained by the warrior clans. Primary authority in Ammerand City rested in the hands of the *triumviri ultima*. The three members of the ultimate triumvirate were the supreme baron, justice advocate, and prime minister, and they governed from Ammerand Palace.

The palace was built into the side of a mountain overlooking a large bay. Created from a stone similar in texture and tone to jade granite, the facade was staggering, rising three hundred yards from the ground. Nearly the entire front of the building had windows facing the bay before it, and light from the Mercatorum sun reflected off them every evening.

"Wow!" Conrad exclaimed as the group walked toward the palace. "What is that?"

"Ammerand Palace," Tiana said. "It is our destination."

They entered the palace foyer and were stopped at a reception area. Alex approached the receptionist.

"Good day to you all," the woman said. "May I help you?"

"Yes," Alex replied. "We're here to see Baron von Goren."

"Is he expecting you?"

Alex threw a glance at Tiana, who nodded her head in the affirmative.

"Yes, he is," Alex replied.

The receptionist closed her eyes tightly. *"Baron,"* Conrad heard in his head, *"there are visitors here to see you—two men, a tall woman, and a boy."*

Several moments elapsed in silence—both physical and mental. Conrad knew there was a reply because the receptionist was nodding her closed-eyed head rapidly.

Finally, he heard, *"Very well, Baron."*

When the receptionist opened her eyes, she first looked directly at Conrad with a strange expression.

"The baron will see you now. Ninetieth floor." She pointed to her right and behind the reception desk. "Take that elevator. It's express."

The group had begun to walk toward the elevator when the little woman said, "I'm sorry, I wasn't clear. You may all go up but the boy."

"Why not the kid?" Alex asked.

She shook her head slightly from side to side. "I have no idea, sir. Baron's orders."

Conrad was dismayed. He felt disrespected once again, and now from the unknown leader of an entire planet. He felt worthless.

Tiana touched his shoulder. *"Stay here and learn."*

He looked up into her face. Her eyes were the color of robin's eggs, and she had a great smile.

"Okay, then," he said. "I'm not a real fan of elevators, anyway. Say hi to the baron for me."

As the other three left Conrad in the lobby, he tried hard to keep smiling. He was very unhappy even though Tiana's thoughts had reassured him. He wanted to be with his companions, but some old, mean dictator refused to have him in his presence. *Screw him*, Conrad thought.

He found a comfortable chair across from the reception desk and plunked his derriere in it. While sitting there, Conrad marveled at his surroundings. He remembered visiting the Empire State Building in New York City when he was younger; he thought it was when he resided with the Thompsons, but he couldn't be sure. As a young boy, he was impressed by the great lobby. Many people were visiting that day, and he remembered the art deco relief on the wall behind the reception desk. It was a metal-and-cloisonné scale replica of the building itself. Just beside the information desk and sculpture was a bank of elevators programmed to rise rapidly to the observation deck on the eighty-sixth floor.

He recalled his heart pounding while riding up to the observation deck, not because he was scared or claustrophobic, which he would tell you emphatically he wasn't, but instead, it was caused by pure excitement. He loved the anticipation: rising floor after floor, feeling the acceleration and velocity in his feet, then exiting the car to the outdoor observation deck into a bright-blue-sky-lit day.

He tried to look down to the ground below that day, but it was difficult to see through the safety fencing. But oh, what a day it was. He remembered hoping it would never end, because for a brief time, he felt worthy and connected to the world. He had felt like he actually belonged there.

Even with all those wonderfully thick memories flooding in, Conrad could not help but be even more impressed with the lobby he sat in now. When he had taken the chair in which he currently sat, he thought it was merely steps away from the reception desk. Now, looking at the receptionist, he was sitting at least a football field away. The lobby was gargantuan. Conrad thought someone could park several jumbo jets in it with space to spare. He smiled at the thought of wings and fuselages taking up most of the area. *How is that possible?* he thought to himself. Perhaps the same laws of physics in effect on Overworld were in effect on Mercatorum as well. And Conrad had been away from Earth for long enough to know that things don't always seem as they appear.

As he continued thinking about this, he began noticing all of the people walking through the lobby. Maybe "people" was an incorrect description. Surely many of them were human beings— or at least humanoid—but there were just as many others one would be hard pressed to describe as "people" or "human."

There was one kid—and Conrad only thought he was a kid because he was holding the hand of an older, taller version of himself—whose head inflated as he entered the building. It continued inflating until it was at least ten times its normal size. When the inflation was completed, this "kid's" head floated off his shoulders, followed by a thin strand of neck. After about a yard of neck had wound out, the "kid" grabbed hold of the neck meat with his right hand and continued walking through the lobby with his head balloon in tow.

He also saw a two-headed being wander through. The two heads—one appearing male and the other female—were carrying on a conversation.

"You are so insensitive," the female said.

"And you are a complainer," the male retorted.

The female swung the arm she controlled in an attempt to slap the male's face, but he responded by grabbing her wrist with the hand he manipulated.

"Why do you always try to hit me when we disagree?" the male asked.

"You just make me so mad," the female said with tears in her eyes.

"I'm sorry," the male said. "Let's try to make the best of the day."

The female smiled through her tears, and this beast with two heads hugged itself.

Chapter Seventeen

To say that the baron's office was lavish would have been the understatement of the millennia. The walls were paneled with alternating bands of gold and platinum. Adorning the walls were original artworks from all over the galaxy: *Las Meninas* by Diego Velazquez, *Study of a Tuscan Landscape* by Leonardo da Vinci, *Atroplocaucus* by Zim Xolocuintle, and *End of Eternity* by Mas Mxlqpivn, just to name a few.

The baron's desk was ten yards long by six yards wide, and it sat upon a riser, lifting the baron nearly fifteen feet above the floor. Someone standing before the desk would be unable to view his face without the photo-reactive viewing screens attached the front of it. Several yards away were three comfortable armchairs positioned in a semicircle.

Nash, Alex, and Tiana were seated in the chairs, and Baron von Goren's visage was presented on the viewing screens.

"Welcome, my friends," the baron said. "To what do I owe this unexpected but appreciated visit?"

Nash prepared to answer, but Alex beat him to it.

"We're here to find Nathaniel Turner," he said.

Von Goren's jovial mood changed. "I thought as much," the baron replied. "We have searched high and low, and we have been unable to find him here on Mercatorum."

Alex stood. "That's impossible, Your Excellency. We *know* he's here."

Von Goren's demeanor soured even further with Alex's challenge. "Just what are you implying, Mr. Sine? You know I can have you arrested for that stunt you pulled last season."

Alex was about to retort something about the baron's mother and her choice in mating partners when Tiana lightly touched his sleeve. Alex immediately regained his composure.

"Please forgive the insolence of my companion, Your Excellency," Tiana announced. "It has been a long trip, and we have yet to be refreshed."

Von Goren smiled slightly again. "Well, Master Tiana, no harm, no foul, but as I indicated, our intelligence suggests Nathaniel Turner has either not been here on Mercatorum recently or he is no longer a visitor here."

Tiana stared intently at the viewing screen for several seconds. Von Goren's image on the screen blinked several times and shut its eyes momentarily.

When his eyes reopened, he said, "You see I am not being false. I am sorry we can be of no further help, but you are welcome to stay in the palace while you are here. Compliments of the counsel."

It was now Nash's turn to speak. "Thank you, Your Excellency. We accept your gracious offer. Good day."

Von Goren's image on the viewing screen watched as they left. When the door closed behind them, the image of von Goren on the screen winced in pain, and a deep, dark voice said, "Very good, Baron. You have done well."

Once the pain had subsided, von Goren replied, "A sentinel will not be deterred. She will find him."

The voice laughed. "We shall see."

Chapter Eighteen

Conrad was getting bored sitting and waiting. As interesting as watching all the different species walk by was, how many three-eyed sloths can one see in a day and not be infected with tedium? He sat in the same chair, comfortable as it was, that he was in when the landing party proceeded to the ninetieth floor. Now, however, he was sitting slouched, kicking his left foot up and down and tapping the floor slightly on each rebound.

The elevator opened and Tiana exited, followed by Alex and Nash. They were having a very heated conversation, but Conrad was too far away to hear anything. He closed his eyes and concentrated on trying to hear Tiana's thoughts. There was nothing. He didn't understand this because usually it was easy for him to hear them.

As they continued their path through the lobby toward Conrad, Tiana held up her right hand and shouted, "ENOUGH!" Her voice echoed through the cavernous lobby. Tiana stopped herself when she realized she had allowed Alex to get the better of her emotions.

"Alex," she said. "I do not know what it is that I felt. I only know I felt another presence in addition to the baron's. Accept it as such."

Tiana resumed her progress through the lobby, but Alex grabbed her arm and pulled her back slightly.

"I just need to know," he said. "If it is him, you will tell me if you confirm it?"

Tiana was looking at the ground and then slowly lifted her eyes. Conrad could see that her eyes were glowing amber.

"Yes," she said. "I will tell you when I confirm. But I will also tell you if it is not him."

As the threesome approached, Conrad jumped out of the chair to meet them. "About time," he said. "I almost died from boredom."

Tiana managed a strained smile and then placed her hand on Conrad's shoulder. "My apologies," she said. "There was much to cover with the baron. Next time you can join us, okay?"

Conrad regarded Tiana. Try as he might, he could not hear her thoughts now, and the lack of communication troubled him.

"Did you find out anything about my father?" Conrad asked.

Tiana looked at him. Her eyes were now brilliant blue. She said nothing, but Conrad heard in his head, *"Not yet, but we will."* Hearing Tiana's thoughts, after being unable to do so, actually startled him momentarily. Tiana noted his surprise. Once again, she touched him slightly and said, "I will explain everything when the time is right."

As the four of them stood in the grand lobby, there was a brief uncomfortable silence. Finally, Nash broke the tension by asking, "So what's the plan?"

"I say we try Valposta," Alex interjected.

Tiana shook her head. "Not at this time. I must analyze what has happened today."

"So then we're just going to give up and leave?" Alex asked sarcastically.

Tiana replied, "He who is ignorant of his enemy will remain in grave peril. And I will not place him at unknown risk." She motioned toward Conrad when she said "him."

"All right," Alex said resignedly. "Nash and I will prepare the ship for the trip back."

"Do as you will," Tiana said. "But I will take Conrad home to Overworld."

She then removed her token from her belt, tapped a few keystrokes, and replaced the token . A bright point of light appeared before them in this grand lobby of the Ammerand

Palace. It then lengthened vertically, finally opening as a bright rectangular doorway. The air in the lobby began to move and rumble as the doorway opened. Tiana held out her hand for Conrad's acceptance, and this time he simply grabbed hold of it without resistance. They stepped through the doorway and disappeared.

When the doorway collapsed on itself, everyone in the lobby was staring at the remaining members of the quartet.

Alex scratched his head and said, "Life is getting stranger and stranger, eh, folks?"

Chapter Nineteen

Conrad and Tiana landed in his room on the thirty-fifth floor of Turner Manor. Conrad stumbled again upon landing, as he always did, but something was different this time. Although he felt a little nauseated, he did not actually feel the need to purge. He stood, slightly bent over at the waist, and smacked his lips together for a few moments to be sure he wasn't experiencing a delayed reaction of some sort. Vomiting uncontrollably was humiliating enough, but doing so with no warning could be the ultimate embarrassment.

Conrad considered what would occur in such a situation while he was speaking to someone, anyone, after what appeared to be an uneventful teleportation landing, and then having projectile vomitus spew all over his cohort. *Especially if it was a girl I was talking to*, he thought.

Tiana smirked when she considered every thought Conrad had regarding his teleportation sickness. He caught her smiling.

"What?" he cried.

She simply shook her head and let out a quiet chuckle. "Get some rest," Tiana advised. "Afterward, a small meal, and then meet me in the training facility." Tiana retrieved her token and began programming a new destination.

"Wait!" Conrad shouted. "Can we talk about what happened—or what didn't happen—on Mercatorum? Where's my father?"

Tiana's demeanor changed instantly from jovial to serious. "We will debrief," she replied. "But get some rest first."

"But I'm not the least bit tired," Conrad complained.

"You will sleep," Tiana said into his mind. *"You might even find some answers there."*

The air rushed in to fill the void where Tiana was standing just a moment before.

Conrad exhaled a big sigh. He thought he might as well get some sleep because Tiana was generally right about things. At least here on Overworld she was. Well, actually, she was correct, or nearly so, everywhere, including back home in California, and here on Overworld, and on Mercatorum. And a boy Conrad's age had no chance at all fighting city hall, so he might as well do what she'd asked and get some shut-eye.

He looked around the room for his pajamas. There was a neat stack of several pairs placed strategically on the storage chest at the foot of the bed. He sorted through the stack and settled on a pair that was multiple shades of blue with gold piping and thin vertical gold stripes.

He began removing his clothes. When he removed his shirt, a whiff of a rancid odor violated his nasal passages. Did he have body odor? Conrad raised his right arm and took a deep sniff near his armpit.

"Whoa!" he exclaimed. *So that's what BO smells like. I better take a shower, too.*

Conrad felt completely refreshed after his shower. He dried himself completely, put on the blue-and-gold pajamas, and returned to the main part of his bedroom. He then sensed a slight rumbling in his belly. A small snack was in order before calling it a night.

"Twix?" Conrad thought.

Twix appeared with a crackle. "You called, Master Turner?"

Conrad felt something funny inside; a feeling of relief or calm washed over him immediately upon Twix's appearance, and he smiled to himself.

"Yes, Twix," he said. "I would like something to eat before bedtime. What do you suggest?"

Twix cocked his tiny head to the side for a moment. "Cookies and warm milk," he replied.

"Great idea," Conrad said, and a plate of snicker doodle cookies, a blue mug of slightly frothy milk, and a snack tray beneath for support appeared hovering in the space in front of Twix. Twix grasped the ends of the tray, walked beside the big bed, and placed the tray on the nightstand.

Conrad took a cookie from the tray. It was warm to the touch. He placed it in his mouth and took a bite. The sugary sweetness, enhanced with the slight cinnamon flavor, enveloped his taste buds. Cookies were the only true comfort food, in Conrad's estimation. He washed down the delicious morsel with a big swig of the perfectly warmed milk. He unconsciously licked and smacked his lips and smiled. Twix smiled, too.

"Will that be all, Master Turner?" Twix asked.

"Don't go yet," Conrad replied. "Please?"

"Very well, sir," Twix said. "What shall we talk about?"

Conrad related the story about his trip to Mercatorum. He described in detail the *Doppler Magnum*, the control center, the acceleration through light-speed, and everything he could remember. He intentionally avoided discussing the simulated battle with Tiana, but he had a suspicion Twix already knew something about it.

"How did you like Mr. Sine?" Twix asked.

"Alex or Nash?"

"Why not tell me about one and follow with the other?"

Conrad told Twix he thought Nash seemed like a nice man, but he was much quieter than his brother. Conrad thought for several moments trying to recall what he had observed about Nash, and he realized he hadn't observed much. He made a mental note to be more diligent in the future about observing people and things better. He did recall that Nash seemed extremely competent at planning space travel and operating spacecraft. He also seemed to be an expert navigator.

Alex was different. He was very sure of himself, and seemed a little boastful, but there was something about him, something Conrad couldn't quite put his finger on, that intrigued Conrad. He would even say he liked Alex. But he also knew, or had a sense, that Alex could be reckless, and that trait could lead to danger. He had sensed Tiana's anger and disapproval at several different moments during the trip. And he also saw how Alex reacted when Tiana disagreed with his opinion, direction, strategy, or tactics. Alex resented being undermined by anyone; however, Conrad had sensed actual fear in Alex only once, and that was when Alex directly challenged Tiana.

Tiana. Conrad wasn't completely sure what to make of her. He did feel that she was meant to protect and mentor him—he was certain of it. However, there were many things she did or said that simply baffled and confused him. She spoke in riddles most of the time, and when he asked her to explain her meaning, she would answer with another conundrum. It was maddening, and Conrad felt, at times, put down by that behavior.

But then again, he also felt that Tiana had more respect and admiration for him than he had for himself. She described Conrad as part of a great universal power, a great triumvirate destined to bring order to the universe. Yet, most of the time, Conrad felt powerless to even control his own life. He shook his head, thinking about that prospect. He, orphaned and alone, was part of a great and powerful group that, together, would one day change the very fabric of the universe? It couldn't be possible, and he wanted to get back to California, back to his mundane existence, and face the reality of his life: he was nothing and would never amount to anything.

"Sir," Twix said, startling Conrad. "I think you should get some sleep. Everything will be better in the morning."

"What?" Conrad said after being jolted back into reality.

"Negative thoughts don't solve anything, Master Turner. Try a more positive outlook, and I am sure you will see the truth."

"Really, Twix?" Conrad replied. "And what is the 'truth' as you see it?"

"Sir, what I see is a bright and talented boy who has been beaten down by life, but one who, given the chance, can accomplish anything he puts his mind to. That is how I see it." Then Twix stood still and said, "Perhaps it will all become clearer in the morning. Good night, Master Turner, pleasant dreams."

After Twix had disappeared, Conrad's eyes filled with tears. He wouldn't allow himself to completely breakdown, but there was a great sadness within him. His life before the fire, before meeting Tiana the rat and coming to Overworld, was one peppered with heartbreak, sadness, and stress. Thinking about it could be overwhelming, so he tried to avoid doing it.

He pulled back the comforter and blanket on the bed and slid between the sheets. He pulled the covers up to his neck and closed his eyes. Before he fell asleep, he thought, *Okay, then, show me what I need to know.* Then he took in a long, deep breath, smoothed the top of the down-filled comforter, and settled in for the night. Within minutes, he was fast asleep.

Chapter Twenty

In the dreamscape, Conrad was running. It was dark, and he was running on a path that was faintly lit by the full moon above. The trees on either side of the path simply swayed in the midnight breeze. As he proceeded, he came upon a small house in the woods. It could be more accurately described as a cabin, being that it was simply constructed of four walls and a roof. Smoke was escaping from the chimney, and there was the flicker of candlelight in the windows. Outside, in the front, there was a tall, thin man dressed in denim overalls, a gray button-down shirt with the sleeves rolled up over his elbows, and a pair of well-worn leather boots. He was chopping wood on the right side of the cabin; he raised his ax above his head, swung it down hard, and split a small log as it rested upon a larger stump.

With one last powerful blow, the ax head came to rest on the stump, and the man gathered up the split wood, carrying it to the woodpile to the right of the cabin's front door. When he turned, Conrad thought he looked a lot like Abraham Lincoln, but there was something not quite right about the look. *What is it?* Conrad thought. And then it hit him. Lincoln wore—at least in the most universally accepted version—a beard without a mustache. This man was wearing a neatly trimmed goatee and mustache.

When the man saw Conrad he said, "Well, young fella, what brings you to these parts?" Conrad shrugged. "Dunno. I was just running on the path."

"I see," said the man. "Well, son, if you don't know where you are going, how will you know when you arrive?"

Conrad thought, *Great! I can't even avoid these riddles in my dreams!* But rather than insult the man on the off chance he actually was Abraham Lincoln, he replied, "Yes, I understand. Do you know where this path goes?"

The man scratched his head and then stroked his beard before answering, "A' course I do, but you are the one who needs to find out. Remember to keep on the path. If you do, you will always be safe. If you don't..." The man wrinkled his face as if he were thinking really hard and then continued. "Let's just say you might not like where you end up."

Conrad nodded his head in acknowledgment, said good-bye to the pseudo former president, and continued his trek down the path.

After a while, the sky grew darker, and the wind picked up. The trees along the path began to resemble goblins with glowing eyes and pointed teeth and clawed, boney fingers. They seemed to reach out to capture him, but Conrad avoided each attempt. In fact, he was actually proud of himself because he seemed to anticipate every move the goblin trees made and counteracted or parried their attacks.

Continuing along the path and avoiding the attacks gave Conrad a great sense of accomplishment. As he rounded a bend, he stopped suddenly. As he stood motionless, he listened intently. There was a deafening quiet. He looked around in a complete circle. Something wasn't right; he felt it.

Finally, as a whisper, he heard, "You do not belong here."

"Who is that?" Conrad yelled.

There was no reply.

Conrad was getting angry. "Show yourself, coward!" he yelled.

Suddenly, on the path before him, a figure materialized. It was over nine feet tall, black, with glowing reddish-orange slits where its eyes should be and pointed black teeth in its mouth. Conrad's heart skipped a beat, but the adrenaline was still flowing through his veins.

"I'm not afraid of you!" he screamed.

The beast flew at him in the blink of an eye, knocking Conrad to the ground.

In his dream, Conrad was angry. The beast laughed at him while he lay upon the ground, and a fury rose up within him as never before. But what could he do within this dream?

He felt something pressing against his thigh, and when he looked down, he saw his scepter was there, attached to his waist. He smiled to himself, and then he jumped to his feet, collected himself into a battle stance, and motioned to the beast to try it again.

"Come on!" Conrad yelled. "Let's see what you're made of."

An ungodly shriek came from this minion of the darkness, and it leaped at Conrad. This time, however, Conrad anticipated the charge, withdrew his scepter from his belt, and activated it a millisecond before the beast struck. Conrad swung the scepter's glowing thread in a figure-eight arc and landed it just above the thing's broad shoulders.

The black head rolled for several yards before it came to rest. As it did, Conrad saw that the red-orange eyes glowed brighter still from the shock of his counterattack. When the head came to rest, it whispered in a coarse voice, "This isn't over, boy. We shall meet again."

Then the head burst into a blue-white flame, which fully consumed it within seconds. Conrad turned his attention to the now decapitated body, but to his surprise—and slight relief—it, too, had disappeared.

Conrad deactivated his scepter and reattached it to his belt. An almost overwhelming sense of satisfaction overcame him. It was the first time in his life he hadn't felt fear during a confrontation. He saw the threat and met it head-on.

Chapter Twenty-One

When he awoke, he still had minor trouble wrapping his head around what had happened and, more importantly, what his dream meant. Did Tiana know he was going to have that specific dream, or did she have another ability? Could she possibly be able to enter into another person's mind and program his dreams? And what about his father? She'd implied, before they'd left for Mercatorum, that Conrad would finally meet his father after all these years.

So many questions were being raised in his mind that Conrad began to get a slight headache. Still, he was incredibly proud of himself for standing up to the orange-eyed beast and vanquishing him. Perhaps Tiana was right about him; perhaps Twix was correct, too. Perhaps Conrad was part of a trinity of souls destined to bring order and peace to the universe. Perhaps he wasn't the loser he, and others, always considered himself to be. The possibility that he was more, much more, than he ever expected gave Conrad great comfort and joy, and he decided to believe it for now.

After he got dressed, Conrad summoned Twix.

"Yes, Master Turner?" Twix said when he materialized. "How did you sleep, sir?"

Conrad told Twix he slept very well and that he felt completely refreshed.

"I see," Twix replied. "I am glad. Did you have any dreams?"

Conrad was stunned. "How did you know?" he asked.

Twix exploded in his high-pitched laughter. "Oh, Master Turner, I know nothing. I was just curious."

Conrad told Twix about the dream, about Abraham Lincoln, about the winding path he was running along, about the little cabin in the woods, and about the orange-eyed beast.

"What do you suppose it means?" he asked Twix.

Twix shook his head. "Master Turner," Twix began, "I know much about many things—things having to do with service to and care for others—but I also know what I do not know. Perhaps Master Tiana will have better insight for you."

Conrad couldn't fault Twix for not having a clue as to the meaning of his vivid dream. He himself was confused by it. He thought that the monster represented danger, in general, and that perhaps his bravery in the face of that grotesque creature signified that he was turning the corner on his fears.

He also considered the vision of Abraham Lincoln. Lincoln, he had learned in school, had overcome a childhood of adversity when his family had lost nearly everything. He also knew Lincoln was known to be proficient with an ax and as a wrestler. But he remembered that all the photographs of Abraham Lincoln showed the former president either clean shaven or with a beard and no mustache. The Lincoln in his dream had a mustache and beard.

Twix is probably right, Conrad thought. *Tiana will help make sense of it.*

"Twix," Conrad said. "Do you know where Tiana is right now?"

Twix laughed again. "Oh, Master Turner," he replied. "You still do not understand how it works."

Twix reached up as far as he could toward Conrad. Even with his arms fully extended, he could barely touch Conrad's hands. When Twix touched him, Conrad sensed something. There was strength in Twix's hands, but there was also something else, something he could not quite put his finger on.

Twix turned Conrad to face the big open window of his room. Conrad saw there were very few lavender clouds in the sky today. Twix placed Conrad's hands to his sides, palms facing toward his legs.

"Close your eyes, please," Twix requested.

Conrad closed his eyes.

"Picture Master Tiana," Twix continued. "Once you have a clear picture of her, think *Take me to her*, and you will find her."

Conrad pictured Tiana: tall with a deep-brown complexion, wearing her battle outfit, boots, halter, coat, and her omnipresent utility belt. As usual, her scepter was at the ready, hanging from it. Conrad saw that she was smiling. He liked her smiling better than any other way. Finally, Conrad saw that her eyes were the color of robin's eggs. *Take me to her*, he thought.

Chapter Twenty-Two

Conrad felt as if someone had punched him hard in the stomach. All the air was knocked out of him; he was having trouble inhaling. Just as he was beginning to panic, Conrad opened his eyes. He was in the warrior arts training facility again. He looked around, and for several moments, which felt to Conrad like several minutes, he was alone in the room.

Suddenly, Tiana materialized before him, her hair pulled into a tight bun atop her head and her eyes like two blazing emeralds. She was dressed in her black combat training uniform.

"I didn't know we were training," Conrad said. "I didn't dress properly."

Tiana stared at him, her eyes beaming bright green. He looked down and saw that he was now dressed in his black uniform.

"What…how?" he stammered.

Tiana laughed. "You are beginning to understand, but you must make faster progress. That is why we are training today."

In quick succession, Mindy, Matthew, and Matilda all entered the facility with flashes of light and a crackle of the air popping behind them as they teleported into the room. Atticus appeared several moments after the others, and he entered with such force that he fell, face-first, onto the training mat. Matthew and Matilda snickered at Atticus's graceless teleportation. Mindy walked over to help Atticus up, and Conrad made the assist.

"Good to see you again, Conrad," Mindy said as they both lifted the massive Atticus.

Once righted, Atticus said neither "thank you" nor "piss off." Conrad knew he appreciated their help, but he couldn't hear Atticus's thoughts.

Strange, Conrad thought.

Tiana said, "Welcome, class. Please assemble."

Upon Tiana's command, each student teleported to his or her assigned spot. Conrad, however, jumped to his.

"No," Tiana said. "You must learn to teleport effortlessly. Please try again."

Conrad returned to his previous location on the mat. He closed his eyes and thought, *Move to my spot.* When he opened his eyes, he remained in the same place.

"What am I doing wrong?" he asked.

"Tell the class what you thought before your attempt."

Conrad described his steps: closing his eyes, thinking *Move to my spot*, and then opening his eyes.

Mindy raised her hand, and Tiana pointed to her and said, "You have a suggestion?"

"No, Master. I wanted to ask a question."

"Go ahead."

Mindy asked Conrad what he felt when he tried to think his way to his assigned spot in the class.

He thought for a moment and then responded, "I didn't want to screw up."

Matthew and Matilda snickered.

"Silence!" Tiana demanded. "There are no wrong answers here. Criticism without construction will not be tolerated."

"That's your problem, then," Mindy said.

Mindy began explaining how the power to manifest has more to do with *feeling* the thing you want than actually *thinking* it. She started with an analogy:

"Think about the sun shining on your face."

Conrad closed his eyes again. He thought about the summer sun in California. It was hot, bright, and good. A smile crossed Conrad's face. Mindy, who was watching him experience his memory, could barely control her excitement.

"Excellent, Conrad, now tell us what you feel."

"It feels good, and warm, and…safe. I always enjoyed my summer days in California. It didn't matter much what I was doing; so long as the sun was shining, I was happy"

Without missing a beat, Tiana interjected, "Very well, now try to teleport to your place in the class."

Conrad, who kept his eyes closed throughout his second attempt in order to savor the summer memory, changed thoughts. He thought about moving through space in an instant to take his place in line beside Mindy. The thought of Mindy filled him with a joy he had not felt in a while.

He hadn't noticed the double crackles that had punctuated his movement from one place to another in the blink of an eye. What he did hear was the applause of his classmates. He opened his eyes, and he was standing on the mat in between Mindy and Atticus. Atticus slapped Conrad on the back, nearly knocking him off balance.

Conrad regarded his classmates. They all seemed genuinely impressed with his teleportation. They were all smiling, laughing, saying words of encouragement and congratulations, and Conrad felt he belonged again. He looked up at Tiana and saw that she was not only smiling from ear to ear, but he also saw a glimmer of pride in her now turquoise eyes. Tiana nodded her approval for all the class to see.

After several congratulatory minutes, Tiana said, "Okay, class, we are all proud of Conrad's accomplishment, but there is much work to do."

As the class was settling down from the excitement, Tiana walked up and down before them in silence, allowing them to regain their composure. Once they were silent, she continued.

"Today we will begin working on our Q-energy transference protocol."

Upon her uttering these words, there was a muttering of excitement coming from the students. Matilda raised her hand.

"Yes, Matilda," Tiana said.

"Master, we were told Q-energy training was reserved for upperclassmen."

"Yes, that is traditionally the case. However, there has been a severe shift in the balance. We must expedite our training because each of you may be asked to join the warrior clan sooner than any of us expected."

Tiana regarded each of them after this pronouncement. She also took inventory of their individual emotional responses. Matthew thought, *All right! Finally, I get to do something.* Matilda's reaction was more tentative. She was thinking about the unknown: *What or who will we be expected to battle? Will anyone die?* Atticus, whose autism did not define him as a person, was thinking in the linear manner many people on the autism spectrum exhibit. He thought about his favorite movie, *Harry Potter and the Chamber of Secrets.*

Finally, when Tiana's scan reached Conrad, she grew confused and briefly concerned. Conrad's thoughts were generally clear and concise to her. However, for some reason or another, she could not quite focus in on what he was thinking at this particular moment. She concentrated more strongly, attempting to get a better fix on Conrad's thoughts. She had to be cautious, though, because too focused a probe could fry his brain within moments.

As she refocused, maneuvering through the various thought frequencies, she finally landed on Conrad's. His thoughts were relatively calm: *I can do this. I am, after all, Trinity-Two, or so I've been told.* Tiana saw Conrad smile, and she smiled back at him.

Tiana composed herself again, and reconnoitering the warrior training facility, she began.

"Conrad, Mindy, move across the mat opposite Atticus and Matilda."

Conrad and Mindy did as Tiana had directed and quickly teleported into their assigned positions.

Tiana continued, "Matthew, move with them, if you will."

Matthew looked befuddled. He was nearly always paired with his twin sister. "Master, I don't understand."

Tiana glared at Matthew with raging violet eyes. "Question not my directions, Matthew." Dejected, Matthew followed Conrad and Mindy to his place.

When they were all lined up across from each other, Tiana explained how Q-energy transference worked. She told them there were three important factors required to successfully transfer one's physical energy. The first requirement was a proper stance. Tiana sunk down into a very sturdy horse stance with her feet shoulder length apart, knees bent, and toes pointed forward.

She then explained the second criterion: proper breathing.

"Always inhale through the nose and exhale through the mouth," she directed. "And your tongue should lightly touch the roof of your mouth. This will maintain the alignment of your seven energy vortices."

Next, Tiana put her hands in front of her body. Her left was at chest level, with the palm of her hand parallel to the ground. Her right was positioned under the left, near her belly. Her right palm was point up toward her left.

"The final process is providing a place for your Q-energy to coalesce," she said. "Watch and learn."

The student warriors watched with great interest and concentration. Tiana, set in her deep horse, breathing in though her nose and out through her mouth, began to produce an effect in the space between her hands. In the center of her opposing palms, a ball of blue-white light materialized.

As she continued breathing rhythmically, running her palms over and around the ever-intensifying light ball, its intensity grew geometrically. Each of the students gasped when the light ball reached a crescendo of brilliance. It was so bright now that they could barely look at the ball without closing their eyes briefly; so star-like was its glow that some of them actually felt pain when looking directly at it.

Matthew, however, was trying to suppress a nervous snicker. He didn't know why he found the exhibition of Tiana's power ball so amusing, but a nearly uncontrollable impulse to laugh out loud was welling up within him. He tried in vain to hold it in because he knew Tiana would not appreciate any levity. However, his will proved too weak, and Matthew let forth a huge belly laugh.

Tiana was monitoring each student's reaction to her demonstration. She wanted to gauge each one's particular disposition, level of acceptance, and yes, even fear or trepidation. She knew before Matthew began to laugh what was about to transpire, so when he lost complete control, she pointed her toes in Matthew's direction. When his first laugh reached its apex, Tiana quickly snapped her wrists so that her palms were rapidly pointed toward Matthew. All the potential energy contained within the blue-white ball of light was flung at Matthew with unfathomable momentum.

The ball hit Matthew, center chest. The energy released lifted him completely off the floor and sent him flying toward the opposite wall. When he hit the wall, the air was knocked out of him, and he collapsed to the floor in a heap. He sat immobile for a while, and his classmates observed in disbelief.

Finally, Matthew shook his head from side to side to regain his orientation.

Atticus began laughing uncontrollably. "Funny," he said.

"Shut up, Atticus," Matilda responded. "Are you all right, Matt?"

"Of course he is," Tiana said. "Remember, nothing can harm you while you are training here."

Tiana stopped to watch Matthew pull himself to his feet. He was clearly embarrassed by what had just transpired, but he remained unwilling to acknowledge it. She walked across the mat to help Matthew regroup. When she approached him, he initially brushed her hands away. She placed a hand on each of his shoulders, leaned in, and whispered something to him. He closed his eyes as she did, and moments later, he was smiling again.

Tiana stepped back from him, removed her hands from his shoulders, wrapped her left arm around his upper back, and they both walked back to rejoin the group.

When Matthew took his place beside Matilda, she asked in a low voice, "Are you all right?"

Matthew simply nodded affirmatively and smiled at his sister. Matilda reached out to him, and Matthew grabbed her hand and squeezed lightly. Both of the siblings then came to attention.

Tiana instructed the students to perform the Q-energy transference protocol pursuant to the instructions she had given. Each one lowered him or herself into a solid horse stance. Conrad followed suit, and he looked to Mindy for assurance.

Within moments, the entire class had a glowing ball of intrinsic energy floating between their opposing palms. Each one glowed a different color, and the student warriors found this difference to be remarkable. When asked, Tiana explained that each being's intrinsic Q-energy vibrated at a different frequency, the same way light does.

Matthew's energy was a brilliant blue-green color. His sister's was similar but of a lesser intensity. Atticus was holding a ball of energy with a reddish hue. Mindy held before her a bright-blue ball. She was moving it up and down between her palms as if it were bouncing between them. Conrad laughed to himself when he saw this.

All of the students carried a ball of energy between twelve and eighteen inches in diameter. Try as he might, Conrad could not manage to create a ball greater than six. It floated between his hands, a deep-purple rotating sphere, and there was something else that differentiated Conrad's Q-energy from the others. Conrad's energy ball was humming.

"Now I want each of you to direct your Q-energy across the mat," Tiana instructed. "I want you to direct it at your partner, carefully."

After observing what had happened to Matthew, everyone exhibited a little trepidation, especially Matthew.

"Matthew has already experienced a Q-energy attack," she continued. "So it is his turn to attack me."

"Master Tiana?" Mindy asked. "Should we wait for each other before attacking our partner?"

"No, I want you to experience a simulated battle sequence. Fire at will!"

The student warriors let their Q-energy ball fly at their respective adversaries. The training facility was filled with mini explosions of color as each student sent his or her energy flying across the room. Nearly everyone one missed his or her target on the first attempt.

Matthew, however, hit Tiana, center mass, knocking her back several yards. She did not fall to the ground, but remained planted firmly upright. She then reconstituted her own energy ball so fast that Matthew had no time to react, and he was pummeled again as before. This time he jumped back to his feet and returned the volley. Tiana was pleased.

Conrad, meanwhile, was experiencing some difficulty. It seemed Atticus's autism allowed him to focus strenuously on the task at hand. Although his first volley missed Conrad, his follow-up hit Conrad in the face. The sting caused Conrad to collapse for a moment. It reminded him of a slap across the face he had received in one of his foster homes.

"Get up and defend yourself. This is no place for self-pity," Conrad heard Tiana say in his head. He jumped to his feet, dropped quickly into a perfect horse stance, created his violet energy ball in a millisecond, and launched it at Atticus. Atticus bobbed to his left to avoid the ball, but it seemed to behave differently from the other students'. When Atticus moved to the side, Conrad's energy flew by him a few feet, but then it doubled back, striking Atticus in the back. The impact was so impressive that Atticus was launched forward, falling on his face, and was pushed the entire length of the training facility.

All the students stopped and watched as Atticus, crumpled at the bottom of the far wall of the room, slowly pulled himself to his feet. His back was facing the rest of the class, but they saw him shake off the disorientation. Conrad stared at his hands, glanced up to see where Atticus was thrown by his Q-energy, and looked back down at his hands again.

Conrad heard the sound of loud applause beginning to build in the training facility. He looked up and saw that Tiana was leading and encouraging the other members of the class to acknowledge what Conrad had just accomplished. Not only was Atticus nearly eighteen inches taller than Conrad and twice his weight, but Conrad's energy ball seemed puny compared to the other students'.

"Bravo!" Tiana exclaimed. "Bravo to both of you. Atticus, you took the attack and returned to your feet without delay."

Tiana then moved over to Conrad's side.

"And you, Conrad. You faced your fears and prevailed in the face of a more powerful adversary. You have much to be proud of this day. Class dismissed."

Matthew and Matilda popped out first. Atticus, still slightly woozy from his encounter with Conrad's Q-energy, stumbled a few steps before vanishing with a crackle. Mindy waited a few moments, hoping to be able to leave with Conrad.

Tiana, knowing and hearing these thoughts said, "Conrad is staying for a while, Mindy. He will meet with you later."

Mindy frowned and popped out in a flash.

After all the others had left, Tiana said, "We have much work to do, and you have many questions for me. Come, let us begin."

Chapter Twenty-Three

Tiana took Conrad to the center of the training facility. *"Are you ready to be a leader?"* her voice reverberated in his head.

He shook it from side to side. *"No, I'm not a leader—far from it."*

"You are and will be." She knelt down in front of him. "And do you know why?" she asked. He just shook his head again.

"Because you are Trinity-Two. This is not a choice; this is destiny."

Conrad looked into Tiana's eyes. They were the color of dark-blue sapphires, and there was something else contained within them. He saw a true caring and admiration for him there. She saw something in him that no one else had—at least not since his mother was alive.

As he continued to look at her, a question welled up inside of him: *What if she is wrong or mistaken?* What if he ended up being the same disappointment to Tiana that he'd been to every other person he cared about since the accident? Sometimes he just wished his mother had stayed home that dreadful night. Perhaps she would still be with him now. And although he hated to admit it, there were times, dark times, where he'd wished he'd gone with her that night. Then they would be together—somewhere.

Tiana stood up. "I will show you the way and prove to you who you are and who you are meant to be. There is much you need to know and precious little time in which to teach it. Therefore, I will give you my knowledge."

"Give me your what?" he asked.

"I will transfer all of my knowledge to you. All of my skill, all of my warrior training, all of the lessons I have learned in battle, and everything you need except for one thing—confidence. You must build that within yourself."

Conrad's head was spinning again, but by now, he was getting used to the sensation when he was around Tiana. "How in the world are you going to do that?"

"Conceptually, it works the same as downloading data files or programs into a computer. Take my hands."

Tiana held her hands before her, and Conrad reached out, taking them in his.

"Are you ready?" she asked telepathically.

He swallowed hard one time and then nodded in the affirmative. She closed her eyes. When he saw her do this, he slowly closed his as well. Unfortunately, it was a gesture in vain.

Conrad felt something run through him like electricity. His teeth clenched together as if each one was attempting to crush into obliteration its opposing tooth on the opposite jaw. All the muscles, sinew, tendons, ligaments, and cartilage in his body was being stressed and brutalized by a force he had never felt in his short and, by all current accounts, soon-to-end life.

Conrad was certain Tiana was electrocuting him. The last thought he remembered running through his mind before he fell unconscious was that he would finally be with his mother, and that made him happy.

Chapter Twenty-Four

He awoke in his bed in his room in Turner Manor. He opened his eyes several times, but each time only slightly. The room seemed indescribably bright, and it hurt. After several minutes of this eyelid fluttering, he managed to fully open them.

Twix was standing next to his bed. He was wearing a stethoscope and holding two of his stubby fingers against Conrad's wrist. "Pulse normal," Twix said.

It was then that Conrad saw Tiana. She was seated toward the bottom of the bed. She had a slight look of concern on her face, but she also seemed to be enjoying Conrad's predicament.

"Are you all right?" Conrad heard in his brain.

He wanted to answer her mentally, but when he tried, he felt a huge stabbing pain behind his right eye. "What did you do to me?" he asked weakly.

Tiana inhaled deeply as she stood and walked closer to Conrad's side. Her eyes were so black that he could not distinguish her pupil from her iris. He could not remember her eyes ever being that color before.

"I beg your pardon, Conrad," she said softly. "I made a mistake. In trying to accelerate your training and knowledge of the warrior arts, I miscalculated your ability to absorb it." She lifted his hand into hers and gently stroked the back of it with her fingers. "I would never willingly hurt you, and I am truly sorry that I did."

Conrad smiled as best he could and said, "It's okay, Tiana. But what happened?"

Tiana explained that, although she could not be certain, she believed that she overloaded his synaptic network with data. Since his brain could not accept the amount of information she was trying to transfer to him, his mind simply shut down.

"And because of this, I have some decisions to make. I may have to return you to California."

Conrad sprung forward in his bed. "What! Why?" he stammered. "You said you would always protect me. You said that. Why do you want to abandon...ugh...return me to them?"

Tiana held his hand more firmly and replied, "Because you will be in danger here." Tiana released Conrad's hand and told him she would see him later.

"Where are you going?" he asked.

"As I said, I must decide how best to protect you. I require several hours of meditation and reflection. I will return to you when the answer becomes known to me."

She then walked toward the bedroom door. At the door, she turned around to address Conrad.

"You should go out and have some fun. Your classmates are heading to the town arcade. You should join them."

Tiana smiled radiantly and then disappeared into a bright flash of light.

Chapter Twenty-Five

After her exit, Conrad changed into some casual clothes: shorts, a bright-orange T-shirt, and gray-and-white New Balance cross-trainers. He left the manor and headed for the town arcade. Twix gave him directions, so finding it was easy. It was actually only a block and a half away from Blasto's.

When he arrived, he looked into the first booth. There were several kids playing a panel game. The object of the game seemed to be inflating a balloon until it popped, but unlike such games at home where water was shot onto a target, here the participants had to use their telekinetic ability to inflate and win the game. Conrad thought someone required great confidence in his or her ability before attempting such a game.

Down the line of booths, he ran into Atticus. He was standing in front of a game that had a large brass base plate on the ground before it. The base plate was attached to a vertical panel that rose fifty feet off the ground. Conrad knew this because the panel was marked off in one-foot increments. On the base plate was a round pad approximately eighteen inches in diameter.

Atticus was standing before the pad holding a large wooden hammer above his head. As Conrad approached, Atticus said, "Watch this."

He swung the hammer down against the pad with all the force he could muster. Upon slamming the pad, Atticus was launched straight up into the air, nearly to the top of the vertical panel. All the way up, he vocalized his complete enjoyment of the aerobatic trip.

He landed with a thud in the exact same place he was launched.

"You've got to try that," he said to Conrad.

Conrad thought about it for a microsecond and said, "Maybe later. Where are the others?"

Atticus pointed to a movie theater down at the end of the street. "Matt and Matti are there," he said. "Not sure where Mindy is."

"I'm right here," Mindy shouted from behind them.

Both boys were startled by her surprise entrance, but Conrad felt a great sense of joy when he turned and saw her face.

"Hey, Mindy," Conrad said. "What'cha been doing?"

Mindy grabbed his hand and said, "Lots. Come on, I'll show you."

She pulled Conrad down the arcade row as he waved good-bye to Atticus.

When Mindy and Conrad reached the theater, there was a small line of likeminded teenagers waiting to enter. The marquee indicated a double feature was playing: *Goldman and Filigree* and *Don't Ask Me Why.* Tickets were seven dollars and fifty cents apiece.

"I don't have any money with me," Conrad said.

"It's my treat" was Mindy's reply.

Her smile was so big all her teeth must have been wiped when she pulled back her lips. Conrad noticed how white they were and how beautiful Mindy looked when she was smiling. This thought brought a smile to his face as well, even in light of his slight discomfort at being penniless.

As they approached the box office, Mindy withdrew her wallet from her purse and presented the ticket girl with fifteen dollars. They were issued two tickets, which Mindy collected and handed to Conrad.

"You can give them to the usher," she said coyly.

Conrad held the two tickets out for the usher to take.

Dressed in black slacks, black-and-white saddle shoes, a red satin vest, and red pillbox cap, the usher received the tickets presented by Conrad. The usher snapped the tickets in half with a quick tug, leaving the stubs in Conrad's hand.

"Enjoy the show," he said as Mindy and Conrad entered the theater to find some seats.

Halfway down, Mindy spotted two seats in the center.

"Look," she said as she pointed to them. "Can we sit there?"

Conrad just smiled at her, grasped her hand tighter, and led her to the seats she'd claimed from the aisle.

"Excuse us," Conrad said as they maneuvered by a few already seated people.

"Pardon us," Mindy added.

Once seated, Conrad asked Mindy if she was comfortable. She told him she was. He asked if she wanted anything from the concession stand.

"Why didn't you ask when we were in the lobby?"

"I dunno. I thought you're supposed get seated first and then get the popcorn and stuff."

"You're funny," Mindy said. "And I like you, you know."

Conrad blushed slightly. "Yeah, I guess I do. I'll be right back." He took a step, but stopped abruptly. He turned back to Mindy. "Can I borrow some money? I promise I'll pay you back…someday."

Mindy removed a ten-dollar bill from her wallet and handed it to him. He acknowledged her kind generosity with a quick nod before he turned around to exit the aisle.

The lines at the concession stand increased in length in the short time from when Mindy and Conrad entered until he returned. Waiting in line, Conrad thought about where he was at that very moment. He was no longer a castoff kid being raised by uncaring, detached, or reluctant foster families. He was beginning to feel he was finally somewhere he truly belonged.

He was also feeling pretty good about his blossoming relationship with Mindy. Yeah, she was hearing impaired, but so what? She was pretty, smart, tough, thoughtful, and funny. Thinking about her made him smile, and he really thought, for the first time in a long, long time, that things were going to be good. He liked thinking this way, and he hoped it would continue forever.

Someone tapped Conrad's shoulder, and the gesture brought him back to reality. His contemplation of the growing feelings he had for Mindy caused a several-yard gap between him and the people in front of him in line. Conrad moved up quickly to close the gap. Once the line continuity was regained, Conrad looked behind him to apologize to the person who had notified him of his faux pas.

When he turned to look back, though, a lump grew in his throat. Standing behind him was Amanda and her ex-boyfriend Peyton. However, by the way Peyton's arm was wrapped around Amanda's shoulder, they appeared to be no longer exes.

"Well, I should have known!" Peyton exclaimed. "How're you doing, little man?"

Amanda elbowed Peyton in the ribs and said, "Hello, Conrad."

"Hi," Conrad replied, rubbing the back of his neck while avoiding eye contact.

Amanda pushed Peyton's arm off her and continued. "Are you here with friends or by yourself?"

Conrad looked up at her briefly. *Why do you want to know?* he thought, squinting slightly.

"I'm here with a friend" is all he said.

"Your protector, no doubt," the Neanderthal interjected.

Amanda could see where this was going. "Okay, then," she said. "Maybe we'll see you afterward."

Conrad did not respond. He turned toward the front and approached the now open concession stand. He completed his order, and while waiting for the concessioner to gather everything together, he stood nervously, tapping his right foot.

When everything was delivered, Conrad paid, gathered his goodies, and exited to the left side of the counter as fast as he could move. Amanda followed him with her eyes as he did, and Peyton's disdain for Conrad continued with an audible grunt of disapproval.

"Why do you treat him that way?" Amanda asked.

"He's a punk weakling, and I hate his kind," said Peyton. "Besides, he tried to move in on my girl."

Peyton grabbed Amanda around her waist, pulled her to him, and kissed her deeply. Amanda's grimace said more than words about how she felt at that very moment, but there was no end to Peyton's depravity. As he withdrew, he licked her face from chin to forehead.

"Eeeuuwww," Amanda said. "Gross!"

Peyton laughed his insidious laugh.

Chapter Twenty-Six

When Conrad finally returned to his seat, he handed Mindy the tub of popcorn, a large soda, and a handful of napkins. He then sat down beside her and watched the screen. The movie hadn't started yet, but the coming attractions were being shown. Mindy knew something was upsetting him because he was completely silent in watching the screen.

"Are you okay?" Mindy whispered.

Once again, Conrad noticed the nasally tone of Mindy's speech, the "okay" sounded like "oh-ay."

"Fine," he said in reply.

"Really," Conrad heard in his mind, *"why don't you tell me what's going on?"* Mindy was in his head, and the shocker was her telepathic speech was tone perfect.

"You can project your thoughts, but you can't hear mine?" he asked.

"Yes. I don't know why, but I can."

"And your speech is perfect in my head."

Mindy gave him a look like he was some ignorant peasant. "Of course it is, silly. I didn't learn to use my mouth and tongue properly since I was born hearing impaired, but thought is not speech. So are you going to tell me what's wrong?"

Conrad told her how he ran into Amanda and Peyton at the concession stand. He explained how he had met Amanda at Blasto's House of Tonsorio, how they had sat together experiencing the Tonsorio effect, how they had walked and talked together afterward, and how Peyton had come upon them in the street. He left out the part about the fight.

"So what?" she said.

"Peyton's not a nice guy," he said. "He wants to beat me up, thinks I'm trying to take Amanda away from him."

Mindy's voice then took on a more serious tone. "Is he right?"

"Is who right?" Conrad asked.

"Peyton. Do you like Amanda?"

Conrad swallowed hard.

Yes, at the time, he did have an attraction to Amanda. After all, he was a red-blooded American teenager, and when a pretty girl gave one of those some attention, of course he would develop some feelings for her. For Conrad, after so many years of feeling worthless, weak, unwanted, and miserable, the mere indication that someone, anyone, especially a hottie like Amanda, found him interesting, if not good looking, was as natural as falling off a stopped bicycle.

"Yes," he admitted to Mindy. "I did like her, sort of. But that was then."

Mindy pulled in her bottom lip slightly and then shook her head once. "I see. So what about now?"

She was looking at her feet in the dark theater, the only illumination cast from the intermittent changing of the scenes on the screen.

Conrad touched the back of her hand lightly. "Nothing now," he said. "I'm a one-girl guy." Mindy smiled widely.

Chapter Twenty-Seven

After the movie, they waited and watched the credits roll. When lights came up in the theater, they were alone but for a few other stragglers like themselves. The got up from their seats and exited.

Outside the theater building, there were people milling around. The little bar and grill across the street, Chuck's Bucket, was lively with moviegoers seeking après film sustenance.

"Are you hungry?" Conrad asked.

Mindy answered by grabbing his hand and pulling him toward Chuck's.

They sat at the end of the service counter, and each ordered a cheeseburger, fries, and Diet Coke. They talked about the movies they had just seen. Mindy wasn't keen on the cop drama, *Goldman and Filigree*. She thought the cinematic device of a male and female police partner team was overused. Conrad said mostly it was done for the sexual tension, trying to get the audience interested in whether or not the two partners would consummate their relationship. Mindy thought it was a trite ruse that underestimated the intelligence of the audience. Conrad realized he couldn't argue with that evaluation.

They both agreed the comedy, *Don't Ask Me Why*, was most enjoyable. They both liked the idea that the male lead, Justin, claimed to be suffering from amnesia whenever the female lead, Constance, his live-in girlfriend, asked him to do something for her.

Mindy said, "I thought he was faking the whole time. What about you?"

"I wasn't sure," Conrad replied. "Sometimes I thought he was faking, and other times I really believed he couldn't remember things. Geez that would be great, huh?"

"What would be great?"

"Not remembering certain things, bad things, you know?"

Mindy frowned. "I don't know about that. I think everything that happens to us, every life experience, makes us who we are. I think forgetting parts of our life would be sad, even the 'bad' parts."

Mindy smiled slightly and touched the back of Conrad's hand. He did not look up from his plate because he knew she was right, but some of the painful episodes in his young life didn't seem to have any purpose—at least not that he could tell.

They finished their meals, adding a hot-fudge sundae that they shared, and Conrad once again realized he had no money.

He was patting his pockets unconsciously when Mindy said, "I told you it was my treat. You can pay next time."

He liked the idea of a "next time" with Mindy. She did like him, something about him clicked for her, and he liked her a lot, too. *Things are looking up*, he thought.

They left Chuck's and walked toward the arcade entrance. On each side of the main thoroughfare, the game operators were closing down for the night. Nearly halfway to the entrance, they saw Matthew and Matilda walking with Atticus. Each was holding a blue-and-gold soft-serve ice cream cone. Conrad noticed that the melting ice cream wasn't falling to the ground. Instead, each droplet rose up toward the dark sky.

"Hey, you two," Matthew shouted. "You're looking very cozy. What's the haps?"

Conrad immediately felt his face flush.

Mindy must have sensed his discomfort because she replied, "Nothing much. Great show at the Bijou."

"Yeah, Matti and I were going to go, but Atticus doesn't like the theater, so we just hung with him. Where are you going now?"

Conrad looked at Mindy, who returned his glance.

"Home," she said, and she placed her hand in Conrad's and they walked off toward the exit. Conrad turned around and waved good-bye to the others as they did.

They continued walking until they reached a little parkette down the road.

Mindy looked at Conrad and said, "Are you real tired?"

He shook his head. They reached a small bench under a large oak tree. The wind was lightly rustling the leaves in it. They sat for several minutes in comfortable silence. Conrad developed a smirk over the course of the elapsing minutes. Then he let out an audible snicker.

"What's so funny?" Mindy asked.

"Nothing," he said.

Mindy gave Conrad "the look" and waited for him to continue.

Stammering slightly, he did. "I'm just really happy—for the first time in a long time." He paused for a few seconds, staring at his shoes, then with a revised attitude he said, "I just hope it doesn't end."

Mindy picked up his hand in hers and squeezed it tight. "I see good things for you, Conrad Turner. I most certainly do." She kissed him on the forehead, stood up, said good-bye, and disappeared with a crackle.

Conrad considered Mindy's prognostication. Things did seem to be on the road to repair ever since the night at the

Best Western on the Pacific Coast Highway, the night when he first encountered the rat with the glowing emerald eyes. Yes, there had been some trials and tribulations, if you must know, but overall, he felt happier than he had been in a long time.

He got up from the bench under the spreading oak and started to walk out of the park. He stopped after several steps and began laughing out loud.

"Man, you are slow, Conrad," he said to the empty night and the tree. "Just teleport home."

He had closed his eyes to visualize his bedroom in Turner Manor when he felt something hard hit him in the right side of his jaw, sending him flying off his feet. He landed on the grass nearly ten feet from where he was previously standing. He opened his eyes and, in a disoriented stupor, looked around in the dark to see what could have knocked him down.

Conrad pulled himself up off the ground, but at the exact zenith of his rise, he was once again struck by something. This time he was smacked in the solar plexus, and all the air was knocked out of his lungs. He fell to the ground, huddled in the fetal position struggling for breath.

Conrad heard a familiar voice say, "I told you, you were dead. And now your mommy's not here to protect you."

The hairs on the back of Conrad's neck stood straight up when he instantly recognized the voice as Peyton Campbell's.

But where was he, and why and how was he attacking him like this?

Conrad started pulling himself up, but also, he acknowledged the voice, saying, "Peyton, why are you doing this? What did I ever do to you?"

Peyton walked in from the dark recesses of the night. Conrad saw him standing there with his black outfit interlaced with chains, a chain-mail vest, motorcycle boots, and a sneer from some forsaken dark place of the world. He regarded Conrad with a contemptuous look and replied, "Because I don't like you." Then he kicked his right foot toward Conrad's rising ribcage.

Amazingly, Conrad varied his assent just slightly enough so that Peyton's leg missed its mark. The sudden lack of a properly positioned target forced Peyton's leg to continue farther in its trajectory, thereby forcing the rest of his body to become unbalanced. By the time Peyton realized this fact, Conrad was far enough along in his trip back to standing upright again that he planted both his feet firmly, bent his knees slightly, grabbed the back of Peyton's right heel, and with a slight push, added enough momentum to send Peyton falling forward and toward the ground.

When Peyton hit bottom, he was furious.

Conrad, however, was remarkably calm. He set himself in a firm battle stance and said, "Peyton, it doesn't have to be this way."

Peyton lifted himself off the ground and, in a snarling rant, charged Conrad with both of his open hands thrust in front of him seeking Conrad's throat.

As Peyton got within range of him, Conrad instinctively shot both of his hands up and out to block Peyton's outstretched arms. He then quickly twisted his right hand, striking Peyton in the neck with a hand sword; grabbed the back of Peyton's neck, pulling him down to the ground on top of him; and then shot his right foot out, striking Peyton in the left hip and sending him flying over his head. Conrad curved his back so the impact energy would dissipate over a wide area when he hit the ground.

Peyton, however, flew several yards away, crashing into several bushes near the park's entrance. He pulled himself onto all fours, looking very doglike. He shook off the disorientation from his flight. When he finally arose and turned to see his foe again, Conrad was crouched in a deep-ground rex stance. Between his hands floated a humming purple ball of energy.

Peyton's anger at the sight of Conrad, unhurt, goading him into attacking again, ran through him like a plasma cutter through cold-rolled steel. *Who did this punk kid think he is? He is a nothing, a zero. Try to steal my girl? NEVER!*

Conrad could see that Peyton was committed to trying to attack him again, but he felt compelled to try to dissuade him one more time.

"Listen, Peyton," he said, "I can see you are very, very angry, but anger won't solve anything. Please don't make me hurt you again."

"Punk!" Peyton screamed. "I'll show *you* what hurt is!"

Peyton launched at Conrad, full bore. Before he could close the gap between them even two yards, Conrad threw his Q-energy ball directly at him. When it struck, all the neurons in Peyton's body short-circuited. Unconsciousness overcame the brute instantly, and the remaining energy sent him flying fully across the street, knocking down several trash cans, mailboxes, and a ceramic garden gnome. He finally landed against the front stoop of a small house across the street from the park. He did not move a muscle.

Conrad watched the entire thing play out. When Peyton came to rest, Conrad held his breath for several seconds. He then began hyperventilating. *What just happened?* he thought. *Did I do all that?* He waited for several moments to see, first, if Peyton was alive and, second, if Tiana had anything to do with this battle scene.

When neither Peyton moved nor Tiana appeared, Conrad really became scared. Had he just killed someone? But it was self-defense, right? Peyton surely would have killed him if he hadn't defended himself. Conrad felt panic envelope him. There was too much to consider at the moment. How had he managed to beat Peyton? He was older, bigger, stronger, and less merciful than Conrad. Even though Conrad had begun training in the warrior arts, too little time had passed, and too little practice had been done within that limited time to make Conrad a fighter of the caliber necessary to win against such a foe as Peyton.

Then it struck him. Perhaps Tiana was wrong when she thought her knowledge download had not worked. Maybe he had the reaction he did not because his mind had overloaded, but perhaps he had shut down from sheer exhaustion after the transfer. Conrad considered this theory for a moment until he caught site of the unconscious and unmoving body of Peyton Campbell.

He had to find out if it could be true. He had to talk to Tiana. He needed her advice now more than ever, but could he, or should he, leave Peyton's body here? Although it was distasteful, he knew he had to be sure whether Peyton was living or dead.

He walked over to where Peyton lay crumpled against the apron of the house. Conrad moved in closely with great caution. He had seen too many movies and television shows where the good guy, or the bad guy, played possum, feigning death, only to spring up at the last moment and overcome the rival.

When he was close enough to check, Conrad pushed Peyton with his foot. The body moved from the jolt and returned to its previous position. Conrad tried to see if he could make out any breathing, but it was too dark to identify any rising and falling of Peyton's chest. Finally, with no other option left, Conrad moved closer, protecting his most vital areas as best as he could, and felt for a pulse on the side of Peyton's neck. A grand relief overcame him when he felt the slight, but steady, beat of Peyton's heart.

He hadn't killed him, but when Peyton awoke, he would be madder than a hornet and ready to take on Conrad once again. He needed to speak with Tiana as soon as possible. He needed her advice. He thought about his room in Turner Manor, followed by, *Take me there*. The next thing he remembered was the flash of light.

Chapter Twenty-Eight

When he arrived back in the relative security of his bedroom, See-Two was sitting at the bottom of Conrad's bed cleaning himself as cats do. The teleportation burst caught See-Two's attention, and he ceased his cleansing ritual.

"Welcome back, Master Turner," he said. "We have been busy, have we not?"

"What?" Conrad said.

See-Two stood up on four paws, took a big stretch, placed his two front paws on the footboard, leaned forward so that his nose and whiskers were mere centimeters away from Conrad's face, and said, "Do not presume what I do and do not know."

See-Two leaped off the bed, and when he landed on the carpeted floor, he did something Conrad had not expected:

See-Two stood up on his back two legs and began pacing around the room, upright.

"I suppose," See-Two began, "that you are confused and somewhat frightened by what occurred between Mr. Campbell and yourself?"

"If you mean because I thought I killed him…well, then yeah."

"Do not be so impertinent. I am attempting to assist you in understanding what is happening here. You have two ears and one mouth. Please use them in the same ratio."

Conrad was feeling frustrated. Who did this cat think he was lecturing him? He could have been killed and nearly killed another this evening. Conrad just wanted to talk to Tiana. He wanted to speak with her and then go to sleep. He felt haggard and his energy level was waning. He didn't know for how much longer he could attend to See-Two's lecture.

Conrad marched around See-Two toward the bathroom. He closed the door behind him. He undressed in the bathroom, replacing his street clothes with a pair of sweats and a T-shirt, both of which were hanging on the back of the bathroom door. He brushed his teeth, urinated, flushed, and went back into the bedroom. See-Two was still standing there, arms folded, tapping his right back paw on the floor.

"What?" Conrad said, smirking.

See-Two shook his head in disbelief. "You must be ready to hear what I am about to tell you. Are you ready?"

Conrad's smile faded. The cat meant serious business.

"Honestly, I don't know," he said.

"Fair enough," See-Two said. "Would you prefer Master Tiana?"

Conrad's eyes widened. "I would like to speak with her," he said, and after several seconds added, "too."

"Very well," See-Two said. Then the big cat closed his eyes.

Within seconds, a vertical line segment of light appeared, expanding into a doorway, and Tiana walked into Conrad's bedroom.

Conrad felt a nearly overwhelming impulse to hug her tightly, which made his face flush at the thought of it. Tiana smiled at his impulsive affection for her and his bashfulness. She sat in one of the two large armchairs that were situated near the wall opposite the foot of Conrad's bed. Once seated, with both of her arms comfortably placed upon the upholstered armrests, she looked at both Conrad and See-Two.

Several moments elapsed in complete silence, until Tiana said, "Well, one of you should tell me why I was summoned here."

Conrad tried to explain what was happening. He wanted to tell her he had been able to defend himself without her help, that he had done it without fear, without effort; he wanted to tell her he thought he had killed Peyton and how that thought had brought fear and revulsion back. He wanted to tell her how relieved he had been when he'd discovered Peyton was indeed alive, and he wanted to tell her he was proud of himself. He wanted to say all of these things to her, but alas, he was unable.

"I...I...I," he said, and from there, his stammering progressively worsened.

See-Two then interjected, "Master Turner has discovered his warrior soul."

He went on to describe in full detail, as if he had been present during the battle, Conrad's confrontation with Peyton. He told Tiana how Conrad had attempted to avoid the engagement; how he had been attacked in the dark; how, once focused with determination, he had acted in defense only; how he had given his adversary several opportunities to withdraw into a mutual armistice; and finally, how he had accurately and effectively focused his Q-energy to defeat his foe.

Conrad watched See-Two describe the battle with complete incredulity. How did this feline, a cat who was not anywhere near the park, anywhere near the arcade, know what he knew?

"Boy," See-Two said, interrupting Conrad's thought process. "You are developing many of your warrior skills. I beg you to work on listening." See-Two jumped off the bed, spinning end over end several times, landing upright on his two back feet. "I am your tutor, your teacher, your conscience, if you will. I know everything that has happened to you."

See-Two paused for a moment, clearly contemplating his next sentence. He walked over to Conrad, and looking up at him from the floor said, "I know things that would make your hair fall out, and one day, if you're lucky, I will bestow all of my knowledge on you, Master Turner. Farewell, you two."

And then See-Two ran toward the open window and jumped out. A slight *pop* indicated his teleportation.

Conrad continued staring out the open window. When he turned his head back to face Tiana, she was standing next to him. He was slightly startled by her close proximity.

"That is something else on which we must work," she said.

"What?"

"You must develop your senses to a greater degree. Only when they are working clearly and crisply can they offer the greatest protection."

Conrad's head hurt. "What are you talking about?"

Tiana folded her arms and regarded him. She used her eyes like a scanning machine, looking over every visible part of him. For what was she looking?

Finally, after several minutes, Conrad said, "Enough. What are you doing?"

"I am looking for changes," she said.

"Changes?"

"Yes, changes. If See-Two's analysis is correct—and I have never known him not to be—you have changed in the time you have been here."

"How so?"

Tiana described her impression of Conrad when they'd first met. She considered him a scared and lonely little boy, completely unaware of neither his power nor his destiny. She indicated that although his first training session in the warrior arts was challenging, to say the least, he had a remarkable ability to absorb the instruction. Now, it seemed, she was incorrect in her initial assumption that her attempt to download all of her warrior skill had failed.

"It appears the download was successful," she said.

"Well, that's a pretty good understatement," Conrad said. "I kicked his butt."

Tiana bent at the waist so that her face drew close to Conrad's. "Do not be proud of injuring another being," she said. "Always attempt to do no harm, and do so only if your opponent leaves you with no alternative." Tiana stopped, straightened up, and listened intently.

"What?"

Tiana held a hand up to Conrad's face. She then pointed to her ear with a finger on her right hand, pantomiming for him to listen, too.

Conrad focused all his attention on his ears, but try as he might, he could only hear the soft wing beats of a flight of pteranodons in the distance and a light breeze blowing in from the coast. He looked at Tiana for permission to speak. She withdrew her hand and indicated he could do so.

"I didn't hear anything."

"Yes, I know. We must work on that as well. Come."

"Where are we going?" he asked.

"You need more training before we embark on your first mission."

"Mission! What mission?"

Tiana held Conrad's shoulders and said, "We must return to Mercatorum shortly. Do not ask any other questions now. I will brief you when the time is right. For now, however, I believe it is time for you to meet the other sentinels."

Tiana removed her token from her belt and tapped a few buttons. They both jumped through the gateway, and it popped closed behind them.

Chapter Twenty-Nine

When they landed, Conrad felt nauseated, as he always had before. This time, however, he did not regurgitate. He considered it a great improvement and felt he was getting better at the whole teleportation thing.

He looked around to get his bearings but did not recognize the place. Tiana and he were standing in a circular building with no walls. The ceiling appeared to be supported by nothing; however, it did not fall on them. *Good thing, too*, Conrad thought, *because the hemispheric ceiling and roof would have crushed them into dust.*

In the center of the room were five wooden armchairs, each with an ornately embroidered seat and arm cushions. The chairs were carved from a reddish-brown wood resembling mahogany. The intricacy of the carved designs belied the apparent strength and resilience of the construction. Behind each chair was a small oriental rug, each one having a different color scheme and pattern.

Numerous questions arose in Conrad's mind, but he was learning to wait before asking. The air in the circular arena became very still. Then a vibration began. Low and slow at first, then building in intensity. Finally, Mindy, Atticus, Matilda, and Matthew appeared in the room, and with them were a crow, an eagle, a gorilla, and something Conrad had not seen before—a dragon.

Each of the students took a seat in a chair, and each animal either stood behind a student or perched itself upon the back of the student's chair. When all were in position, each animal transformed into a person—two women and two men. Each one, as different as the day is long, was standing, waiting patiently.

Behind Mindy, the crow converted into a tall, thin man with dirty-blond hair and bright-blue eyes. His skin was tan and his muscles sinewy. His attire was appropriate for a surfer: tank T-shirt, board shorts, and sandals. When he smiled, the whiteness of his teeth was nearly blinding. Conrad knew this was Donovan. But there were others present who were new to him.

The golden eagle metamorphosed into a lean, attractive platinum-blonde woman with green eyes. Her hair was kept shoulder length, and she was wearing a royal-blue mini-dress with a silver belt. She was also wearing a pair of black Mary Jane's. She stood behind Atticus with her hands placed upon his broad shoulders. Her name was Harlow.

The gorilla reorganized into a frail-looking old man with a long white beard. He was called Meinhard. He wore a loose-fitting tunic, belted around the center, and held a six-foot-long walking stick in his right hand. His eyes were jet black and were so intense one would be loath to underestimate their owner. Meinhard stood behind Matilda, gently patted her on her head, and smiled.

Finally, the dragon transmogrified into a woman who could be Tiana's sister. She was tall, muscular, and radiantly beautiful. She was wearing the same type of battle armor as Tiana, but her boots were shorter, and the articulated regions seemed to have a metallic quality. The main difference between Tiana and this woman were hair and eye color. The dragoness's hair was deep-red burgundy in color, and her eyes were nearly translucent gray. She took her place standing behind Matthew. This was Atara.

When everyone was in place, Tiana began the introductions.

"Welcome, all," she said. "Welcome, warriors and sentinels. We have much to discuss and accomplish, but before we begin, introductions are in order." She placed her hand on Conrad's shoulder and said, "Sentinels, this is Conrad Turner."

Once the introductions were complete, Atara said, "I am pleased we are all now as one, yes. Conrad, I await your counsel at a later time." Atara then looked directly at Tiana and said, "What quest is to be laid before us?"

Tiana explained that the entire group would be going to Mercatorum. She briefed everyone about the previous trip, how they had information that Conrad's father, Nathaniel Turner, was there, how Baron von Goren had not seemed quite right, how he had reacted when Nathaniel's name was mentioned, how the baron had denied Nathaniel had been on Mercatorum, and how Tiana had sensed an additional presence in the baron's office but could not identify it.

"Who or what do you think it was?" Atara asked.

"I am not positive," Tiana said. "But I have my suspicions."

Meinhard stepped forward and said, "I know your suspicions. Is it possible? He has been gone a very, very long time."

"Who?" Harlow asked.

Donovan started laughing.

"What is so funny?" asked Harlow.

"You sound more like an owl than an eagle, that's all," Donovan replied.

Mindy and Matilda giggled at Donovan's goofiness, but Tiana threw her hands up to stop the levity.

"This is not the time," she said. She started pacing around the room. "Although I am not convinced it is him, if it is, the entire sector could be in danger. That is why we must all go to Mercatorum."

Mindy put her hand in the air.

"There is no need for that, Mindy. You are a warrior now. What is it?"

"When do we leave, and for how long will we be gone?"

Tiana's head bobbed up and down slightly. "Yes, very good questions." Tiana moved back into her original position facing each of the chairs with their respective occupants. "We leave within the hour, but alas, I do not know for how long. Pack only what you need, say your good-byes, and meet in the cathedral."

All of the students looked at each other with various states of shock and disbelief upon their faces. This was for real. They were all going into battle for the very first time. Would they return safely? Each sentinel tried to assure their individual charges that they would protect them. And after all had popped out of the room, Conrad's head remained filled with questions, insecurities, and trepidations.

"Conrad," Tiana said. "You have made great strides on your quest thus far. Do not forget from where you came, and remember, I will always be with you."

Conrad looked up at her, tried to smile, and nodded his head.

"Good," said Tiana. "I will see you in an hour."

Tiana touched her token without removing it from her belt and disappeared in a point of light.

Once again, Conrad was alone. He had many emotions floating and colliding within him at that moment, and he felt unusually energized and excited at the same time. He was a long way from home in Redondo Beach, and where he was, where Overworld existed, he really wasn't sure. He was now about to embark on a journey—"a quest," as Tiana had put it—and by all accounts, there would be danger. What would become of him? What if he did not hold up his end? What if he let everyone down? What if he died?

These thoughts and others troubled him, but as he deepened his reflections, he discovered something unexpected. He was less troubled than he remembered being in the past, but there was something else, something he couldn't quite put his finger on. Even though he was uneasy about all of the unknowns connected with the upcoming quest, he had a sense of exhilaration, too. He was actually looking forward to it, and the anticipation filled him with positive energy.

He smiled, thinking all of these thoughts. Perhaps Tiana was right, and he was now on a good path. He closed his eyes and thought, *Take me to my room*. There was a slight hesitation and then the sound of rushing air as he disappeared into a point of light.

Chapter Thirty

Once his backpack was filled, Conrad swung it over his shoulder. He threaded his arms through the shoulder straps and grasped them one in each hand. He inhaled deeply, closed his eyes, and began to think about popping over to Tiana's chamber when See-Two crackled in.

See-Two's entrance startled Conrad.

"All ready for your next adventure?" See-Two said.

"Y…y…yes, I guess," Conrad said. "What are you doing here?"

"I wanted to discuss a few points with you before you left. Can you spare a few moments?"

"Um…okay…" Conrad said.

"There are things about to happen"—See-Two paused for a moment—"not necessarily to you, but around you, that you will not fully understand. In time, you will, but remember, not everything is as it seems."

Conrad stared blankly at See-Two. "What are you talking about? Why do you and Tiana have to speak in riddles?"

"My dear boy," See-Two said. "Once again, we are suffering a failure to communicate. Did you not listen when I visited you after your battle with Peyton Campbell?"

Conrad slowly nodded his head.

"I know everything about you—past, present and..." See-Two trailed off and stopped.

Conrad's mouth opened in disbelief. A small drop of drool was beginning to trickle down the left side of his mouth, but he caught it in time with his tongue and licked his lips to be sure nothing more would drip out.

"Do you know my future?" he asked.

See-Two frowned, walked over to Conrad, and stood on his hind legs. Even standing fully erect, See-Two was much shorter than Conrad. Conrad knelt down so they could both look eye to eye. See-Two extended his paw, which Conrad gratefully accepted.

Then See-Two said, "My boy, whether I do or do not is unimportant. The road you travel does not matter. What matters is that you embark upon your journey."

With that, See-Two released Conrad's hand and dropped down on all fours.

"But I want to know," Conrad said.

"No, you do not. You merely think you do."

Conrad shook his head. "Don't tell me what I do and do not want."

"Really," See-Two said, "you think knowing everything about your future will give you peace, power, comfort, and security? It would yield none of those things."

"But at least I'll know," Conrad said.

See-Two stared at Conrad for several seconds before he spoke again, and when he did, he said, "Conrad, my boy. If you knew everything about your future—what will happen during your next trip to Mercatorum, when you will find your father, when you will die—you would not be happy. Quite the opposite would be true. When someone knows his or her future to an absolute moral certitude, their reason for living evaporates. Life would have little or no meaning. You must believe me as your tutor, mentor, conscience, and friend; you are better off knowing as little as possible about your future."

Conrad thought for several moments. His thoughts went off into a very dark direction, and before he could stop it, a single tear slid down his cheek.

Upon seeing this, See-Two said, "Dear boy, there is nothing to fear. You have been doing so very well in conquering your fears and anxieties. Keep up the good work."

"But I…I…I'm afraid I might die."

See-Two looked up from the floor, stood upright again, and said, "Of course you will die…someday. But worrying about it will neither stop it from happening nor change the time and place. Go forth and have your adventure."

See-Two smiled a Cheshire cat grin and disappeared with a pop.

Conrad felt a great relief once he'd absorbed what See-Two had said. *Right*, he thought. *I'm gonna die someday. So what? I have things to do now.* He closed his eyes again and thought of Tiana in her study. Seconds later, all that remained of him in his room was a flash of light and some movement of the air left behind.

Chapter Thirty-One

Once he arrived in Tiana's study, Conrad stumbled as usual, but the impulse to throw up was absent. He ran his hands down the legs of his pants, smoothing the fabric. Upon completing this grooming task, he began to realize something was awry. Scanning his surroundings, he recognized what it was: He was alone. This had not occurred before. Generally, when he pictured Tiana in planning his teleport, she was standing there, either waiting or at least available. But now she was absent.

He inspected her study, looking for clues. Tiana's desk was neatly arranged with a blotter, penholder, wooden in-box, and crystalline paperweight with a hologram contained within. He touched the seat of her chair to test for warmth. He had seen that on a cop show back in California, and the detective indicated it could tell you if someone had been sitting in the chair during the last few minutes. Conrad found no warmth on the seat. He unconsciously scratched his head, and then he sat down in Tiana's chair to contemplate his next step.

When he sat down, he looked around the large study from this new angle. After several minutes, though, he grew tired of this futile attempt to locate her, and he resigned himself to simply waiting until she returned. He took a piece of paper from a small stack on the corner of the desk and began making a list.

Things to talk to Tiana about:

1. Everything happens – What? I think I know but ask to be sure.

2. I must decide my destiny – What if I'm wrong? I need help with this one.

3. Does Gunter Went have anything to do with my father's disappearance?

As he was writing, something caught his attention. On the wall opposite the large desk, hanging on either side of the doorway into the study, were two large and ornate mirrors. The one on the right side was reflecting something flashing periodically. He stopped writing his list and looked directly at the mirror to see the light. Once he raised his head, he saw nothing. Conrad couldn't quite understand this, so he looked back down at his list, intending to resume. The light flashed again.

Conrad quickly looked up at the mirror again, waiting for the next flash. Again, there was none. Frustration was beginning to rise in him. He returned to his list, and out of the corner of his eye, he saw another flash. Keeping his head in position, he shifted his body, thereby giving himself varying perspectives of the reflections in the mirror, and then he saw the flash over and over again.

He saw that it was coming from somewhere on the wall behind Tiana's desk, so he tried to get a fix on its exact location by glancing at the reflection and then immediately searching the wall for the source. After several attempts that yielded nothing, he eventually found a seam next to the grandfather clock. He tried to look through the seam in order to see what was beyond, but the borders were too tightly fit together to render any substantial view.

Conrad figured there must be a room or some other sort of chamber behind the clock. After all, the training facility was located behind the alcove on the left side of Tiana's desk. He grasped the side of the clock and pulled toward himself, but the clock did not budge.

He thought for a moment about his first experience with the training facility. He remembered Tiana clapping her hands together before the alcove revealed the entrance. He clapped his hands, hoping the clock would reveal its secret chamber behind it. Nothing happened. He clapped again. Again, nothing.

He regarded the clock again. He noticed that the two carved wooden pillars on the front had different patterns etched into them. Upon closer examination, he noticed each had a similar oval-shaped pattern near the top of the pillar. He touched each of the ovals with his two thumbs and released. The clock suddenly rose vertically up the wall several meters, revealing a doorway leading to a spiral staircase. There was a faint light coming from the bottom of the stairs. He swallowed hard and plunged into the darkness.

As he descended the staircase, he heard a low-frequency hum coming from below. As he continued, it became more intense. After two and a half twists, he reached the lower level.

There before him was Tiana, but she seemed unaware of his presence. She was floating above the floor in a seated position with her legs folded in front of her. Her hands were pressed against each other at chest level, and she was chanting. Before her was a rectangular portal comprised of swirling colors.

Conrad did not know what to do. He didn't think it would be right to interrupt her meditation, but he was curious and many questions filled his head. He thought, *What else is new? I've had more questions here than answers.*

"Perhaps," he heard, *"questions are more important for you than answers."* He knew it was Tiana, but he wasn't sure if he was hearing her thoughts or if she was speaking to him.

Tiana gently descended to the floor. When she reached it, she disengaged her folded legs, stood, and faced him.

"Questions," she said, "generally lead to more questions and, therefore, more knowledge, whereas answers are finite."

"That makes no sense," he said. "If all I have are questions, how can I know anything?"

"How can you, indeed," she said. "Close your eyes."

"What?"

"Do it."

Conrad did as Tiana commanded. He felt her move behind him, placing a hand on each of his shoulders.

"What do you see?"

Conrad focused on the dark and black places we all see when we first close our eyes. After a while, something began to coalesce within the pitch. At first, there were simply gray shadows and threads resembling fine smoke. Eventually, the focus corrected and the vision came into view.

"I see my class," he said. "I see the warrior students standing shoulder to shoulder."

Tiana smiled. "Very good," she said. "What else do you see?"

Conrad concentrated again. The vision became more distinct and converged. "They are preparing for battle."

"Do you know why?"

Again, Conrad paused to reflect and examine the vision. A small lump rose in his throat, and he said, "They want to help me find my father."

Tiana turned Conrad around so that he was facing her. He opened his eyes as she said, "Are there any more questions now?"

Conrad shrugged his shoulders slightly and shook his head from side to side.

"Good," Tiana said. "Let us join your friends and classmates and begin the next part of your adventure."

Tiana removed her token, tapped out a destination, and returned it to her belt. The portal appeared as it always did, and they stepped through together.

They landed in the warrior training facility. The students were already preparing for their journey. Mindy and Donovan were making a written inventory of numerous items before each one was placed into a backpack or a duffle bag. The placement of each item was precise and meticulous.

Harlow was filling Atticus's backpack while Atticus was counting and sorting various spherical objects of different sizes. At one point, Harlow called to Atticus, asking if a boomerang-shaped item was necessary for the trip. Without looking up from his project, he grunted in the affirmative. Harlow then walked over and redirected him to the bags she was packing. She asked him to verify that everything they would need was contained within his backpack.

Atticus looked into it for less than three seconds and said, "No, we're missing a toothbrush, stensor oil, and four pieces of droplino." He then returned to his marble-sorting activity.

Matthew, Matilda, Meinhard, and Atara had completed their packing chores prior to Conrad and Tiana's arrival. The four of them were now practicing in battle drills on the far side of the training room. Meinhard and Atara were playing the aggressors, while Matthew and his sister defended.

Meinhard stood at the apex of a triangle with Matthew and Matilda at the other angles. Standing there, he appeared to be supporting himself with the walking stick with such frailty that, at any moment, he might fall to the ground in a heap. Then, in the blink of an eye, Meinhard bounded into the air, spinning the walking stick around his body in a vibrant figure-eight pattern. From his apogee, he stopped the rotation of the stick, pointing the end in Matthew's direction. A bolt of bright light flashed from the stick, exploding directly where Matthew was standing just moments before. Matthew dove to his left microseconds before the bolt struck, and he returned the attack with a Q-energy blast from his right hand. Meinhard deflected the energy beam with his walking stick.

"Excellent," Meinhard said. "But next time, make sure you hit me."

As Meinhard and Matthew left the practice mat, Matilda faced Atara. This time, however, the sentinel forged her attack as her other self. Atara converted into a giant red-and-black dragon. A thunderous roar preceded Atara the dragon's attack. She opened her mouth wide, displaying row after row of razor-sharp teeth, and exhaled a barrage of fire headed directly for Matilda. Moments before contact, Matilda erected a force field bubble around herself. The dragon flame enveloped the bubble, obscuring everyone's view of Matilda, and until the flames subsided, no one could see if Matilda was safe, injured, or consumed by the fire.

When Atara ended her attack, and the fire dissipated, Matilda remained within her Q-energy cocoon. Other than appearing exhausted by the ordeal, she was breathing heavily, and her head and neck were lowered. She seemed no worse for wear.

After retracting her force field, Matilda stood up and brushed her forehead with the back of her right hand, wiping away the beads of sweat.

In a deep, guttural voice, Atara said, "Good strategy, Matilda. Very nice, indeed. Next time—"

But before Atara could finish her sentence, Matilda threw both of her palms straight out in front of her, accompanied by a diaphragmatic grunt. Two blue-green bolts of energy radiated out from her palms, striking Atara in the chest and knocking the several-ton creature head over tail. Crashing into the wall behind her, Atara became disoriented from the impact, but she shook it off. Anger rose slightly in her, but as a sentinel, she gained control almost immediately.

She converted into her humanoid form and teleported to Matilda to read her the riot act, but before she could utter a word, Matilda said, "You didn't say *tap*."

All Atara could do in light of her obvious failure to adhere to protocol was smile and laugh.

"Next time, young one," she said. "It will not be so easy to defeat me."

Tiana organized the group. She directed them to place their bags and packs in one area for transport. Then she reviewed the procedure for multiple teleports to the same spot. She was careful to repeat several times that inter-dimensional travel over many trillions of miles was vastly different from teleporting around Overworld, especially when several people and their respective belongings were included. Focusing a group transport to a very precise location without either centrifuging them all into a molecular stew or failing to reconstitute everything at the other end was nothing short of magic.

When the students were lined up in order of height, Tiana walked along the row of them, making sure there were no superfluous articles of clothing, miscellaneous straps, or other bits of matter that might make the whole trip more exacting. She tucked in Atticus's shirttail, and he let out a snicker when she did. Tiana playfully batted him on the back of the head which made him smile..

When the students were all checked out, Tiana said, "Very well, warriors, proceed to the coordinates that have been downloaded into your tokens."

Each student had proceeded to remove his or her token when Atara interjected, "Wait! Tiana, do you think it is wise to have the students lead the expedition?"

Tiana looked at Atara quizzically.

"Don't you think," she continued, "we sentinels should precede them in order to secure a perimeter?"

Tiana shot Atara a look that Conrad knew contained thoughts that Tiana did not want them to hear. He concentrated on Tiana, adjusting his cerebral tuner to connect with the frequency of Tiana's thought. When he did, he heard, *"Yes, if you feel it is so, the sentinels will teleport first. Thank you, sister."*

"Student warriors," Tiana said. "We sentinels will transport first to Mercatorum. I am certain our landing zone is safe, but you are all too valuable to risk any possible calamity. You will follow us as I instructed. Is that clear?"

The students nodded their understanding.

Conrad's nod was clearly less enthusiastic than the others'.

"You have a concern?" Tiana said in Conrad's mind.

"What if I can't do it? It is a long, long way."

Tiana knelt down next the boy, placing a hand on each of his shoulders. "You can do it," she said quietly. "But the token will remove any doubt. I will see you over there."

Tiana stood and walked over to where the sentinels were assembled. They were also in line according to height. Atara, being the tallest, was at the front and would therefore teleport first. She removed her token from her belt, tapped in the destination sequence, and returned the token to its holder. She waited for the gate to open. After several moments had passed, a strange look began to grow on everyone's face. Atara removed her token again. She reset the device and then repeated the sequence for transport. Once again, after several seconds had elapsed, nothing happened. You could cut the incredulity in the room with a knife.

"Let me see it," Tiana said, extending her hand.

Atara handed her token to Tiana, who turned it, flipped it, pressed several buttons, and even held it up to her ear. She handed the token back to Atara and removed her own token. Tiana pressed the coordinates into the control plate on the device, tapped the backing plate lightly, and looked up in front of her. After several seconds had passed yet again, it was clear to everyone that the ability to teleport using the tokens was offline.

Tiana told everyone else to attempt teleportation with his or her own personal token. Every student and sentinel in possession of a token followed the transport sequence, only to achieve the same result as both Atara and Tiana. None of the tokens were working.

All the sentinels looked perplexed by this transport failure, but the students looked downright concerned. Well, all except for Atticus. He was examining his token and attempting to open its seamless one-piece chassis.

Conrad raised his hand.

Tiana gestured to him, thinking, *"Ask."*

"Why aren't the tokens working?"

"That is a very good question," Tiana replied. "The answer must wait. First, we need to find a new method of transportation to Mercatorum."

Tiana closed her eyes and concentrated. After several moments, and facial gyrations, she said, "Good. The *Doppler Magnum* is available. Does everyone know how to get to her?"

All the students nodded yes.

"Very well. The question remains whether our inability to teleport is limited to interplanetary travel or if the entire system is offline."

She then closed her eyes and disappeared with a crackle. After seeing what seemed like a successful local transport, each of the remaining students and sentinels visualized the *Doppler Magnum*. One by one, the students disappeared into points of light, followed closely behind by the sentinels.

They all landed in the *Doppler Magnum*'s hangar as a spine-tingling sequence of noises was emanating from Seks. The robot was positioned in the same place he always was—attached by his torso to the main control console. However, his head was turned severely to the left, and the cacophony of beeps, tweets, squeals, and clicks blasting in Alex's direction indicated Seks was experiencing a greater than usual level of frustration with Mr. Sine.

"Okay, okay," Alex said back in Seks's direction, trying in a vain attempt to interrupt the android. Finally, when Seks ceased his castigation, Alex said, "Wow, you'd think we are married or something. Sorry to say, Seks, but you're not my type."

Seks resumed the concert of accusation against Alex as Alex walked away grinning to himself.

Alex continued toward the ship, picking up a small black-and-brown case on his way there. Tiana, observing the commotion upon their arrival, teleported to the extended loading ramp of the *Magnum*. Conrad watched carefully as Tiana requested information from Alex in pantomime. Every so often Alex would laugh loud enough for them all to hear, and then Tiana would ask another silent question to which Alex would answer in silence.

"What do you think they're talking about?" Mindy asked Conrad.

"Dunno, but I'll bet Alex is just being Alex."

"What do you mean?"

"Do you know Alex very well?"

Mindy shook her head.

"He likes to do things his way. Unfortunately for him, sometimes his way rubs Tiana the wrong way."

"Do you think they ever fight about it, and I mean *really fight*?"

"No way! Alex is tough, but I saw him back down already when he pushed Tiana just a little too far."

"She's amazing, isn't she?"

"Yes..." Conrad stopped mid-sentence to contemplate the gravity of what Mindy had implied.

Yes, Tiana was amazing and talented and powerful and...beautiful. He didn't think he should tell Mindy that last one. He thought he should just leave it as an agreement between them.

"Yes, she is amazing. And I am fortunate to have her as my sentinel."

Tiana walked back to the group, leaving Alex with the ship.

"All right, everyone," she said. "We are just about ready to embark. Be certain you have everything together, because once we leave, we will not be back for quite a while."

The student warriors regarded each other when she said "a while," but each one's sentinel assured him or her that everything was as it should be.

The student-sentinel groups gathered their belongings and proceeded toward the *Doppler Magnum*'s loading platform. Conrad waited with Tiana.

"You can board the ship with your classmates," she said.

"That's okay. I want to be with my sentinel."

Tiana smiled and said, "You are learning quickly, but I always knew you would."

She picked up her duffle bag from the ground and watched as Conrad gathered his backpack and other things together. Then the two marched off, following their comrades toward the ship. In silence, they walked, comforted in their reflections and anticipations.

Chapter Thirty-Two

Overworld shrunk in size as the *Doppler Magnum* left the planet using contragrav propulsion. When the ship reached the relativity perimeter, the supralight engines engaged, flinging the ship into hyperspace. Conrad was careful not to stare at the photic flare again, and this time his sight did not diminish.

Once safely in hyperspace, the passengers released their retention harnesses and began moving about the cabin. The artificial gravity regulators automatically calculated the mass variances and adjusted the force. Alex and Nash remained in their seats, making adjustments to the autopilot controls. Even in this most mundane task, the brothers disagreed incessantly.

Conrad stood and stretched his arms above his head.

"I didn't stare at the stars this time," he said to Tiana.

"Yes," she replied. "You do learn from your mistakes. Never underestimate the benefits of that ability."

While he continued his stretch, now reaching down to loosen his lower back muscles, Mindy came over.

"Out of shape?" she said.

"Very funny. Just keeping myself flexible."

Conrad reached out and poked Mindy in her midriff. "You're a little soft, too. Maybe some sit-ups?"

Mindy stuck her tongue out and gave Conrad a raspberry.

Alex Sine got out of the pilot's chair and turned to address the group.

"The flight to our destination should be uneventful," he said, "but does anyone want to explain what we are doing? I mean, we were just on Mercatorum and Nathaniel was nowhere to be found."

Tiana stood to respond to Alex, but just before she could utter a word, Alex continued, "Did you confirm that he is there?"

"I have no confirmation," Tiana said. "It is only a hunch."

Alex did not appreciate this response. "We're traveling seventy light-years on a hunch?"

Tiana's eyes were glowing brightly, and they were the color of deep-green emeralds.

"A hunch is all I have," she said, "but I do believe it is time for a briefing."

Tiana walked to the front of the main cabin. Nash was still in the navigator's seat listening to the conversations, but continuing his duties.

"Nash," Tiana said, "will you join everyone in the gallery?"

He nodded affirmatively and moved to the back of the flight deck.

Tiana began by reciting select history—some known and some obscure—to bring every member of the team up to speed. She asked who had heard the legend of Myrddin and Dualoc. Nearly everyone raised their hands. Atticus did not, but when Tiana asked him directly if he knew the story, he said he did.

"What happened to Myrddin?" she asked.

Matthew and Mindy shot their respective hands into the air.

"Matthew," Tiana said, "what happened?"

"Dualoc banished Myrddin from reality," he said. "And legend states that he is caught between reality and shadow."

"Very good, Matthew. That is what the legend states, but with what you know of the physical universe, does that seem to be a correct assumption?"

Matthew shrugged his shoulders.

Mindy was still waving her hand in the air, and Tiana pointed to her.

"I had heard," Mindy said, "that Dualoc placed Myrddin into a deep sleep, and one day, he will awaken and destroy Dualoc."

Everyone including Conrad looked at Mindy incredulously.

"Bravo, Mindy," Tiana said. "Yes, that is truly what happened, but there is more to the story."

Tiana continued by explaining to the group what she had told Conrad previously. Before Myrddin was entranced, he foretold that three beings would one day bring order to the universe and chaos would disappear forever. This group of three, the Trinity, was comprised of extremely powerful and good incepts, and their alliance would render all other dark incepts powerless.

"The forces of the dark cannot afford to allow the Trinity to complete itself," Tiana said. Then she looked directly at Alex and said, "That is why we are traveling seventy light-years."

Alex looked back at Tiana disdainfully. "That is why?" he said. "You said nothing about why we are going." Alex started pacing back and forth.

"Are you implying that the…What did you call them? The Trinity? Are you saying they are on Mercatorum? I thought we were going to find Nathaniel Turner."

Tiana was just about to speak. She was ready to tell them all that Nathaniel was Trinity-One and that their classmate Conrad was Trinity-Two. She was preparing to say it aloud when she heard in her mind, *"No, please, please, please, don't!"*

When she heard Conrad's plea, she turned her gaze, looking him straight in the eye. Her eyes were now a soft amber color with barely any phosphorescence. There was no pity, no sympathy. She only felt remorse for the fact that this wonderful, talented, and clever boy could not accept his predestination, and he continued to have trouble believing he was more than he appeared to be.

"Let it suffice, we are going to Mercatorum to help bring order to the universe."

Alex was not satisfied with the explanation. He never did accept vagueness or ambiguity from anyone, but he decided to let it go for the moment.

"What's the plan to accomplish this order in the universe?" Alex asked.

Tiana's eyes began the oscillating green glow she exhibited when she was ready to do battle.

"First," she said, "we will investigate the disappearance of Nathaniel Turner."

The meeting ended and everyone returned to the main cabin. Conrad watched Tiana's every move as she stopped to speak to each student warrior. He saw how she placed one hand on Matthew's shoulder while speaking to him, hugging Matilda to send her on her way. He saw how she tousled Atticus's hair, and although Atticus did not look directly at Tiana, a smile grew on his face as she did.

Just before Tiana left the gallery, Conrad sent a thought to her. *"Thank you,"* he thought.

Tiana turned her head around. She was smiling at him with eyes brilliant blue. *"You are welcome, T-Two"* was the response as she walked into the main cabin.

Her addressing him in the abbreviated form for Trinity-Two seemed less formal, less obnoxious. He turned the acronym over in his head several times, but he couldn't shake the happiness he felt. Whenever Tiana had addressed him as Trinity-Two before, a lump rose in his throat. A lump comprised of one part embarrassment, one part humiliation, and one part curiosity. Now he felt neither embarrassed nor humiliated, but the curiosity remained. *T2*, Conrad thought. *I think I like that.*

Conrad sat down in a chair, put both of his hands behind his head, and closed his eyes. He was smiling widely while he reflected on all that had happened to him recently. The last few years had been very trying for the boy. Never feeling he belonged anywhere since his mother died, he took solace in the fact that, once he turned eighteen, he could strike out on his own. And although not all of his foster families were cruel or abusive to him, none had ever been able to make him feel he belonged. It was as if everything was working toward making him not feel he belonged anywhere. Conrad's eyes popped open. Maybe he wasn't supposed to feel like he belonged simply because he did not belong, not only in California, but perhaps he didn't belong as part of all existence.

Now he felt a connection for the first time in a long time. He felt like the pieces of his life were finally falling into place. He believed that his purpose in the world was rapidly coming into focus with laser-like precision. He was T2, and he was starting to feel something he hadn't ever felt before. He felt pride.

"What are you thinking about?"

The question caused Conrad to spring up from his chair, disoriented. When he did, his legs were wrapped around each other so he fell to the floor. He looked up to see the question had come from Mindy, who was now looking down at him, laughing slightly.

"I'm sorry I startled you," she said.

Conrad picked himself up off the floor, and said, "I thought I was alone. How long have you been here?"

"I never left," she said.

Once Conrad regained his seat, Mindy took the one to his right.

"So, what were you thinking about?" she asked.

An awkward sense of nakedness crept up in him. He knew he wasn't speaking his thoughts aloud, but was it possible that Mindy had heard them?

"You don't know?" he asked.

Mindy frowned mildly. "Sorry, Conrad, but I can't hear your thoughts. I can only give you mine."

"Oh, yeah. Why can't I get that?"

He was still trying to get a handle on this telepathy thing. Not everyone on Overworld could read minds, and those who could did not necessarily have the ability to read everyone's mind all the time. Some telepaths could only hear the thoughts of specific individuals, and others could only hear the thoughts of animals or plants. Keeping track of it all was mentally exhausting. Conrad had decided not to think thoughts, or at least attempt to not, for which he would be embarrassed. But he remembered that Mindy was an empath.

"Do you know what I'm feeling?"

Mindy closed her eyes for several seconds. And when she reopened them, she shook her head.

"I was thinking about home," he said. "And everything that has changed since I came here."

"Well, what's changed?" Mindy asked.

Conrad explained his situation at home in California. He didn't go into great detail about the horrors just after his mother's death, but he began with his first foster home.

When he moved into the Dennison's' house, he was so overcome with grief and fear that he could not be sure at times whether he would survive the heartbreak. Judy and Peter Dennison were nice enough folks. They had no children (Conrad had heard that Peter had some sort of accident), but they seemed content in their life together. Conrad thought he would be able to stay with the Dennisons indefinitely, but it was not to be. Several months after he moved in, Judy

Dennison nearly overdosed on sleeping pills, so Peter found another home for Conrad.

The Cabelas were the next family in Conrad's young life. Tino, Marie, and their twin daughters, Cara and Sara, lived in Torrance. Their house wasn't big enough for an additional person, so they put a small bed and some miscellaneous furniture in the garage to give Conrad some semblance of a home. He was with the Cabelas for three weeks when Marie Cabela found Cara and Sara in Conrad's "apartment" playing a game of "you show me yours and I'll show you mine." It was all the girls' idea, but that explanation was ignored by Marie and Tino.

The next seven homes were merely foster homes set up and monitored by the California Department of Children and Family Services, or DCFS, and each one was a bigger nightmare for Conrad than the previous one.

When he was living in each, Conrad assumed the families were simply bringing foster kids in for the five hundred dollars a month they received for the children's care. He was certain of it. It was during this time that Conrad had lost all remaining enthusiasm for life, and he anticipated the day when he could be on his own and no longer need the services of other people. He even considered emancipation when he reached his fourteenth birthday. He would have done it, but then he moved in with the Petrarcas.

Bob Petrarca had dated Veronica Harper when they both attended UCLA. Bob had planned to marry her after graduation, but something changed the summer after their freshman year. Veronica cut classes many days during sophomore year, and she ended up on academic probation. However, the most painful thing to Bob was how aloof Ronnie had become toward him.

He confronted her once regarding her absenteeism and her recent rejection of their relationship. Ronnie cried when Bob proclaimed his love for her and his previous intention to ask her to become his wife. Once she composed herself, all she said was that what was happening was beyond her control, that it was her destiny, and that she was truly sorry to hurt Bob in any way. Veronica also told him that they could never see each other again.

Bob had no idea at the time that Veronica had met Nathaniel the previous summer, and her life would be tied to his from that moment forward. Bob also had no inkling during their breakup that Veronica was already expecting a child, Conrad himself.

Mindy listened intently to Conrad. Despite her hearing deficit, she had taught herself to actively listen to conversations while watching the person's lips. This way she not only had auditory information passed to her through her cochlear implants, but the information was augmented with visual confirmation by lip reading. Sometimes, however, the muffled sounds transmitted to her inner ear combined with the visual cues produced by specific lip and tongue position were not enough to give Mindy complete comprehension. In those instances, she used her metaphysical powers. As she tried to tune into Conrad's thoughts at that moment, she found she remained unable to tap into his exact frequency. She did catch several small thought fragments, but her frustration grew. She decided she had to ask questions.

"Do you know what happened to Bob?"

"I'm not sure. I heard Beverly and he separated for a time after I left, but that might just be a rumor."

"Did you ever try to tap into his frequency to find out?"

"No, I never thought about it." Conrad thought it was creepy to tap into someone's thoughts like that. He wasn't sure he would if he could. "Have you done that to anyone?"

Mindy thought for a while. "Not really. I find it uncomfortable to do it. I only did it once or twice in order to save myself or someone else."

"Really? What happened?"

Mindy looked at Conrad with a serious look uncharacteristic for her personality. "Let's see," she began. "It was after I arrived on Overworld, and I had only been here a few weeks. Donovan was teaching me to hone my telepathy skills. It was difficult at first."

"Difficult how?"

"Because I don't hear sound very well, the first few times I 'heard' someone else's thoughts in my head the volume seemed unbearable."

Conrad nodded as if he understood what that would be like.

"After some practice, I learned to control the intensity. Anyway, there was another girl here, Tasha Grigorieva. Tasha was older than I, but we became close friends."

Mindy paused for a few moments. She turned her head away from Conrad, and he saw her move the back of her hand across her eyes. Without returning her head to Conrad's direction, she continued.

"Tasha disappeared one night. There were no clues in her room, and no one remembered seeing her after dinner. So I took it upon myself to seek her out."

Mindy stopped again for several moments. After waiting for her to continue, Conrad could no longer endure the suspense.

"Yeah, so what happened?"

Mindy turned her head around, tears streaming down her cheeks. "I saw her die, and it was the most terrible thing ever. It was almost like it was happening to me, too."

Mindy grabbed Conrad, buried her face into his shoulder, and began sobbing deeply. Conrad hesitated at first, but then wrapped both hands around her, holding her closer.

After a few minutes had passed, Mindy regained her composure. She began pulling back, and Conrad released his hug so she could sit up straight.

"I'm sorry," she said.

"Nonsense, I'm the one who's sorry. I had no idea." He looked down at the floor and then back up to Mindy. "Can I ask one last question?"

Although Mindy knew what he was going to ask, she nevertheless nodded affirmatively.

"What happened to Tasha?"

"I don't know. Her body was never found, but what I saw...heard...felt...was a blackness, a vicious, violent dark force, and I heard Tasha's scream and then silence. It was awful."

Conrad gently placed his hand on Mindy's shoulder as a gesture of comfort.

Suddenly, an explosion rocked the ship, throwing both Mindy and Conrad to the floor. A second and third explosion continued the gyrations until the alarm klaxon sounded red alert. ANN's synthetic voice indicated battle stations as red lights flashed and the ship's altitude stabilizers strained to regain level flight.

Once the ship renewed proper altitude, Conrad lifted himself from the floor and then helped Mindy to her feet.

"Are you all right?" he asked.

"Yes," she responded, "but I think we better get onto the flight deck."

Dazed, Conrad grabbed Mindy's hand and quickly led her toward the front of the ship. He barely noticed the sound of energy weapons exploding outside the ship now that the *Doppler Magnum*'s shields had been raised. He opened the flight deck door, and the two walked through.

The command deck was buzzing with activity. Alex and Nash were manning the control console as they normally did, but now there were other stations being operated. Along the side bulwarks of the command console, four stations hovered above the floor, attached to the ceiling. The sentinels were controlling these ancillary stations.

"Maintain deflector array at seventy-five percent," Alex commanded.

ANN responded nearly instantaneously to protect the ship from the onslaught outside.

Tiana gestured to Conrad and Mindy, who were frozen in the doorway watching. *"Secure your seats,"* Conrad heard in his head.

Even from as far away as he was from her, he could see that Tiana's eyes were two glowing emeralds. He grasped Mindy's hand tighter and directed her to two empty passenger chairs. They sat, secured their harnesses, and continued observing.

"Nash," Alex bellowed. "Escape vector?"

Nash's fingers rapidly played the buttons on his control console like a piano. "Calculating," he said.

"Make it snappy," Alex replied.

The ship was buffeted by the dozens of concussions blasting against its deflector array. The sentinels were each returning fire from their respective battle stations. As they did, their stations traced severe geometric patterns through the air. To Conrad's eye, it looked like a sort of cosmic ballet.

"They're sending multiple PEP fighters at us," Atara said.

"Target their photon collectors," Alex said.

"I know their weakness, Alex," Atara said with disgust.

Alex laughed and said, "Pretty girl."

The *Doppler Magnum* flew a serpentine course through a cloud of the small, nimble fighters. As it traversed space where the battle was erupting, it appeared to be moving rapidly through a storm filled with electric rain. Millions of tiny red-and-yellow energy bolts filled the battle zone like shrapnel from an explosion. As the bolts impacted the deflector array, the ship's systems transferred energy to the affected area in nanoseconds, protecting it from further damage.

From inside, Conrad watched the virtual viewing screen from his seat. He felt a strange sensation because the monitor indicated that the ship was making a path similar to that of a great roller coaster. Up, down, sideways, and through several loops the *Magnum* traveled, but there was little or no sensation inside the ship due to the artificial gravity holding the passengers to the floor.

"Nash!" Alex screamed. "I need that vector now!"

"I'm calculating, but it's almost as if they know our moves before we do."

"What are you talking about? How is that possible?"

Tiana closed her eyes briefly. "Someone, or something, is scanning us," she said. "We are exposing our tactics to our enemy."

"So what do you suggest?" Alex asked.

Tiana closed her eyes again. "Nash," Tiana said. "Clear your mind while plotting the vector."

"How do I do that?"

"Think a repeating thought."

Nash renewed his keyboard manipulation, his fingers flying over the control console as the ship continued its circuitous path through space. The sentinels also managed to return voluminous fire, knocking out multiple targets; however, the PEP fighters continued the onslaught, seeking any weakness in the *Magnum*'s defenses.

After several minutes, Nash said, "Vector calculated."

"Great," Alex said. "Initiate escape vector."

Nash paused.

"What?" Alex asked.

"ANN suggests using the PCG."

"I don't know," Alex said. "What about the power drain?"

Nash returned to his console, selecting several buttons. "We can proceed at sub-light with the collector deployed. Estimated time to ninety percent power is two hours."

Alex thought for several moments before he nodded his assent. "Everyone," Alex said, "make sure your retention harnesses are secure. Sentinels, secure your battle stations and return to the passenger gallery. We are about to deploy the phased chaos generator, as suggested by ANN."

Conrad looked at Mindy. "Do you know what he's talking about?"

Mindy shook her head.

Conrad turned his attention to Tiana. *"What's going on?"* he thought.

"I will explain later, if necessary" was the response.

The sentinels' battle consoles dropped to the floor, securing themselves to the bulkhead. Each sentinel then joined the others in the gallery. Suddenly, a strong explosion rocked the ship, sending Harlow to the floor and staggering the others. An alarm sounded and a rapidly flashing red light illuminated on Nash's console.

"We're losing a deflector."

"Deploy the PCG—now!" Alex barked.

As Nash renewed his control symphony and the sentinels returned to their seats, secured themselves, and prepared for the next event, Conrad's head was spinning. So much was happening so rapidly that he couldn't quite grasp the gravity of the situation. He knew there was danger because the tension in the cabin was tangible. You could cut it with a knife.

The ship creaked and groaned as the PCG extended from its mooring. Once it was fully enabled, the ship began a corkscrew path through the battle zone. Hundreds of PEP fighters continued their barrage on the *Doppler Magnum*'s defenses. Energy bolts and blast charges exploded and ricocheted off the remaining deflectors. The enemy craft were as thick as bees near a hive. The little unmanned craft were relentless in their pursuit of their quarry.

The *Magnum*'s helical flight path perfected, the PCG began spinning in a complementary arc. Within seconds, the PCG began emitting a fusillade of multicolor bolts. With uncanny accuracy, the bolts found their targets, destroying the PEP fighters one after another until the space around the ship was void of any remaining threats. Once the barrage was completed, the PCG returned to its docking station, and the ship returned to straight and level flight.

The occupants released a collective sigh of relief as the danger passed. Everyone applauded the command crew's efforts in bringing them all to safety. They all began releasing their retention straps in order to move about the ship. Once Alex was able, he moved back to the passenger gallery to address them.

"That was exciting, wasn't it?" he said. Nearly every one of them simply stared at him.

"I thought it was great," Matthew said.

"No you didn't," Matilda said. "You were as scared as the rest of us."

"True, but it was fun."

Matilda punched her brother in the arm.

"Should we continue at sub-light," Tiana said, "or is it more prudent to simply stop while the systems power up?"

"It won't make much difference either way. We're still nearly a parsec away from our destination. Two hours of sub-light won't make a dent, but most passengers feel better when the ship is moving."

Alex looked over his shoulder toward the command console. There were several rows of lights glowing with several flashing randomly.

"The ship has sustained some damage, but the repairs are being completed currently." Alex smiled and looked back at Tiana. "I leave the decision to you since this is your show."

Tiana considered the options momentarily. She closed her eyes and said, "I believe the more prudent course is to stop while the ship recharges and completes any necessary repairs." She stood again to address the student warriors and the sentinels. "I would suggest each of you partner up and practice battle scenarios."

Each student and his or her respective sentinel joined together and exited from the flight deck to find a suitable training area.

Afterward, only Alex, Nash, Tiana, and Conrad remained. The four stood in silent contemplation. Alex knew Nash and he had responsibilities at the command station, but he wanted to speak with Tiana about the fundamental goals of their quest. He tried to tune into Tiana's frequency to retrieve a clue but was unable to glean one.

After several moments had passed, Tiana said, "Come, Conrad, we should train with the others," and she led Conrad toward the rear exit from the flight deck.

"Wait!" Alex shouted.

Tiana and Conrad turned.

"Can I have a word with you?" Alex asked Tiana.

"Of course you can. Conrad, please go ahead and wait for me."

"Where do you want me to go?"

"Find an empty cabin where we can train. I will be there shortly." She looked at Alex. "Will this take long?"

Alex shook his head that it would not.

Conrad left the deck through the main access door.

When he closed the door behind him, he stopped and pressed his ear to the door, hoping to hear something. As he placed his ear to the door, a thought ran through his head: *Just listen to her thoughts*. He pulled back from the door and linked to Tiana.

Chapter Thirty-Three

On the command deck, Alex was pacing back and forth. Tiana, standing with both arms folded, watched him intently. After several laps, she said, "I assume you want to discuss something urgent."

Nash, who the whole time had been monitoring the repairs and regeneration, turned and said, "Will you say something, for Pete's sake?"

Alex shot Nash a look, and he stopped pacing.

"I want to know what you know."

"What I know about what?"

"About Nathaniel's disappearance."

"I do not *know* much, but I sense several things."

It was clear Alex was becoming perturbed. "Tell us everything. I think we have a right to know."

Tiana began by reviewing their last trip to Mercatorum. She told Alex and Nash that she felt Baron von Goren was not being completely honest when the matter of Nathaniel Turner arose.

"Yes, you said that then," Alex interjected. "But there is something more, right? I mean, you wouldn't place the lives of five kids, one of whom is Nathaniel's son, in jeopardy based on the fact that a politician was being less than candid, would you?"

"Your sarcasm is neither appreciated nor helpful. Yes, there is more, but I hesitate to discuss things for which I have scant evidence."

"The time has passed for being coy, Tiana. If I'm going to help on this quest, I need to know what you know, think, feel, and expect." Tiana acknowledged that Alex was right.

Conrad was completely spellbound by what he was hearing in his mind. When they were on Mercatorum previously, Tiana had asked Baron von Goren if he knew where Conrad's father was. The Baron denied knowing anything, but Tiana sensed there was another presence in the baron's chamber at the time. She had a suspicion that this other presence was controlling the baron, or if not controlling him, exerting great influence upon him.

There were spots in the telepathic information Conrad received that were silent, and he assumed this represented the times when either Alex or Nash was talking. After a very long pause, Conrad heard that Tiana thought someone had returned. He did not receive the name of this someone, but he could tell that neither Alex nor Nash nor even Tiana knew a name.

Then something happened.

Conrad heard Tiana think, *"Do not go there, Alex."*

A long pause followed, which Conrad knew meant Alex was off on another one of his tirades. Waiting seemed forever, and Conrad began to get anxious. He wanted to think, *Oh, come on already*, but he knew if he thought it, there was a great likelihood Tiana would intercept it.

After several long, painfully boring minutes, Tiana thought, *"I do not know if he betrayed Nathaniel."*

"Who?" Conrad thought without restraint. The instant it left his mind he knew he was caught. Tiana gave him a moment to soak in his crime, and then she thought, *"You and I will speak about this."* He moved away from the doorway and sat down against a bulkhead. He placed his head in his hands and sat, waiting for Tiana's wrath.

About five minutes later, Tiana walked through the door from the flight deck and gently closed the door behind her. She walked over to where Conrad sat, slowly and with deliberation. He could see nothing but her boots because he refused to look up at her for fear her eyes were glowing red with anger. He looked at her boots until she said, "Look at me, Conrad."

He slowly lifted his head, already accepting of his fate. When he looked at her face, she was smiling softly, and her eyes were the color of robin's eggs.

"I am not angry, but we must discuss the proper use of your developing gifts."

Conrad understood what Tiana said about "invading" the privacy of another being. He knew firsthand that privacy was precious; when you lived in a house occupied with many other people, like most of the foster homes in which he'd resided, privacy was a commodity that should be cherished. Now he found himself in the position of usurper of Tiana, Alex, and Nash's privacy.

"I'm sorry," he said, "but I just wanted to know what was going on."

"Your apology is accepted. In this instance, I believe it was necessary, but take heed in the future. Your self-sought desire for knowledge might sometime need to be put away for the greater good," Tiana said. She extended her hand to him and helped him stand up. "Shall we practice some of your battle skills?" She smiled brightly at Conrad.

"Yes," he said. "I think I need lots of practice."

Chapter Thirty-Four

While sentinel and student practiced battle maneuvers, ANN completed repairs, and the ship's systems recharged. The ship then reentered hyperspace, continuing the trip to their destination. They arrived at the Mercatorum system several hours later.

Upon arrival, the *Doppler Magnum* slowed from supralight speed, exiting hyperspace, well outside of the deceleration zone. However, seconds after they slowed, two planetary attack vessels positioned themselves on either side of the ship.

"Attention, *Doppler Magnum*," a voice said from the transceiver. "State your destination and purpose."

Alex said, "This is Captain Sine. We are proceeding to Ammerand. We wish to see the supreme baron."

Several seconds elapsed before a reply came from the escorts. Finally, a broadcast said, "Since you have come uninvited, please follow us. We will escort you in."

"That's really unnecessary," Alex said. "We were with von Goren—"

An explosion outside the ship rocked everyone inside the *Magnum*.

"What's the big idea?" Alex exclaimed.

"Follow us in, Captain Sine, or your ship will be destroyed. This will be your only warning."

Alex looked over at Nash. He was planning to call their bluff. He was also planning to teach Baron von Goren a lesson when he got his next opportunity.

"Now is not the time, Alex," Tiana said telepathically. *"Pretend inferiority and encourage arrogance."*

Alex nodded his assent.

The two attack craft entered the atmosphere at a severe angle; however, their astrodynamic design allowed the acute angles necessary for fast and agile maneuverability during dogfights. The *Doppler Magnum*, on the other hand, was designed for intergalactic travel and the transportation of goods and passengers. The sharp decline was buffeting the ship intensely.

"Skin temperature is reaching critical," Nash said.

"Can you slow the descent enough to offset the atmospheric friction?"

"I can try."

Nash began running his fingers over his command console like a prodigy playing Rachmaninoff. The sound coming from the engine room notched down several points in frequency, and the majority of the buffeting subsided. The ship slowed to a point where the two escorts were no more than two dots on the horizon when viewed through the virtual windshield, but the ship was automatically following them just the same.

The two attack ships had already landed at the Ammerand Spaceport by the time the *Magnum* reached the destination.

"Landing protocol," Alex said, and the ship's autonomous systems took over control.

The landing struts were deployed, the sub-light engines were deactivated, and the gravity drive was activated nearly simultaneously. As the ship landed, it rotated ninety degrees to ensure that the passengers could exit without being directly impacted by the prevailing surface winds.

The *Doppler Magnum* landed on the surface, and the landing strut shock absorbers set it down with a subtle thump. Finally, the disembarkation gangway extended to allow easy egress. The ships cooling ports spewed forth condensed vapor from the relativity and gravity drive conduits. Through the mist, several uniformed troops approached the ship with weapons drawn, and they aligned themselves in control formation.

Inside the ship, Alex rallied the students and sentinels to prepare to defend themselves. It was clear the students were anxious about being involved in a battle so shortly after they had arrived. Mindy grabbed Conrad's sleeve, and he looked over at her, touching her hand with his.

"It will be okay," he said.

"You think so?"

"Yes. Don't worry."

But he was worried, he just didn't want Mindy to know. Why should he burden her, this sweet, caring, courageous, disabled girl with fears that were irrational anyway? If a confrontation with the troops positioned just outside the ship was inevitable, they would either be victorious or not. Agonizing over it would not help in the least. It would be a much better use of their time now to focus on a solution or a battle plan.

He reached out to Tiana with his mind. *"What are we going to do?"*

Tiana looked over at Conrad and replied, *"Trust your instincts."*

Conrad was not comforted by this response, but nevertheless, he knew Tiana was a better judge of these situations than he. Trusting in Tiana hadn't let him down yet. He pushed the thought *But there's always a first time* out of his mind.

Tiana walked up to Alex. She placed her hand on his shoulder and said, "No, we will not confront them now. We will pretend to be ineffective, incompetent, submissive."

"Why would we do that?"

"Because we should assess the situation carefully to determine any potential risk to our group."

"So we're going to just walk out there and surrender?"

"It is not surrender if it is our intent to evaluate the situation in order to consider options."

Alex's mouth had been hanging open slightly, the words forming just behind his teeth. However, he thought about Tiana's ability to evaluate, analyze, and formulate, and his lips snapped together before any new protest exited them. "Okay, you're in charge. I'll follow your lead."

The group marched out the egress port, down the loading ramp, to be greeted by two squadrons of soldiers. Some of these troops held their energy weapons at the ready, and others had them trained upon the passengers exiting the *Doppler Magnum*. Tiana felt a shudder from one of the students laced with a tinge of panic, but with the telepathic bandwidth completely congested with thoughts, fears, agitation, and aggression, she found it difficult to hone in on whose mind was losing focus. She telepathically screamed, *"STOP!"* in hopes it would quell the concerned. After several moments, she realized she was successful since the airwaves were then free from the transferred thoughts of panic.

As they reached the bottom of the gangway, one of the soldiers stepped forward to address Tiana. His uniform was of a different cut and color from the others, and it was clear from his confident stride and demeanor that he was in charge. He quickly two-stepped to within a yard of Tiana, his feet landing together side by side, and slapped the sides of both of his legs with his hands as he stood ruler straight.

"Welcome to Ammerand," he said, looking directly at Tiana. "I am Colonel Guerrero. You will all come with us…please."

Alex could barely restrain himself. He tapped the handgrip of the disrupter pistol he had hidden in the waistband of his pants. "Welcome?" he said. "You call this a welcome?"

The colonel's eyes narrowed as he turned his gaze to Alex Sine. "Yes, just as I expected, Captain Sine." The colonel snapped his fingers and two troops circled behind Alex with weapons drawn. The colonel moved close to Alex and said, "Give me a reason."

Alex watched the colonel's face with his peripheral vision, realizing his impulsivity would, one day, cause him great pain. Alex was going to offer an apology when Tiana interjected.

"He is sorry, Colonel. We will do as we are told. Take us where you will."

The colonel led his troops with their "guests" to Ammerand Palace. They entered the palace through an underground passageway adjacent to the overlook attached to the rear portion of the main building. The forward squad proceeded down the access ramp first, followed by the students and sentinels. The second squad brought up the rear. Once the group was belowground level, a soldier waved his hand over a biometric measurement plate. A muffled grinding noise began as a metallic-plated gate closed off the opening to the passage.

At the end of the passageway lay a dead end. As the soldiers neared it, they stopped, turned around in place, and presented their arms before themselves at chest level. The students didn't know what to think about this maneuver. They also turned around, but seeing the second squad simply stop and display the same weapons presentation as the other soldiers caused their stress levels to increase. Donovan and Meinhard moved in front of the students, facing the first squad. Harlow and Atara moved slowly to face the second. It was clear they were preparing to defend their charges under the proper circumstances.

Suddenly, the floor of the room began moving. Everyone could feel the sensation, and indeed, they were rising in the cavern. Lights flashed periodically as they rose up into the palace above. Conrad grabbed Tiana's arm and held Mindy's hand tightly.

When the elevator stopped, a large door opened to the side of them. The colonel walked toward the open door, turned slightly, and invited them all to walk through into the next room. They followed the command as if their collective will was no longer their own. And when the last one walked through the doorway, it closed behind them.

The holding chamber was festooned with many of the comforts of home. There were several rows of chairs that resembled movie theater seats without armrests. A long oval table was positioned near the far wall. Eight chairs adorned the table, but the space between each chair looked odd to the casual observer. A table this large would be better suited with twice the number of chairs present. The walls were covered with tapestries from an ancient time, and interspersed between them were paintings created by some of the Dutch Masters.

"You, you, you, you, and you," the colonel said, pointing at each of the students, "sit over there." The colonel was directing them to take a seat in the gallery.

"Sentinels," he continued, "please join me at the board." The colonel then looked at Alex and Nash. "You two," he said, "find a seat where you can."

The students went to the movie seats. Matthew and Matilda sat in the first row at one end. Atticus sat in the last row, center. Mindy took a seat in the second row while Conrad watched her. She sat down, smiled at Conrad, and tapped the seat next to her with her hand. Conrad smiled back and joined her.

The sentinels followed the colonel to the board table. The two men sat on the far side of the table while Atara and Harlow sat on the near side. Tiana stood waiting to see what the colonel would do. He stood near the head of the table adjacent to a door. When he noticed Tiana remained standing, he indicated she should take the seat at the opposite table head. She did. Alex and Nash took the two remaining seats at the board table. Alex sat directly to Tiana's left, while Nash was at her right.

There was an eerie silence in the chamber. Each sentinel was looking directly forward, not moving a muscle.

Conrad and Mindy watched this, and he thought, *"I bet they're planning something."*

Tiana looked over at Conrad. *"Careful"* is all he heard.

Mindy grabbed his hand and squeezed it hard.

After many minutes had passed, a door opened near where the colonel was standing. As it did, all the soldiers snapped to attention. The colonel followed suit, and he turned slightly. Baron von Goren walked through the door, and it closed behind him.

The baron was dressed in full military attire with epaulettes on both shoulders. His charcoal-gray trousers were pleated with blood red stripes down each out seam. His shirt was the same color as his pants but was adorned with hemispherical gold buttons along the body in two parallel rows. A sword and scabbard hung from his waist along his right leg, and his black overcoat was long, running nearly to the floor in back.

"Welcome, my friends," the baron began. "To what do I owe this surprise visit?"

Alex turned his head to regard Tiana's reaction to von Goren's plainly sarcastic remark. He wanted to withdraw his blaster from its holster and end the insult permanently. Tiana gently touched the back of Nash and Alex's hands before standing to address the baron.

"Baron von Goren, your troops have insulted us greatly. We have been treated as prisoners of war when in reality we are here, on Mercatorum, for a humanitarian cause."

"Really?" von Goren said. "And what, pray tell, would that cause be?"

Tiana scowled at him, her eyes burning emeralds. "We are here to find Nathaniel Turner."

"I told you before, Turner is not here, and from what my intelligence service can gather, he hasn't been here in many, many years. Trust me."

The right side of Tiana's mouth turned up slightly. "Forgive me, Baron, if I do not trust the word of a politician."

Von Goren's visage changed at the challenge and insult. He was clearly becoming upset and angry. Just as he was about to respond with his own invective, Tiana interrupted.

"Let us go, or you shall bear the consequences."

Von Goren regarded his troops, two squads of his most highly trained soldiers—soldiers with years of training, battle experience, and temper. These men were part of his elite fighting force. Certainly this ragtag band of children, metamorphs, a scalawag, and his brother were no match for them, especially under the command of Colonel Leo Guerrero.

"I think you overestimate your chances, Master Tiana. However, if you believe this course is best…"

Von Goren scanned the chamber with his eyes. He looked first at the sentinels seated at the table, then Alex and Nash, and finally, he turned his attention to the gallery. The student warriors were each in different states of anxiety, fear, and repose.

Conrad looked over at Mindy, who was beginning to hyperventilate. He said quietly, "Are you okay?"

Mindy nodded affirmatively, and Conrad saw a slight smile on her face.

"Is this fun for you?" he whispered.

"It's what we trained for," she replied in his head.

Conrad couldn't quite get over the fact that although Mindy's speech voice had an odd quality due to her hearing loss, her thoughts were crystal clear, without accent.

Von Goren completed his overview by returning his gaze to Tiana, who the entire time kept her eyes on him.

"Very well," he said. "Remember, I am not responsible for this. This is your doing."

"You are wrong, Baron," Tiana said. "I do and will hold you responsible for whatever is the outcome."

Baron von Goren swallowed hard, and he tried to camouflage it by turning his head to the left. He turned completely around and exited the room through the same door from which he came. The door closed behind him with a shudder.

As the baron left the chamber, the soldiers watched him go and then turned their attention to Colonel Guerrero. They were awaiting orders. The colonel thought for a few moments before issuing the attack order, as he was an honorable man of warfare, and the seemingly senseless slaughter of innocent children was distasteful to him.

However, being a career soldier, he knew duty was before honor, and therefore, he had no choice but to follow the command of his supreme commander, Baron von Goren. Colonel Guerrero had committed a fatal error, however, because in his brief time of contemplation, the opposition forces rallied.

"Havoc!" Tiana yelled, and the sentinels went into action.

Meinhard metamorphosed into a giant King Kong–esque gorilla. He stood nearly twenty feet tall, and he immediately began pounding his chest with both of his fists. Several of the colonel's troops took aim at Meinhard, but before they could fire any shots, Harlow, who had transformed into a large bird of prey, swooped down, grabbing the guns in her large talons.

Meanwhile, Atara, now a dragon with iridescent scales, large teeth, golden eyes with vertical pupils, and razor-sharp claws on all four feet, let out a tremendous roar that shook the chamber to its foundation. She took a position in front of the gallery, thus protecting the student warriors from an assault by the troops, and with several energy blasts exploding near her and some deflected off of her scales, she opened her mouth wide, brandishing her teeth, and let loose a counter attack on the troops—with fire.

The flame shot from Atara's maw, running along the floorboards, radiating toward the attacking troops. Try as they might to avoid it, several were consumed before they could react. The others avoided the conflagration by pushing the board table on its side and hiding behind it. This tactic, however, only postponed their inevitable fate.

Rather than allow her inflammable sputum to ignite the entire chamber, thus killing everyone therein, Atara inhaled the remaining fire. When the flames dissipated, Tiana and Donovan drew their scepters, activating them fluidly. Two of the troops hiding behind the board table let fly several energy bolts. Tiana deflected one with her scepter, sending it careening into the wall above the overturned table. The second landed harmlessly on the floor.

"Warriors," Tiana said to the students. "It is time."

Matthew and Matilda withdrew and energized their scepters first.

"Meinhard," Matilda said. "Be my second?"

Meinhard pounded his chest with both palms and let out a substantial roar. Matilda ran toward him to fight at his side. An energy bolt flew past her, but she was able to anticipate its flight. She dropped to the floor, rolled, and it missed her, exploding in the opposite wall. Meinhard located the soldier who had attempted to shoot his charge, and leaping toward the man violently, he landed, extinguishing the threat.

Matthew stood beside Atara. She dropped her head close to his face, her giant golden eye looking directly into Matthew's.

"I know," Matthew said. "We all appreciate it. Let's finish this."

Moments later, it was finished. The room filled with a smoky haze, Matthew, Matilda, and Mindy, together with Meinhard the ape, Harlow the eagle and Atara the dragon, stood back to back to back surveying the situation. Then they began the distasteful task of counting the remains. From their preliminary count, it appeared several soldiers had managed to escape immolation somehow, and the body of Colonel Guerrero was also unaccounted for.

The battle had been won, but there was a palpable sadness in the air. Victory was never simple to accept when lives were lost on either side; however, there was also acceptance that all other options were taken from them by the baron.

Certain the threat had passed, Meinhard, Harlow and Atara returned to human form. They approached Tiana, who was also looking over the results of the assault.

"We are not out of this yet," Atara said. "How will we get everyone out of the palace?"

"I am working on that," Tiana said.

She removed her token from her belt, punching buttons on its faceplate as she did. She examined the device, turning it over in her hands. She tapped the back of it, then held and released a button along its top edge, rebooting it. She manipulated the screen icons with several repeating patterns. After several attempts, Tiana shook her head with incredulity.

"Something, or someone, is preventing a leap once again. Does anyone have any idea how we can leave the palace?"

"I say we just go back out the way we came in," Alex said.

"That is an option, but I suspect that way will be flooded with forces loyal to the baron."

"So what? We beat them once. We can do it again."

"Alex, every battle brings a risk of loss or defeat. I do not wish to risk the safety or lives of anyone here if there is another way."

Atticus, standing at the back of the group, slowly raised his hand.

"Atticus," Tiana said. "You have an idea?"

"Why don't we leave from the roof of the building?"

"Really?" Matthew said. "I suppose we'll all just jump over the side."

Atticus, staring down at the floor, drew slow circles with his right foot. "Atara and Harlow can fly us all down to safety," Atticus replied without making eye contact with anyone in the group.

Tiana smiled broadly. "Well done, Atticus. That is what we shall do."

Tiana led them to the roof. As she opened the main door to the board chamber, she withdrew her scepter once again. She did not activate it immediately, however. She simply wanted it at the ready in the event that a stray soldier, or a squadron, was awaiting them outside. None were. One by one, they exited into the hallway, following Tiana's lead.

Conrad, who by this time was thoroughly confused and slightly disoriented, pushed through the group to get to Tiana at the front. As he moved past Alex, he heard him say, "How do we get to the roof?"

Tiana shot her right hand into the air, indicating an all-stop. Everyone followed her symbolic instruction, and they all moved instinctively against the wall. Tiana used her token's locater function to give her a layout of the palace's passage diagram.

Conrad took the opportunity to rush to the front to be nearer to Tiana. He arrived by her side just as the passageway map fully manifested on the screen. Tiana indicated the stairwell to the roof was less than fifty yards ahead, but she told everyone to be cautious just the same. On her mark, the group returned to their endeavor.

When they reached the stairwell door, Tiana swung it wide, holding her deactivated scepter in front of her. Fortunately, there were no troops waiting to spring a trap. Tiana made her way up the stairs toward the roof, all the while holding her scepter ahead of her in case its use was necessitated. The others followed behind like the cars behind a locomotive.

When they reached the top of the stairway, there was a large wooden door laminated with a shiny, metallic substance. There was no door handle with which to open it. Instead, to the right of the door was small round recess covered with metal meshwork. Tiana examined it, and having determined it to be a sonic receiver, she once again enlisted the help of her token.

Tapping several factors using screen icons, she held it near the receiver. Multiple tones emanated from the token as it made the necessary calculations. Moments later, the sound of a mechanism unlocking erupted from the door, and it disengaged from its locked position. Tiana pushed the door open, and bright sunlight flooded into the stairwell.

Always careful, Tiana was first to exit, checking all the flank positions, including behind the now open stairwell door, for danger. As inconceivable as it was, there was no one waiting for them on the roof. However, Tiana knew that caution was not to be foolishly cast to the wind, and until she had delivered them all to safety, she would remain so.

As they all streamed out into the daylight, Tiana place her hand on Conrad's back.

"I know you are confused," she said. "Once you are safe, I have some things to share."

She smiled at him, and Conrad noticed her eyes were again robin's egg blue.

Atara and Harlow morphed into their animal counterparts. Mathew, Matilda, Atticus, and Mindy climbed aboard Atara's back. When Mindy secured her position, she waived to Conrad, indicating she wanted him to sit with her. Conrad looked up at Tiana. It was clear he wanted to fly to safety with Tiana by his side, yet something inside him told him to be with Mindy.

"What should I do?" he thought to Tiana.

"Trust your instincts."

Conrad joined the other student warriors, and once he was seated, Atara let out a roar and leaped off the palace roof. She dropped several stories before flapping her giant wings to gain altitude. Conrad looked back at the palace to make sure the others were following. He saw the sentinels climb onto Harlow's feathered back. She flapped her wings gently, moving a few feet off the roof, and then she gently grabbed Alex and Nash with her talons before launching off the building.

Atara and Harlow flew their passengers over Ammerand City toward the Klisto mountain range. As they flew, Conrad looked out and down, taking in all the terrain. In the city, there were many people looking up at them, pointing. Some even ran for shelter and safety thinking the great bird and dragon were some evil harbingers of doom.

Outside the city, and just before they reached the mountains, there were several open ranges of land. There were trees, running streams, fields of grass, and a few small dwellings scattered here and there. Conrad saw some farmers working the fields look up at the two gargantuan flying beasts. They reacted, not with fear or dread, but with genuine interest and curiosity. They seemed to be more focused on their work than on a haphazard dragon and giant eagle sighting.

Conrad looked over at Mindy, who was seated next to him. She had a big smile on her face and, with her eyes closed, was enjoying the sun shining on her cheeks. She let out a small giggle.

"What?" Conrad asked.

Mindy, opening her eyes said, "Nothing, I'm just happy."

"Happy? We were almost killed!"

"Almost, but not quite. Isn't this nice, though?"

Mindy grabbed Conrad's hand in hers and gave it a big squeeze. Fighting the urge, but unable to in the end, Conrad smiled back. He had always liked and appreciated Mindy's attitude. She never really seemed to be bothered by much of anything. And yet she had had many challenges in her life. Conrad was glad Mindy was part of his life.

Soaring over the mountain peaks, Atara and Harlow located the city on the other side—Valposta. It lay before them beautifully. Valposta was a different kind of town from Ammerand. There was no large edifice like Ammerand Palace giving focus to the place. Instead, the city was laid out in concentric circles. In the center circle were several buildings in a row. Outside that was the business district. Farther out were dwelling places for the residents. Finally, completely outside the concentricity was open farmland.

The two leviathans dove out of the sky toward an open meadow on the outskirts of Valposta. As they approached the landing area, Harlow dropped Alex and Nash in a large patch of overgrown alfalfa. They both landed with a subtle thump. Alex murmured something about thanking Harlow for nothing. Nash stood up and dusted himself off.

Atara and Harlow landed concurrently, and their passengers offloaded themselves. Once all were again on solid ground, they returned to their human forms. The sentinels converged to discuss their strategy while the students looked on, wondering about the plan. Some of them were more on edge than others.

Matthew whispered something into Matilda's ear causing her to say, "Stop it, Matt. I hate it when you're a negative thinker."

"What did he say?" Conrad asked.

"Nothing. He's just being a dimwit."

"You know," Mindy began, "we're all in this together, and I don't think we should have any secrets from one another."

Matilda stared at Mindy, at first with slight contempt, but ultimately in understanding and agreement. They were in this, whatever it was, together, and they would need to support and rely on one another.

"He just said he didn't want to die waiting for the sentinels to decide what to do."

Conrad and Mindy looked at Matthew, who had a ridiculous smirk on his face.

"What?" he said.

Conrad and Mindy just shook their heads.

After a while, the sentinels turned toward their charges and approached them. Each sentinel took position beside or in front of his or her respective student warrior. Tiana stood before them preparing to announce something.

"Warriors," she said. "First, we want to tell you all how very proud we are with your first real-time battle performances. Bravo."

The sentinels hugged and shook the hands of their respective students. Conrad looked around at everyone else, and he realized he was too far away from Tiana to have any meaningful interaction with her at that moment. Sensing this, Tiana walked to him and gave Conrad a great big hug. She then held his face in her hands and looked into his eyes. Upon releasing his face and patting him affectionately on the back, she returned to her place at the front of the group and continued.

"We know the battle was stressful, but you should be proud of your accomplishments." Tiana's face grew more severe.

"However, that battle is in the past, and we have a far greater one ahead."

She looked over the students to gauge their reactions before continuing. Then she looked over her left shoulder. In the near distance, there was a small cottage with a thatched roof, smoke billowing from its chimney.

"Let us all go there for some comfort, rest, and sustenance. Later, we will discuss the plan of attack for the next confrontation." Tiana led the way toward the cottage, with everyone else following behind.

The cottage was small but had a comfortable interior: four walls and a roof with a kitchen along the back wall, minimal furnishings, and lots of space. There were several rolled mattresses stored in a utility closet to the right of the kitchen, along with other items suitable for construction of a makeshift bed. The students assembled sleep areas using the available materials.

After a brief discussion about the day's adventures, each student changed into sleep attire and bedded down for the night. The sentinels lay next to their student wards and prepared for a few hours of sleep as well. However, as a sentinel, each was always prepared to protect his or her charge if needed.

Conrad lay in his bed with both hands behind his head. A smile grew on his face as he thought about the day.

"A penny for your thoughts?" Tiana asked from his side.

"I was just thinking about today. Even though we could have been killed, I've never felt so alive."

Tiana smiled. "Yes, it can be exhilarating to come close to death, but life is precious, as are you. Get some rest because I believe we may have more trials ahead."

Conrad sat up slightly and looked at her. He could see the light emerald glow of her eyes.

"Do you think the baron will follow us?"

"I am certain he will. Rest now, young one, and practice your warrior arts in your mind."

Conrad rolled over. He rubbed his closed eyelids lightly, scratched his nose, and yawned. Before he could think another complete thought, he was fast asleep.

Chapter Thirty-Five

As morning broke, Conrad was awoken by Tiana. She was kneeling beside his slapdash bed constructed of rough-hewn muslin covered in an Egyptian cotton sheet. His pillow was a small bale of newly harvested rough cotton, and his blanket was the tanned skin of some bearlike creature, dark brown and thick. He thought he had never felt so warm a blanket in his life.

Tiana held a small lamp in her hand. It contained a small floating luminescent ball the size of a large marble. With every motion of the lamp itself, the glowing marble moved with the inertia, then regained its place in the center.

Only a dim twilight was entering through the windows of the cottage. Someone had built a roaring fire in the large fireplace on the far wall. As Tiana knelt beside Conrad, her eyes were green and did not glow with their own light. She was smiling and asked if he had a good night's sleep. Conrad said he had, but that he also had some very strange dreams.

"Tell them to me," Tiana said.

He thought for several minutes because dreams have an uncanny ability to fade from memory the more intently we attempt to recall them.

"I wish I had written them down sooner, but here is what I can remember. I was running through the woods on a very narrow path, breathing very hard. So hard, in fact, that I could feel my lungs straining for breath, even in my dream." He ran his hand across his chest to ensure that he had no actual wounds there.

"Continue," Tiana said.

"I came to a clearing in the woods where there were several paths. I stopped there because I heard a voice calling to me. It was a man's voice."

"What did the voice say?"

"It was faint and not very clear, but I think it said, 'Come to me, Conrad. Come to me.'"

"What happened next?"

"That's all I remember because then I woke up. What do you suppose it means?"

Tiana considered it several different ways. She asked him if he could recall how many different paths diverged from the clearing.

Conrad thought about it for a while before saying, "twelve."

Tiana nodded and stood up.

"What do you think?" Conrad said.

"I think it is time for breakfast." She walked over to the kitchen area where there were two plates with eggs, bacon, fried potatoes, and a thick slice of obviously homemade bread with lots of butter melting over its top. Conrad sat up on his makeshift bedding and finally smelled the freshly cooked breakfast foods. The smell made his mouth water because he also couldn't remember the last time he had been so hungry. *Perhaps running in a dream increases the appetite*, he thought.

He stood from his bed and walked over to where Tiana was doling out silverware for them. He scanned the cottage and realized there was no one else inside but Tiana and him.

"Where's everybody else?"

"They are all done eating. You will join them shortly."

Conrad happened to glance out the large front window, and he saw everyone else standing in the field in front of the cottage. They were practicing battle processions and working on their fighting skills. Conrad almost lost his appetite because he thought he was intentionally left asleep due to his less-than-adequate performance at Ammerand Palace. When he looked back at Tiana, she was scowling at him.

"You must stop the self-pity. It is unbecoming of a Trinity. Eat a hearty breakfast and then join your classmates."

Conrad pulled up a chair next to Tiana, salted and peppered his eggs, and devoured the entire plateful of food within minutes. He washed down the delicious meal with a large glass of ice-cold fresh-squeezed orange juice, slapped the empty glass onto the tabletop, let out a large belch, and said, "Where are my clothes?"

Once he had changed into his warrior arts uniform, Conrad noticed something different. Upon his belt was appliquéd a single bright-red chevron on both sides of each end. He held an end in each hand, holding them up slightly, and looked at Tiana, questioningly. Tiana, who was putting away the breakfast dishes and utensils, stopped.

She returned Conrad's look and said, "You earned that stripe. And so you shall earn many more in time." Tiana wiped the moisture from her hands with a white-and-blue dish towel and walked over to Conrad. She held each of his shoulders with her hands, strong hands with long, well-manicured fingers, and said, "You will rise to the occasion. Fear not, young one, for in your veins runs a powerful force. You know this to be true, yet I see some doubt remains."

Tiana then knelt lower so her eyes were at the same level as Conrad's.

"As steel is tempered through fire and quenching, so too will your spirit. Go with your classmates, and remember, I will always be with you."

Tiana rose. He watched her, trying to see any sign that she would release him from this next course of action. An extreme sense of fear overwhelmed Conrad, and it sickened him. He swallowed hard, managed a sideways smile, and ran out the front door to greet his classmates.

Chapter Thirty-Six

The warrior arts students were scattered over the long expanse of the field working through maneuvers. Conrad was familiar with some of the moves, but others were foreign and new.

As he approached, he saw Atticus standing alone mid-field, facing the rising sun with his eyes closed. Harlow was situated opposite Atticus's position by over one hundred yards. Harlow ran toward Atticus, jumped into the air, and instantly morphed into her eagle alter ego. With a loud war screech, Harlow the eagle rose higher into the sky, and reaching the apogee, reversed her trajectory, flying at terminal velocity directly at Atticus.

Atticus, however, seemed unaware of Harlow's attack. He stood resolute in the same position, with eyes closed, during much of her rapid descent. Conrad was about to shout out a warning to Atticus when suddenly Atticus withdrew his scepter, activated it, and parried Harlow's attack, all while dropping to the ground and rolling several feet out of her attack zone. When he regained his footing, he held his fully activated scepter in front of him, standing in a forty-five-degree ground-rex stance, ready for any follow-up attack.

Harlow flew back into the sky several hundred feet, reversed again, screamed a shrill "wee-aaaaaa" from her syrinx, and dove again at Atticus. He spun his scepter in his hand like a song leader's baton and reversed his stance so that his empty left hand was now forward, throwing his open palm in the diving Harlow's direction.

An orange beam of light shot at Harlow. She flipped her left wing up just in time to avoid an impact and continued her attack vector, now spinning toward Atticus. He deactivated his scepter, returned it to his belt, and created a Q-energy ball. Harlow was now less than three seconds away from grabbing him; however, Atticus held his Q-energy until she was at the point of no return and then let it fly at her.

The ball knocked Harlow in a ballistic arc, landing her seventy-five yards away. As she hit the ground, she immediately reverted into her human form. Stunned, she rose from the ground after several moments, smiled at Atticus, and held her right arm over her head with thumb extended toward the sky. The rest of the warrior arts students applauded loudly.

"Way to go, Atticus!" Mindy said.

"Yes, wonderfully skillful," Matilda added.

Matthew began chanting Atticus's name, and soon all the others joined in the revelry.

"Atticus, Atticus, Atticus," they sang, and there was a renewed sense of well-being shared amongst them.

Atticus was smiling broadly and would glance at his classmates briefly then avert his gaze. He began clapping for himself and said, "I did good."

Harlow, who had rejoined the group after her thunderous landing, gave him a big pat on the back. She then grasped each of his hands in hers and, turning them over to view his palms, inspected their surfaces. Not seeing anything of concern, she dropped them and said, "Very nicely executed, Attie. But I warn you, next time will be different." She smiled and pinched his chubby cheek before walking over to Atara.

The students and sentinels spent the entire remainder of the day drilling, practicing, focusing, and planning, for they knew the battle to come would be epic and dangerous. Tiana and Meinhard ran through several manifestation incantations as the warrior arts students looked on.

"Remember," Tiana said, "the size of your desire is of little importance. It is the size of your will and your belief that will lead to victory."

She looked out over the class to see if she could spot the student with the least of either. After considering several others, it was clear to her that Conrad needed the most reinforcement.

"Conrad," she said, "please come forward."

Conrad, slightly surprised to be called on, irresolutely stepped up toward Tiana.

With her head held high and still looking at the rest of his classmates, Tiana said, "Is there something, some object, which you desire more than anything else?"

Conrad thought about the question. If she had simply asked what he wanted, he would have said that he wanted to go home, back to Overworld. He would have said that he did not want to risk his life for someone he barely knew, even taking into account that the man was his father. But Tiana was not to be trifled with, and she was very specific with her question: What object did he want? He continued to think about the ramifications of his answer. He considered that the question itself might be another in a long series of tests, and the answer given could forever brand him a coward, an egotist, or worse, a nincompoop.

Conrad lost all sense of time for a moment. He realized it when he finally looked up to see Tiana glaring at him, then heard snickering coming from Matthew and Matilda. He could feel his face flush with embarrassment and tried to regain a semblance of respect by standing up straight, looking over at Matthew and Matilda, and shouting, "Shut up, moron twins!"

Matthew and Matilda immediately stopped their revelry and, with somber faces, looked down, checking their sneakers for discoloration.

"I want a milk shake," Conrad said.

"Very nice," Tiana replied. "Now, manifest it."

Conrad looked at Tiana incredulously. *"How am I supposed to do that?"* he asked telepathically.

"Picture what you want in your mind and will it to be."

Conrad closed his eyes and pictured an ice-cold chocolate milk shake just like the ones he'd ordered back in California on the rare occasions when he was treated to one at In-N-Out Burger.

As he continued thinking, he began to actually smell the chocolate in the air around him. He instinctively held his hand out in front of him, pantomiming holding a paper shake cup. Moments later, he actually felt his outstretched hand getting colder, and finally, he felt something solid in his hand.

When he opened his eyes, he was holding a condensation-covered white paper cup with swaying red palm trees printed on the side and a white plastic straw protruding from the top. Conrad placed the straw to his lips and applied the extra amount of suction required to taste the deliciously thick ice cream shake, and as it reached his tongue, a great big smile spread across his face.

"It's an In-N-Out shake, all right," he said. "Anyone want a taste?"

All of the warrior arts students huddled around him, each dipping a finger into the cold, brown concoction within the cup. They all agreed it was perhaps the best chocolate shake they had ever tasted.

As the sun began to set, the warrior arts students were ending a long day of practice and drills. They ended the session with an exit kata, their hands flying in a synchronized circular motion, feet gliding forward, back, and sideways with varied strikes, blocks, and foot techniques interspersed, ending with a fist salute rolling back to attention. When the exit display had been completed, the sentinels gave the students a hardy round of applause, and they all congregated to discuss the day.

Conrad stared up toward the horizon. There, the setting sun appeared large and orange. He liked the way the atmosphere made the sun appear to shimmy as it disappeared beyond the edge of the world. It made him think of *Star Wars*, the twin suns of Tatooine setting with young Skywalker looking on.

Conrad squinted for better focus. He thought his eyes were playing tricks on him. He rubbed them briefly with his fingers and then looked again. It was there. There was a small black shadow of something silhouetted by the setting sun. As he watched, it grew progressively larger. It was something alive, and moving toward them.

"Tiana!" he shouted.

Tiana looked at Conrad, who was now pointing toward the apparition on the horizon. She turned her head in the direction indicated, and she saw the same thing. There was something, or someone, coming toward them.

"Sentinels!" Tiana said.

The sentinels came to attention, their gazes transfixed on the horizon. Alex and Nash followed suit, but Alex showed more emotion.

"I told you we needed more weapons," he shouted. "We're sitting ducks out here, in the middle of a field, with only a wooden cottage for shelter."

"We do not even know if this is a threat yet," Tiana said.

"What else could it be?"

"It is one being against a dozen. Do those odds threaten you, Alex?" Tiana had an incredulous smirk on her face.

Alex was flustered at first, but eventually, he had to smile as well. "Okay, Chief. What do you suggest we do, then?"

"Let us observe, but also let us prepare."

Tiana told the sentinels to create a perimeter as a precaution. If this being wanted a fight, he, she, or it would get one. She also told the students to keep close to her and to visualize what action they would take if an attack came to them.

As the apparition moved closer, its outline became clearer and more defined. There were two different creatures approaching. The main one looked like a rhinoceros with two heads, and the heads were held far above the body on long necks. At the top of each neck was the head of a snake, their forked tongues flicking in and out. The heads moved rhythmically as the beast progressed, scanning the landscape as if searching for something. On its back rode a man, and it became more distinct the nearer they approached that the man had his right hand raised in greeting.

When the beast was within visual identification range, Tiana said, "It is Went," and she smiled to the others, indicating the high tension of readiness could be released.

Conrad thought, *"Went...Went...How do I know that name?"*

"He is your father's best friend," Tiana responded telepathically. *"You met him briefly on Overworld."*

Chapter Thirty-Seven

Gunter Went was a student at the original Incept Training Academy. His roommate for all five years was Nathaniel Turner. When Gunter and Nathaniel first met, no one could have expected that they would ultimately become the best of friends, because Gunter hated Nathaniel. For many years at the academy, the old legends about the coming of the new Trinity of Souls were passed from class to class like some rite of passage.

Each class would try to identify if one of their members was indeed part of the new trinity. Some had even announced, publicly, that they were. But in the four hundred years that passed, every person who was identified as part of the Trinity of Souls was ultimately denounced—that is, until Nathaniel Turner arrived.

It was clear from the beginning that Nathaniel was different from the other underclassmen. Although the academy granted entrance only to young men and women who could perform astonishing feats, Nathaniel proved he was in a different category from the start.

Since his infancy and throughout his life, stories were told of miraculous things occurring around him. It was legend that Nathaniel's mother nearly died in childbirth because she began bleeding, and the bleeding would not stop. Several doctors attempted to control the blood flow, to no avail.

After several transfusions, administration of clotting factors, and other procedures, the chief obstetrician told the nurses to bring the newborn Nathaniel to his mother for her to say good-bye. The infant was placed in Georgina Turner's arms, and as she stroked the baby's head, kissed his face, and said she would miss watching him grow, the young Nathaniel reached out and touched his mother's lips. Immediately, Georgina's wounds healed, her blood loss ceased, and she rapidly regained her strength. All the medical professionals present were at a loss to explain what had happened. The final official explanation was that the clotting factors had some kind of delayed efficacy, and it was the compound interactions that saved Georgina Turner's life.

Others were not as convinced. When Nathaniel was a toddler, he had rolled out into traffic on his tricycle. A man using a personal communication device while driving his vehicle had failed to see him in time. Several people screamed in warning seconds before the impact, but all closed their eyes to avoid seeing the imminent collision and resulting carnage. The screech of skidding tires on the roadway was all the temporarily vision-impaired masses heard or felt.

When they all reopened their eyes, the car was stopped askew in the middle of the roadway, and young Nathaniel Turner was sitting on his bike on the opposite side of the street, none the worse for wear. No one having actually observed what had happened, everyone assumed Nathaniel had seen the car in time and had pedaled his heart out to avoid being run over.

By the time Nathaniel arrived at the academy, too many other unexplained phenomena had occurred. When he submitted his application, there was already talk in the registrar's office that one of the Trinity of Souls would be attending the very next semester. And Gunter Went was determined to prove that Nathaniel was no more a trinity than was he.

Gunter set about a program to undermine everything Nathaniel tried to accomplish: hiding Nathaniel's homework, destroying his research notes just days before a research paper was due, short-circuiting the battery in Nathaniel's laptop and causing massive data corruption, and stealing several items from a chemistry lab and blaming Nathaniel for the crime.

In each instance, not only had Nathaniel managed to submit his completed homework timely, receive an A+ on the research paper, reconstitute his entire database file on a new laptop, and turn over the stolen property to the chemistry department chair, but Nathaniel in no way lost his composure at any time. In fact, when Gunter admitted to all his transgressions, hoping to incite an emotional response from Nathaniel, he received no satisfaction. Nathaniel simply said, "I know, my friend, and it is all right."

Thereafter, Gunter and Nathaniel were as close as friends could be—closer than brothers, even. They went everywhere together, took all the same classes, and even dated young ladies together. Not the same girls at the same time, but they did double-date quite often—that is, until Nathaniel met one Veronica Harper.

He first saw her after graduation. Gunter and he had decided to spend the summer on the beaches of Southern California; they roamed from Rat Beach in Torrance up the coast to the far north end of Manhattan Beach. All they had with them were two Tommy Bahama backpack beach chairs they had acquired at Costco. Between them, they had less than five hundred dollars cash, but when Gunter expressed his concern that their funds would run out way before the summer would, Nathaniel advised him to have faith.

One fine summer day, the two young men were sitting on their chairs watching several games of beach volleyball being played nearby. Most of the games were played by young men, several were coed, but the game that drew Nathaniel's attention was one comprised entirely of several lean, tall, beautiful young ladies. There were eight of them all told, but one in particular caught Nathaniel's attention immediately.

She was tall, easily over six feet, but from Nathaniel's vantage point, he could not be positive. Her long blonde hair was pulled back in one straight ponytail, and unlike the other girls, she was wearing a fashionable one-piece bathing suit. But her physicality and poise were not what caught the attention of Nathaniel.

While watching her, he could not help but notice that she smiled absolutely. Never was there a moment when her gleaming white teeth were invisible. Even during a difficult volley where one of her teammates allowed an unearned point, she continued to smile, and she even encouraged her dejected teammate.

Her name was Veronica Harper.

She was enjoying her summer away from college with several Chi Omega sorority sisters whom she met while pledging at UCLA. Veronica felt most at home at the beach because, during her parent's bitter divorce, her grandparents took her every summer to stay at their beach house in Southern California.

When their game had concluded, Nathaniel got up and went to speak with Veronica. During his trip across the hot summer sand, her friend, Daphne, commented on the hotness of the young man approaching. The two young women watched closely as he walked purposefully across the steaming pulverized quartz.

"He's staring at me," Daphne said.

Veronica was not convinced, but decided to let sleeping dogs lie.

When Nathaniel arrived, Daphne gently placed herself in front of Veronica and said, "Can we help you?"

Nathaniel did not respond. He simply looked at Veronica, a slight smile upon his face. Daphne was nonplussed.

"We saw you and your friend over there. Care to play a game?" she asked.

Nathaniel did not respond, but continued his examination of Veronica's face. After several minutes, he extended his right hand to Veronica and said, "Would you like to go for a walk?"

Without thinking, she accepted his hand in hers, and the two walked together toward the low tide line.

From then on, Gunter and Nathaniel's paths began to diverge. It seemed to Gunter that Nathaniel was nowhere to be found. Every morning, as he prepared for his beach bum day, Nathaniel was writing in his journal. When Gunter would ask if Nathaniel planned to hang out, Nathaniel inevitably turned Gunter down with a courteous refusal.

At that summer's end, Nathaniel announced he planned to marry the tall blonde vollyballer.

"You don't even know her," Gunter objected.

"I know all that I need to know. She is the vessel."

"What? Vessel? She's a ship? What's wrong with you?"

Nathaniel gave Gunter a big hug. "You will always be my best friend, but there are forces at work here far beyond what you can fathom, my friend."

Nathaniel packed his scarce belongings, said good-bye to his friend, and did not see Gunter again until after Conrad was born.

Chapter Thirty-Eight

As Gunter Went dismounted his beast, he walked over to the where the sentinels and the warrior arts students were congregated. He extended his hand to Tiana, who shook it vigorously.

"This is an unexpected pleasure, Gunter," Tiana said. "To what do we owe this visit?"

"I'm afraid it's not all pleasure, Tiana. I came to warn you."

Gunter explained that Baron von Goren was furious with his defeat at Ammerand Palace. So angry was he that he had summarily executed Colonel Guerrero for his incompetence. This was the modus operandi of all despots: Rule of law was replaced by fear and intimidation. Even now, the baron was amassing his forces on the Valposta frontier. He most likely would not enter the prefecture without permission for risk of violating the Treaty of Begin, now in effect for nearly seven centuries.

"He will find a way to exact his revenge, you know," Gunter said.

"Yes, I am well aware of the baron's treachery," Tiana replied. "We will not remain a target."

Tiana called the sentinels and the students together for a conference. They gathered near the cottage and arranged several tables and benches for the meeting. Conrad wanted to sit beside Mindy, but Matthew dropped in the open place just moments before he could. Conrad paused for a few seconds, looking at Matthew with an air of incredulity. Finally, he cleared his throat in order to draw Matthew's attention to his faux pas. Matthew, being Matthew, ignored Conrad's less-than-subtle attempt to get his attention.

"Matthew, do you mind if I sit next to Mindy?"

"Why don't you sit over there?" Matthew said, pointing to an open place on the opposite side of the table.

Conrad thought about confronting Matthew, but heard, *"Sit beside me,"* in his head. He looked up, and Tiana was staring at him. Her eyes the same light blue he had seen many times before. He walked over to the opposite side and sat down. Mindy watched him, and she elbowed Matthew in the ribs once Conrad sat down.

Tiana stood at one head of the table; beside her stood Gunter Went. She watched the warrior arts students as they continued to fidget, waiting for something, anything, to happen. When she believed they were ready, she began.

"Students, for those of you who do not know, this gentleman standing beside me is Gunter Went. Gunter has long been a friend to the Brotherhood of Incepts, and although no longer one himself, you should respect him and listen to him, for he was once the right-hand man to Nathaniel Turner, Trinity number one. Gunter." Tiana returned to her seat next to Conrad, giving Gunter Went the floor to address the group.

He watched her sit down, swallowed hard, rubbed his right wrist and said, "I am honored to be in your presence. Truly, I am. Although many of you do not know me, I am positive we will all become great friends."

Gunter described what he knew. Baron von Goren, enraged and humiliated at his trouncing by the students and their sentinel partners, immediately executed all the surviving officers. Gunter had heard the baron state that an officer who loses a battle should take his or her own life as penance for the lack of success. He then elevated the captains to colonels, or in some instances, to general. He then started planning his retribution.

"He has amassed an army of five thousand, and he is waiting on the Valposta frontier."

"What is he waiting for?" Matthew blurted. Realizing his faux pas a millisecond too late, he pursed his lips tightly together.

"I suspect he has asked the regional governor for permission to take his standing army across the border. Whether he receives such permission or not is anyone's guess."

Tiana arose from the table, and turning toward the Klisto Mountains, she watched. Conrad looked up from the table to regard her motions. He saw her eyes were emerald green, as they generally were when she was accessing her Q-energy field. They grew in intensity, finally glowing brilliantly.

"The governor has not relinquished control—yet," Tiana said, momentarily closing her eyes. "He is awaiting a payment of tribute from von Goren." She then turned to face the group, her eyes still gleaming. "We have time to strike the baron preemptively." She looked at Gunter. "Can you provide mounts for my warriors?"

"Yes. I was hoping you would ask," Gunter said.

He took a small device about the size of a smartphone from his pocket. After activating the device, he transmitted several muffled clicks and tones that were inaudible to the human ear. When he was done, he returned the device to his pocket and waited.

Within fifteen seconds, there was a cacophony arising from the horizon, the same direction from which they had watched

Gunter Went emerge from the woodlands. The sound grew in intensity. Everyone rose from their seats and looked in the direction of the noises. The trees danced quickly from side to side as something large moved rapidly forward toward the clearing.

Several multicolored tyrannosaurs emerged and ran toward them at tremendous speed—or at least they appeared that way. Five gigantic carnivores approached the group, running probably forty to fifty miles per hour. The behemoths continued, their rows of razor-sharp teeth gnashing and guttural roars sounding like a symphony of death and destruction.

Conrad's heart was pounding in his chest as he watched these ancient predators advancing on them. He wasn't sure if they were doomed or what. No one seemed to be concerned that these five beasts could kill and eat them, all in a matter of seconds. However, he saw Alex place his hand atop his trusty disrupter pistol, and he felt better. Most assuredly, he was not alone in his concern.

As the five dinosaurs approached, they slowed their progress uniformly. As if guided by some form of group communication, the dinosaurs pulled back from their charging stance and, with heads now held high, continued at a trot. Conrad couldn't help noticing that, as the tyrannosaurs, moved they scanned the landscape with their heads and eyes.

Could they be looking for danger around them? If so, they had to have intelligence of some type, no?

They arrived within seconds and stopped on a dime, reared up, and announced their arrival with a roar and flourish. Then they each turned their attention to Gunter, seemingly to wait for a command.

"Will these do?" Gunter asked.

Tiana smiled broadly. "Not exactly what I had in mind, but the effect they will have upon the baron's troops will be much desired."

Chapter Thirty-Nine

Baron von Goren's army was stationed on the outer edge of the frontier. He had mustered the troops with promises of vast land grants on the other side, provided they succeeded in their duty. When asked about the Valposta governor and the independence of the people, von Goren simply lied, as was his pattern, and he told them the interlopers who had barely escaped alive from Ammerand Palace, had claimed the land east of the frontier as their own. Therefore, Valposta was in a state of civil war, and his men had an opportunity to not only vanquish the alien invaders but also to help bring order back to Valposta.

Von Goren felt a sharp pain in the back of his head. He closed his eyes and winced, trying to sooth the ache. Using small circular motions, he rubbed his temples with his fingers.

He stopped suddenly when he heard in his mind, *"Do not fail me again, Baron."*

Von Goren's eyes opened as he scanned his makeshift headquarters searching for the source of the voice. He ran outside when he saw no one else was there.

Outside the portable command center building, troops were milling around making ready for war. A private looked up as the baron exited, and he made the unfortunate mistake of making eye contact with von Goren.

"You, soldier, come here."

The private ran to the baron and stomped his feet together, came to attention, and saluted the commander in chief. Von Goren returned the salute and the private remained at attention.

"Yes, sir?"

"Where you just outside this door a few moments ago?"

The private was perplexed. "Pardon me, sir, I'm not sure what you mean."

Von Goren moved his face to within inches of the soldier's. "I am asking you if you were outside my door. It is a simple question."

"Yes, sir, I guess I was."

"Did you say anything?"

"Excuse me, sir?"

"DID YOU SAY ANYTHING?" von Goren yelled.

"N...n...no, sir. I was walking by. That's all."

The Baron withdrew from the soldier, and as he did, he forced a devious smile upon his face. He had realized that his outburst had taken the other soldiers by surprise, and he didn't want his paranoia to upset them.

"Very well, then," von Goren said to the subject of his interrogation. "As you were." The two exchanged salutes again, and von Goren returned inside.

Von Goren closed the door behind him and leaned back onto it, somewhat relieved. Then he heard the voice again.

"You know who it is."

Von Goren sprung away from the door, into the center of the room.

"What do you want from me, Your Excellency?"

"Do not fail us again. The son of Nathaniel Turner must not return to Overworld."

The baron swallowed hard.

"He is well protected, Your Excellency. We will prevail in the next battle, but I cannot be held responsible if he somehow escapes." The pain returned to von Goren's brain, and he winced in agony.

"We hold you responsible no matter what. Do not fail us."

The pain subsided, and the baron composed himself. He walked to his desk and sat down in the hover chair positioned behind it. Waving his hands over the desktop, he activated the command system. Several virtual displays projected themselves above the desktop. Each display provided the baron with real-time reconnaissance of the vicinity around the command headquarters. He scanned the screens, searching for something or someone. After several minutes, he found his field marshal, Colonel Immanuel Gastineau.

"Colonel Gastineau, come to the command center," von Goren said.

On the screen, von Goren saw the colonel look up, salute, and begin walking in the direction of the command headquarters. When he arrived at the command center, Colonel Gastineau walked in the door, saluted Baron von Goren and stood at attention. Von Goren analyzed and observed Colonel Gastineau with a steely glare.

"Colonel Gastineau, I assume your men are ready for battle?"

"Yes, sir, they are ready. Have we received authorization from the government of Valposta?"

Displeased with his insubordination, von Goren regarded the colonel with contempt. "Let us agree, Colonel, that as your commander in chief, I remain responsible for our relationship with the Valpostan government." Then von Goren stepped around his command station to address Colonel Gastineau directly. "Do not disappoint me, Colonel. Your career rests on this victory."

Being duly motivated, Gastineau saluted his commander, turned on his heels, and exited the command center.

Baron von Goren watched him leave, and moments after he'd left the building, von Goren winced in pain, closing his eyes.

The voice in his head said, *"I do not share your confidence in Colonel Gastineau. Do not disappointment me again."*

Once released, von Goren dropped to the floor, hyperventilating. He shook his head, attempting to regain control of his own mind. Slowly, he pushed himself off the floor, gradually rising to his feet. He smoothed his hair with his right hand and exited his command center. If he had only glanced at the images on his virtual displays, he would have seen multiple contacts flooding into his perimeter, surrounding his troops.

Chapter Forty

By the time Colonel Gastineau had reached his division commanders, the troops were equipped and ready for battle. Gastineau consulted Captain Donnelly, his primary battlefield commander. Donnelly advised they were prepared to move the divisions over the border into Valposta on Gastineau's command. Before he gave the order, Gastineau decided to make a preliminary survey of the battlefield.

He walked out into the cleared field. It was a perfect avenue for his forces to march into Valposta. Wide and unencumbered by trees, the short yellow grasses would provide sure footing for both infantry and cavalry. He bent down, pulled several short blades of dried grass from the ground, stood up, and gently released them to get a sense of the wind direction and velocity. He watched the majority of the blades blow to the south in the direction of his army. However, several of the lighter blades swirled in the breeze and were lifted upward.

Gastineau watched the rising blades, shielding his eyes from the bright sun. When he looked straight up, something caught his attention. The sun briefly reflected off something directly above him. It twinkled momentarily and then subsided. Gastineau repositioned his hand in an attempt to get a better look and identify an actual object or confirm an optical illusion. Seconds later, he received his answer as Atara the dragon landed directly on him, crushing him to the ground. Atara then let out a roar that shook the surrounding landscape with its tremolo.

The warrior arts students, riding their Tyrannosaurus rex mounts, proceeded to attack Baron von Goren's forces. They created a double-envelopment flanking position in an attempt to overrun the soldiers. Conrad and Mindy took the left flank, and Atticus and Matthew took the right. Matilda, along with Nash, Meinhard, Donovan, and Tiana, remained in the center to prevent the baron's forces from escaping. Astride the final tyrant lizard, Alex was with them, twin blaster pistols at his side and a multi-barreled assault cannon in hand. They were all ready for the inevitable rush of enemy combatants, but only Alex expressed it.

"Bring it on, Baron! We're ready for you!" Alex yelled from his position fifteen feet off the ground.

Atara the dragon, fresh from her colonel-crushing duties, advanced before Conrad and Mindy to weaken any resolve of the troops on the left flank. Likewise, Harlow the eagle cleared the way for her charges. With talons forward, eight gleaming razor-sharp claws, Harlow swooped out of the sky, glided over the twin T. rexes, and destroyed several squadrons of von Goren's troops.

Mindy and Conrad rode side by side, frontally attacking two squadrons of enemy soldiers. They weren't really doing anything since the T. rexes were chomping and gnashing the terrified combatants. As they moved closer to the central encampment, a fusillade of energy bolts blasted past them, exploding in the trees.

"We better split up, or we're doomed," Mindy said telepathically.

Conrad nodded his agreement and held his right thumb up in the air. He hoped Mindy would be safe, but as she herself understood, every living thing has a destiny.

Conrad, standing on the back of his T. rex, was deflecting the energy bolts being fired at him from a group of soldiers on the ground. He stood in a modified ground-rex stance as his mount galloped at full speed toward the enemy troops. All at once, a small blast careening off a nearby tree knocked him to the ground. He watched as his T. rex also fell and slid into some brambles nearby. Shaking off the impact, Conrad slowly regained his orientation. As he was lifting himself from the ground, he felt something slamming him back down. He looked up and saw a dark, shrouded being with its foot directly upon his chest. The beast bent down to regard Conrad, allowing him to see that, in the face hole of its hood, there was no reflection.

Instinctively, Conrad reached for his scepter, but he was unable to retrieve it. Then he heard in his mind, *"This is your last day, little one,"* and the beast reached out with both hands to end Conrad's young life.

Before it could, however, Conrad reflexively thrust both of his hands into the creature's abdomen. A blinding flash of purple light emitted, throwing the attacker into a nearby cliff face. As it struck, the beast belched the most horrible screech Conrad had ever heard. Jumping to his feet, Conrad located his scepter lying on the ground. He scooped it up, activated it, and awaited the necromancer's retaliation. The beast watched as Conrad swung his scepter in predefined arcs around himself. The dark creature darted its head looking for an opening.

"Come-on, you devil! Hit me with your best shot!" Conrad screamed. The beast stood silent as if doubtful about its chances, and Conrad relished his newly discovered courage. As the two stood staring each other down, Conrad continued his defensive scepter kata, fully ready to repel any attack directed his way.

Suddenly, the beast raised its gloved hands. Conrad swung his scepter around himself in an attempted parry when he felt every muscle in his body weaken. Black electric bolts ran from the hooded specter's hands and flooded Conrad's body. With all voluntary muscle control now gone, he dropped his scepter, which deactivated as it fell. He then fell to the ground having lost control of his legs.

The beast, now standing above him, continued to inject its dark energy into Conrad's body. The pain being inflicted became nearly intolerable, and it caused Conrad to writhe against the discomfort. He screamed out, "Stop it!" but alas the beast closed in to finish him for good.

As life began to drain from his body, the pain subsided, and he felt an unusual sense of well-being. *It's okay*, he thought. *I'll be reunited with her.* Thinking about his mother always brought joy to the boy. He closed his eyes prepared for the end.

But the end was not to be. Although in a state of shock, he felt the bombardment cease. He slowly regained consciousness. As he opened his eyes to see what was happening, he tried to focus on the area nearby. He saw a figure rapidly flailing its arms. When his hearing returned to normal, he heard the crackles of a scepter filament striking.

Pushing himself off the ground he looked to his left and saw Tiana pummeling the beast against a tree. Every time the beast attempted a counter, Tiana struck it with lightning speed. Another attempt, another failure. This continued for several moments as Conrad continued his recovery. Finally, he thought, *Tiana!*

Hearing his call, Tiana teleported to his side. Her scepter remained drawn, ready, and her eyes were green fire. Protecting Conrad she yelled, "Leave this place, beast, or by Cormallen's Fire I will smite thee!"

The beast, pulling itself up, made a sudden leap toward Tiana and Conrad. Instantaneously, Tiana thrust her scepter in front of her and, with her left hand, summoned a ball of Q-energy.

"Tempt me not, beast. I shall destroy you if you attempt to harm the boy again!"

As she spoke these words, Atara the dragon and Harlow the eagle landed just behind them. Atara's roar and Harlow's screech echoed through the forest. The hooded beast, realizing it would be unable to vanquish this overpowering force of sentinels, folded in upon itself and disappeared.

As a quenching silence befell the woods, Tiana scanned the area visually and psychically. Indeed the hooded apparition was gone. Conrad also looked around. *Where did he go?* he thought. "I do not know," Tiana said. "But something tells me he will be back."

Atara and Harlow returned to their human forms. Each watched a different direction so that the entire hollow woods would be surveyed. "Sister," Atara said to Tiana. "Do you sense to where the beast flew?" Tiana shook her head.

"I do not. Strange, but there is something about this beast that eludes my mind." Harlow quipped,

"So we wait for it to attack again?"

"Of course not, Harlow. It is better to have a plan in hand than to deal with the creature on its terms..." Tiana stopped mid-sentence and concern grew upon her face.

"We must return to the others now. Atara, Harlow, go to your wards. Conrad and I will follow shortly." The two sentinels acknowledged Tiana's words mere seconds before each one disappeared with a crackle.

Conrad looked up at Tiana for reassurance. She placed her hand on his shoulder and said, "Do not concern yourself, T2. We will get to the bottom of this mystery. For now we should return to the others." Conrad nodded in agreement.

"Collect your mount and return to the battlefield. I will see you there," Tiana said as she disappeared into a point of light.

Conrad looked over his shoulder to where his T. rex had collapsed into the undergrowth. The giant dinosaur had returned to its feet and seemed to be sniffing the air searching for something.

"What do you smell, girl?" Conrad said. His mount looked at him and roared.

"It's gone now, but there are other enemies. Are you ready to return to the fight?" he said. Again the giant theropod responded with a bellowing roar. He then teleported directly to her back and seated himself in the saddle. He took a last look around before commanding his T. rex back to the main battlefield.

A large contingent of Baron von Goren's remaining troops attempted to escape through the center of the battlefield. Watching them advancing, Meinhard quickly morphed, and now the harried soldiers were coming face-to-face with a twenty-foot gorilla. Meinhard the ape slammed both of his fists into the ground, stood upright, and pounded his chest, roaring with contention.

A few of the men, unconvinced they could not overcome the gargantuan primate blocking their escape route, opened fire on Meinhard the ape and the others. Flashes of condensed energy careened through the forest, many whizzing by the heads of the student warriors. Explosive concussions abounded causing many large trees and bushes to explode into flames.

Several barrages of energy bolts exploded near Matilda. Meinhard the ape, seeing his student charge in danger, roared out and charged the soldiers. Two soldiers operating a shoulder-mounted howitzer took aim on the approaching giant and fired. Meinhard the ape avoided the first few volleys, but a guided energy beam knocked him to the ground.

Alex immediately reacted to Meinhard's predicament by laying down suppression fire with his rotating energy cannon.

When the energy bolts hit home, the two soldiers responsible for wounding Meinhard evaporated. As Alex continued spraying other escaping soldiers with cannon fire, most of them threw their weapons to the ground and their hands up in surrender. Accepting their submission, Alex disengaged his attack and approached the disarmed troops atop his T. rex.

Atara and Harlow arrived at the battlefield in time to assist with mopping up duties. Atara morphed back into her animal alter-ego as did Harlow. The two giants took to the air to round-up any other miscreant troops.

Seeing two giant winged monsters above them, several soldiers began to run for the forest. Conrad's timing was impeccable as he emerged from the woods to block their escape route. Two of the more recalcitrant soldiers pointed their pulse rifles at Conrad's T. rex hoping to bring the giant down, but they were too late. Conrad shot a purple energy beam from his left hand distracting the men long enough for his carnivore mount to devour them both.

Mindy, Matthew, and Atticus then rounded up the remainder of von Goren's army with Conrad coming from behind them as back-up. The four tyrannosaurs, with riders, formed four points of a virtual capture pen, each one crouching and bearing jaws filled with six-inch razor-sharp teeth. Harlow the eagle and Atara the dragon acted as sentries in between in case any of the captives had the temerity to attempt an escape. Tiana stood before them, scanning for something.

When she identified the most senior officer among the captives, she approached him, asking for Baron von Goren's location. The intimidated captain denied knowing anything about the baron's whereabouts. Tiana quickly searched his mind. He was being truthful, but she also sensed von Goren's presence. She turned toward Conrad and telepathically requested his assistance.

Conrad climbed down from his T. rex and hurried to Tiana's side. He waited patiently while she continued looking in several different directions. Without averting her gaze she said, "I want you to reach out with your mind. Tell me if you sense the baron's presence."

Conrad did not immediately register the request. When it dawned on him that he could be the only likely respondent, he replied, "Me? Why me?"

"The baron is interested in you. I believe he knows what happened to your father, and I think you will be more likely to attract his thoughts than would I." Tiana looked at Conrad, her eyes brilliant robin's eggs, and she smiled subtly.

Conrad closed his eyes, cleared his mind's eye, and thought, *Find the baron.* He immediately saw something racing through a wooded area. He heard someone struggling to catch his or her breath as he or she ran through the trees. The person in question tripped and fell, and Conrad could see the entire calamity. Finally, the running person stopped behind a large tree. In his mind, Conrad's view pulled back to reveal the terrain: a large oak nearly one hundred feet tall surrounded by a dense forest of smaller trees. A man peaked out from behind the wooded colossus. It was von Goren.

His eyes snapped open. The woods provided the backdrop for the command center, and most of the trees were mostly of the same height. As he looked into the distance, he saw one lone tree towering over all the others.

"That must be the one," he thought.

"Good," Tiana replied in his head. *"Are you ready to be a hero?"*

Conrad swallowed hard and stared at the ground. He fought the beginnings of hyperventilation and simply nodded his assent. Tiana reached out her hand to him as she programmed her token with the other. The air around them had begun swirling when Conrad firmly took her hand in his, and he exhaled vigorously. They disappeared with a crackle.

They landed right in front of the monster tree, and for the first time, Conrad neither fell nor was he nauseated. Tiana quickly removed and activated her scepter and stood in a modified bow stance. Conrad followed suit. They stood observing the tree before them for several seconds, while the glowing threads of their scepters hummed and threw sparks periodically into the air.

"We have you!" Tiana said. "Come out, and you may survive this day."

After several moments, von Goren finally stepped out from behind the enormous tree with a smirk upon his face. When fully before them, he outstretched his arms and said, "Here I am, Master Tiana, I surrender." He then regarded Conrad and said, "And this brave lad must be the famous Master Conrad Turner. I wish we could have met under different circumstances, Master Turner. Your father always speaks so highly of you."

Conrad dropped his scepter to his side. "You knew my father?"

"Not past tense, my boy. I *know* your father."

As Conrad heard this, his hand immediately released its grasp on the scepter, which deactivated and dropped to the ground. "Where is he?"

The baron smiled broadly at Conrad's frantic questions. "Close by. Would you like to meet him, finally?"

Without thinking, and as if under a trance, Conrad began walking closer to Baron von Goren.

Tiana watched the entire exchange with great concern, but now she knew it was time to intervene. She leaped in front of Conrad to block his way. When she landed before him, Conrad was jolted out of the trance.

"Conrad, keep away from him! I sense he means you harm."

Conrad watched helplessly as Tiana flew across the forest, slamming into a sycamore tree fifty yards away. When he looked forward again, Conrad saw von Goren standing erect, as if frozen, and behind him stood the dark beast.

The air around became thick and misty. Conrad's heart beat fast and hard in his chest as he tried to figure out what to do. He looked over to where Tiana lay. She was not moving, and Conrad initially feared the worst. He looked at his dead scepter lying on the ground beside him. He looked at von Goren. Everywhere Conrad looked, the dark creature's eyes followed, orange slits tracking Conrad's lead, looking at Tiana, the scepter, and down at the top of von Goren's head.

Panic began to overtake Conrad. Too many negative thoughts clouded his reasoning. *It's over*, he thought. *Tiana's dead and soon you will be too.* The sheer weight of the responsibility for everything started crashing down on him, crushing his confidence, his will, and his resolve. He was beaten.

Conrad fell to his knees and said, "Do what you will, beast." The beast began to laugh. Slowly at first then building to a crescendo. The laughter affected Conrad. Somewhere deep inside him anger arose, and this anger coalesced into a call to action. From deep within Conrad mustered the resolve to fight. He looked directly at the faceless hole in the creature's cloak, staring into the two glowing pieces of coal.

"I'm not afraid of you!" Conrad shouted.

The creature reacted by leaning forward, moving its blank face closer to Conrad's, and when it was just inches from Conrad, a voice from inside the face hole said, "You will be!"

Before he knew what hit him, Conrad was flying backward, propelled by some invisible force. He summoned his determination by thrusting his feet to the ground to stop himself. Once grounded again, he ran back toward the creature as fast as he could. The creature simply laughed at the attempt.

As he got closer to the creature, Conrad held out his right hand with his palm open, and he thought, *Here!* The scepter wavered slightly and then flew into Conrad's open hand. He wrapped his fingers tightly around it, and it activated immediately. Then with it held over his head, he sprung up and performed an aerial Smithson maneuver. He swung his scepter at the creature, and when it hit where its shoulder should be, it let out a bloodcurdling scream that shook the forest to the treetops. The beast fell to the ground, and as it did, so did the frozen body of Baron von Goren.

The creature pushed itself off the ground, a growl erupting from it. It waved both of its arms in the air above its head using a circular motion, and after several rotations, it thrust them in Conrad's direction. A wave of oscillating black energy immobilized Conrad, causing him pain. Dropping his scepter, he screamed out in agony. The pain was interfering with his ability to think, however, on instinct alone he began rotating his hands around each other to generate a purple ball of Q-energy. He threw it at the black energy net around him, and when they connected, the little purple ball absorbed the dark power. Conrad's Q-energy then continued on its course, impacting the creature knocking it to the ground.

And again, it jumped back to its feet and yelled, "You think you can defeat me! Prepare to breathe your last breath!"

Streams of jet-black lightning exploded from the creature's fingertips, flying toward Conrad. Conrad braced his hands, hoping to deflect at least some of the power, but he also closed his eyes and thought, it *is a good day to die.*

Seconds passed, and then Conrad opened his eyes and saw the dark energy ricocheting through the forest. Tiana had jumped between the beast and Conrad and was in full combat position, repelling the vicious attack. The creature drew back and fired yet another battery, which Tiana repelled again. The next time it drew back, Tiana launched a three-foot-wide blue-white energy sphere. The Q-energy flew at the creature, but split into two just before impact, both hemispheres slamming together and trapping the creature within its grasp.

Tiana walked to within a foot of the imprisoned being as it writhed around trying to escape.

"Who or what are you?" she said.

"You will pay for this, sentinel."

"Do not task me. Answer my question."

"Release me, or the boy's father dies."

When Conrad heard this threat, he ran beside Tiana. "Where is he!" Conrad yelled.

Tiana said telepathically, *"The creature is trying to get an emotional reaction from you. Do not let it!"*

Conrad turned and looked at Tiana. *"But it must have my father."*

"We do not know that. It might be playing games."

The beast's orange eyes disappeared leaving nothing where its face should be but blackness. Suddenly, a bright light grew in the forest about fifty yards away from where the creature was imprisoned. Both Conrad and Tiana looked in the direction of the light to see what it was. When the light faded, crumpled on the ground at the foot of a tree was a man dressed in satin robes. Although his face was turned away from them, it was clear his hair color was a mixture of black-and-white strands. The man slowly lifted himself from the ground, and turned his face in their direction. There stood Nathaniel Turner, beaten but alive.

Conrad's mouth dropped open; he couldn't believe his eyes. Was this another dream or was his father actually there before him? Conrad observed the man as he rubbed the dirt off his robes. The man looked up and when he realized Conrad was watching him, outstretched his arms and said, "Come to me, son." Without thinking, Conrad ran to his father.

Tiana, who had her hands full with her captive, saw this and called out. "No, Conrad!" she yelled. "It could be a trap!" Conrad heard none of her warning. He was too overcome with joy at the sight of his father. After fifteen years, he was finally going to meet him in the flesh, and nothing was going to stop or delay their reunion. He was no longer an orphan.

When he reached Nathaniel, Conrad swung his arms around the man. Nathaniel reciprocated the gesture, and they hugged each other for what seemed like hours. Conrad then looked up into his father's eyes, the eyes he had seen in the vision, and said, "Is it really you?"

Nathaniel smiled, his brilliant white teeth glistening. "Yes, it is, and I am so very happy to see you again."

Tiana's concern grew. She was expending most of her intrinsic energy maintaining her energy trap. If Nathaniel's presence was indeed a ruse, she would be hard-pressed to both keep the creature confined and protect Conrad. She reached out with her mind, looking for any clues to assist her decision making ability. *Be careful*, she thought. *This may not be as it appears*. There was no response from Conrad.

Tiana tried again to reach Conrad's mind, to see his thoughts. All she could see was his joy. There was nothing else. Conrad's mind was not analyzing the circumstances; he was not considering the risks involved. He simply wanted to be with his father, with Nathaniel.

Tiana's heart went out to her ward. Part of her wanted to be with him. Part of her wanted everything to go well. Part of her hoped that the union would lead to new growth in Conrad. But her logical side resisted. She looked back at her constricted captive. She tried to enter its mind for a sign, any sign, of collusion and deception, but she was unable to get a clear fix on anything.

Then she noticed that the beast had ceased struggling to break free from its prison. She watched it for several moments, and although its face-hole contained no features save for the two awful eyes, she swore she saw a twisted smile within it.

"What say you, beast?" Tiana said.

"Release me," it replied.

"Why on Overworld should I do so?"

" The boy and his father are reunited. Release me and I will leave them to you."

Tiana considered the request, but her instincts were conflicted. Although she did not sense that the creature was being untruthful, she knew enough to be cautious. She looked again at Conrad and Nathaniel and the joyful reunion they were sharing.

"If I release you, never return," Tiana said. "Do you hear me beast? You are never to return to our plane, our world, our lives." Then she moved to within inches of the creatures face hole, staring directly into the two orange eyes.

"For if you do, or if you ever again harm any member of Clan Turner, I will find you and destroy you."

The creature stared back at Tiana, raised its cloaked head, and nodded to confirm its agreement to the terms. Tiana deactivated the Q-energy prison, and the creature stretched its arms high over its head. It began spinning wildly, discharging thick black smoke. Then it vanished into thin air.

Tiana, still unsure about the wisdom of releasing the creature, went to join Conrad and Nathaniel, however, within a few steps, she was knocked to the ground. Invisible hands trapped her arms behind her back, and she was tossed across the forest floor to rest against a large rock. Conrad looked over in horror just in time to see her roll to a stop.

"Tiana!" Conrad screamed, but his scream was extinguished when he was also thrust up into the air. He fell back to the ground with a sickening thud. As he regained his awareness, he looked at his father. Nathaniel was clearly distressed by what had just transpired, but before he could react to events, Nathaniel's body stiffened, and his face contorted as if he was racked with pain. Conrad watched from the ground as his father writhed and convulsed for a few moments.

"Help me, Conrad!" Nathaniel yelled. "Help me, son!"

I line of light formed behind Nathaniel, ultimately becoming a portal. The wind picked up as the air around them was sucked into it. Even though he tried to hold his place by grabbing onto the ground, the agonized Nathaniel was dragged toward the opening. He tried to crawl away from the portal, but the force of the airflow was overpowering, and he finally succumbed.

As he was torn through the opening, Nathaniel screamed, "Help me, Conrad!" and he disappeared into a point of light.

"DAD!" Conrad bawled.

With the silence of the woods enveloping him, Conrad began to sob. His father had returned to his life, he was no longer an orphan. Now, once again, her was alone in the world. He sat up, pulled his knees to his chest, and cried. He rocked himself to gain some form of comfort for his loss.

So engrossed was he in his misery that he failed to notice Tiana arising from where she had been thrown. Seeing Conrad's sadness, she went to him, wrapped her arms around his body, and hugged him until he regained his composure.

Once Conrad did, he looked up at her. Her eyes were sapphires, and a single tear left a track down her right cheek.

"Are you all right?" she asked.

Conrad did not answer at first. He squeezed her tightly to him.

"I'm okay, but my father..."

Tiana released Conrad and turned him to face her.

"I promise you we will find him."

"How?"

"Do you still doubt my abilities? With all we have been through can you not believe we will find him?"

Conrad's mood changed. She was right. If a rag-tag team of students, sentinels, a scalawag and his brother could beat the army of an entire country, what could stop them from finding one man?

"Ok, what's the plan?" Conrad said

"First, we go home for some well-deserved rest. Then we must discover who is responsible for your father's abduction, and when we do…"

Conrad waited for her to finish her sentence, but eventually realized she was not going to.

"What?" he asked.

"Never mind. Let us find the others. You have quite a tale to tell."

Tiana stood and helped Conrad to his feet. They both began the walk back through the woods. Conrad took in all the sights, smells, and atmosphere of the place for he somehow knew it was a great day. He thought about his father's embrace, and he knew he would be reunited with him again. He looked up at Tiana, who was walking beside him. He smiled at her. She was as she claimed: someone meant to protect and guide him through his adventures. He also felt something else from her, but he was loath to say it yet. She did love him.

Tiana smiled when she saw these thoughts of Conrad's. He was growing into the man she knew he would be. And as they continued walking toward the cabin in the meadow, she threw her arm around his shoulder. He returned her affection and wrapped his arm around her waist. Together, they walked in silence.

THE END

ABOUT THE AUTHOR

James Lee is a native New Yorker living in Southern California.